Searching for Sal

Rob Zaleski

ISBN-10: 1470088290

ISBN-13: 978-1470088293

Book design by Mark Giaimo

To Coach Phil Plautz, who lit the flame;

and to Cindy, who keeps it flickering

1

As they plodded toward the third tee at Turtle Creek Golf Club, so immersed in the moment they didn't even notice the lingering morning chill, Nate Zavoral felt his legs start to quiver.

"C'mon," he muttered under his breath. "This is ludicrous."

Much as he tried, however, there was no controlling his nerves, no diminishing the magnitude of what was about to occur.

Besides, Nate knew that his merciless golf partners—Freddie Luckovich, Tyler Briggs and Harold "Doc" Flanagan—weren't about to let him off the hook. To a man, they reveled in the absurdity of the moment.

"Feel that breeze? It's Sal, man, I'm tellin' ya. He's hovering over us, ready to make history," Tyler deadpanned while depositing his golf bag just a few feet from the rectangular tee box.

"Yeah, I feel it," Luckovich said. "But is that really a breeze—or his nasty garlic breath?"

"One swing and you change the world, Z-man. But hey, no pressure," Doc bantered.

To be sure, this was a complete reversal of how the men had felt just four months earlier. Like Nate, they, too, had been stunned and distraught over the news that their friend and fellow golf partner, Sal Magestro, had died of a massive heart attack just a day after Christmas. They, too, had fumbled for the right words while attempting to console Sal's mother, Sophie, and his younger brother Tony at the funeral.

"Jesus, what do I tell her?" Doc had asked Nate in a panicky voice as they approached Sophie in the long reception line at the Helgeson Funeral Home.

"That the fling her son was having with a 20-year-old waitress was strictly platonic? That she shouldn't think the worst, because I spotted Sal at confession just a few days before this whole insane thing happened?"

But that was back in December.

It was now late April—Saturday, April 24 to be precise—and as the four middle-aged men reached the third tee and squinted at the blue flag fluttering on a hilltop, 172 yards from the middle tees, they had a different perspective.

Yes, of course, they'd forever mourn the loss of their longtime friend, who was as generous and gregarious as they come. But now, four months later, they could at least reflect on his shocking death and, in an odd and perhaps perverse sort of way, smile.

As Nate liked to put it, it wasn't so much that Sal—who'd turned 54 in November—had died that had shaken them to the core. It was the *manner* in which he'd died.

The owner of Magestro's, a popular bar and pizza restaurant on the University of Wisconsin campus—just blocks from the gritty, ethnically-rich neighborhood where he'd grown up—Sal had twice been hospitalized for stress-related symptoms in recent years. But he'd refused to alter his admittedly brutal work load, despite repeated warnings from his doctor and his brother Tony, who conveniently ignored the fact that, at roughly 325 pounds, he was a walking time bomb himself. So it was widely assumed that Sal would probably keel over some frenzied night while barking out orders in his restaurant's inferno of a kitchen.

However, no one was prepared for the news that Tony had relayed the morning of Dec. 27; that Sal had suffered a massive heart attack while he and a "female companion"—Tony's words—were sharing the outdoor hot tub at Sal's mountainside condo in Steamboat Springs, Colo. The female companion in this case being Connie Frataro, a perky, doe-eyed college sophomore who could have passed for Marisa Tomei's little sister and whom Sal had hired to wait tables shortly after Thanksgiving.

The news was all the more jarring because Connie Frataro's parents, Bendito, aka "The Bull," and Maria Frataro, were lifelong friends of the Magestro family. In fact, Doc recalled at the funeral, Sal had actually been present at Connie's baptism nearly two decades earlier.

Moreover, none of Sal's relatives or his inner circle of friends—including his lifelong confidante, Nate—had even been aware that Sal, who'd divorced his wife Tammy over the summer, had slipped out of town for a ski getaway the evening of Christmas day. Or, more unsettling yet, that he'd been romantically involved with Connie Frataro, who, as Luckovich cracked at the funeral, "was probably breaking in her first Big Wheel" around the time Sal was receiving his associate business degree from Madison Area Technical College.

In light of those disclosures, few people were surprised when word seeped out shortly before the funeral that alcohol was a crucial factor in Sal's death. Meaning that, according to the coroner's report, the blood alcohol level in Sal's pink, bloated body was an alarming .027 when police arrived at the scene following Connie's hysterical 911 phone call shortly before midnight on Dec. 26.

Even Tony didn't try to deny the obvious.

"I think it's fairly obvious their thinking was impaired when they entered that hot tub," he acknowledged in his phone call to Nate the morning of Dec. 27. "Police said the water temperature was jacked up to something like 130 degrees. I mean, criminy, you probably could've boiled lobsters in it."

And, of course, two days and nights of nonstop sex probably didn't help either, Tony speculated. "Don't share this with anyone else—especially my mother," he told Nate with disgust. "But police said Sal

4

looked totally exhausted when they found him—like a guy who'd just gone through boot camp."

Even so, police had stressed that there'd been no signs of foul play, Tony said. ("Although there sure as hell would've been," Doc later exclaimed, "had The Bull been aware of his daughter's whereabouts.")

So startling were these revelations that Nate had been discombobulated for days. He was so dismayed, in fact, that it wasn't until the morning of the funeral on Dec. 30—while weaving through the snow-covered countryside just outside Madison in his finicky but still functional 1967 Austin Healey sports car—that he suddenly remembered the frayed document in his wallet that he and Sal had jokingly referred to as "The Pact."

The Pact was nothing more than a two-paragraph statement the men had typed up one evening following one of their inane philosophical arguments about the meaning of life. This particular debate had taken place during a late summer fishing trip to Adams County in south-central Wisconsin in 1999. And this one was even more contentious and personal than the others, fueled in part by a bout of heavy drinking after being skunked for two consecutive days on Big Pike Lake.

Being Italian, Sal was a devout Roman Catholic. So he fully bought the traditional Christian view that not only would there be a judgment day, but that whenever a decent, God-fearing person died, their soul immediately ascended to heaven, pearly-gates and all. No less important, Sal believed, the soul then had the power to influence the lives of loved ones still on Earth.

Naturally, he also accepted the church's conviction that the souls of people who died without having repented for mortal sins they'd committed went straight to hell and were subjected to eternal flames and suffering.

"Phoenix without air conditioning," Sal liked to say.

Nate, for his part, found such beliefs so infantile and illogical that he was flabbergasted anyone with more than a 5th-grade education could embrace them. Like a lot of "recovering Catholics" from the 1960s, he'd abandoned the church by his late teens—triggered in part by the church's rigid opposition to birth control, a stance Nate found irresponsible in a world of six billion people—and had come to view life on Earth much as his father had: Once you're dead and buried, you remain dead and buried. Either that or you re-emerged as a worm and then faced the prospect of some day being attached to the end of a hook and nibbled to death by bluegills.

Still, he was an agnostic, not an atheist, Nate was always quick to point out. His views were similar to Albert Einstein's, he would explain: There might indeed be a Supreme Being, but it wasn't anything like the Supreme Being that traditional religions promoted.

"And if it isn't all just an accident," he'd muse about life on Earth, "then it's probably beyond our comprehension."

He believed wholeheartedly in evolution, of course. As for this daffy notion of a hereafter—of a big, harmonious kingdom where everyone was in a perpetual state of euphoria and never did bad things or, apparently, even had bowel movements—Nate felt it was downright laughable and something that people clung to only because they feared deep down that it was, in fact, just a ridiculous fairy tale.

"And, frankly, it sounds pretty damn boring, too," he would crow, knowing full well it would push Sal to the boiling point—which it always did.

Indeed, Sal found such beliefs not only blasphemous and outrageously cynical, but in Nate's case hypocritical as well. If Nate didn't believe in a hereafter, he would argue, why had he confessed just a few years back—after a half dozen rum and Cokes during a fishing trip they'd taken to Zihuatanejo, Mexico—that he still said his prayers at night?

"I don't know," Nate had limply responded. "I guess the brainwashing was even more effective than I'd like to admit."

What Nate didn't confess—and would never admit to anyone— was that his beliefs weren't as resolute as he let on. For reasons he couldn't explain—again, maybe due to the brainwashing—a part of him *did* fear that deceased members of his family had reunited somewhere in the great beyond and were observing his every move. Including, of course, his stern but beloved Granny Zavoral, who succumbed to Alzheimer's disease when Nate was still a teenager, and whose Catholic beliefs were even more hardcore than Sal's.

It was Granny Zavoral, after all, who had first lectured Nate at age seven about the need to pray before bed each night. Once, for added effect, she'd pressed one of his fingers against a hot stove for several moments so that he understood what the consequences would be if he didn't. Nate's blood-curdling scream, neighbors reported, was heard almost a block away.

But as they drank the night away on Aug. 19, 1999, Sal decided he'd heard enough. Yes, his mind was starting to fog over. And yes, he'd heard the same infuriating arguments countless times before. But he could no longer accept that an otherwise moral and reasonably intelligent guy who grew up in a staunchly Republican household and whose parents were regular church-goers could be so lacking in faith.

How, Sal would ask himself, could a guy who revered Nelson Mandela, volunteered at the local V.A. Hospital, took immeasurable pride in being an English teacher and still adored his wife of 25 years—how could such an individual possibly be an atheist? OK, even an agnostic? It just didn't compute.

"Well, all right then," Sal finally decided over dinner that evening in the tiny lake-front cabin that had been in Doc's family for years, and which Doc had offered to them for their late summer escape. "Guess I'm just going to have to prove it."

Prove it? Nate, who'd just taken a last bite of the delectable rib-eye steak his friend the chef extraordinaire had prepared, looked up and furrowed his brow.

"Prove it?" he said with a smirk. "Now *there*'s a fantastic idea, Salvatore. Yeah, you prove it and I'll tell you what. I'll make it my mission to tell the world we've found the missing link—the answer to the question that theologians and philosophers and all the other elite thinkers have been searching for since ... since forever.

"Hell, I'll personally call the Pope and give him the news. How's that?"

Sal burped out loud, then pushed his chair back from the kitchen table and peered at his friend with bemusement. He wasn't actually drunk, but he was clearly feeling the effects of the half dozen or so beers he and his hopelessly misguided friend had consumed. He got up from the table, stumbled to the refrigerator and pulled out two more bottles.

"Here's the deal," he said, handing a beer to Nate as he walked into the small adjacent living room and plopped back down in a recliner. "We have this agreement—we'll put it down on paper. Whoever dies first sends a signal to the one who's still alive. I mean, c'mon, doesn't get any simpler than that."

"A signal," Nate mumbled under his breath. He was intrigued.

He stood up, staggered into the living room and dropped his torso into a worn black leather sofa directly across from Sal. Then he propped up his boots on the small wood-burning stove just a few feet away and took a swig of his beer. Sal had his faults, Nate often said, but the guy wasn't dull. Or lacking in imagination. It was one of the things he treasured about him.

"I like that," he said finally. "Makes perfect sense. The one who dies first sends a signal to the survivor. Maybe a bolt of lightning that strikes him in the ass and knocks him out of bed. And then we'll know, with absolute certainty, that your dad and my granny and all the other wonderful people who graced our lives—hell, maybe even your old hunting dog, Groucho—are watching us 24/7 to make sure we don't do anything stupid.

"My man, you are—you're a genius!"

Nate took another swig of beer, then leaned back and stared up at the ceiling fan for a long moment. He truly liked the idea—even though it wasn't exactly original. He suspected that other people—mostly happily married couples whose lives were growing short, he presumed—had made similar agreements over the course of time.

But he couldn't recall ever hearing of anyone who actually made a connection with a dead person—other than some oddball psychics. Nonetheless, Nate knew there were people who claimed it was possible. But they were mostly religious zealots—zealots like Sal Magestro, Nate thought, as he peered across the room at his bleary-eyed longtime chum.

As he continued to ponder Sal's proposal, Nate couldn't help but chuckle. Maybe it was all the alcohol he'd consumed, or maybe he just wanted to shut Sal up once and for all, but he began to entertain the possibility that this might work. They could type up the agreement on Doc's old Smith Corona that he kept on a small corner table in the lone bedroom. Just a couple short paragraphs detailing how the signal would be delivered. They could make a copy and sign each one, then store the documents in a safe place till whoever croaked first.

Of course, Nate reasoned, they'd have to share the documents with their wives and a few close friends—their golf partners seemed the obvious choice—when they got home, just to verify the documents' existence.

"So, about this signal—have you figured that part out yet?" Nate inquired with a wry smile.

"Actually I have," Sal said, pausing to remove a piece of steak that had become wedged in his teeth. "Here's the thing. We're both golf fanatics, right? I mean, we've been playing the damn game since we were kids.

"And yet, let's be honest, Z. It's been a couple years at least since either of us even broke 100. I mean, seriously, we're just a couple of aging hackers, right?"

Nate reeled slightly.

"Hackers might be a little strong," he said defensively. "But, OK, so we'll probably never qualify for the pro senior tour. And your point is?"

Sal settled back in the recliner and took another gulp of beer.

"You asked about the signal part. Well, how's this? One of us dies—let's say you. I then go to our favorite course—Turtle Creek—as soon as conveniently possible. Upon reaching the first par 3—which is No. 3 at Turtle Creek—I look up at the heavens, nod once and proceed to hit my tee shot.

"The deceased—in this case, you—intercepts the ball in midflight, regardless of where it's headed, flutters over the green and drops it in the hole for an ace, the most cherished and difficult shot in all of golf. And then—and then we'll know!"

Sal tried to envision the scene in his mind and frowned.

"OK, I'm getting a little carried away here," he conceded. "I mean, I won't actually be able to see you guide the ball into the hole. Ghosts are invisible—everybody knows that.

"Still, think about it, Nate. The odds of a hole-in-one under those circumstances would be—I don't know, maybe 800,000 to 1? Especially for a couple of duffers like us.

"And just in case anyone tries to dispute this bona fide miracle, the guy who's still alive brings along our other golf partners as witnesses: Luckovich, Tyler and Doc.

"So … what do you think?"

Nate snickered but said nothing for a few moments. He gazed straight ahead at the wood-burning stove and pondered his friend's silly, though admittedly creative, brainstorm. Finally he let out a sigh and smiled. Though he was feeling a bit woozy, he certainly was capable of pounding out a simple two- or three-paragraph document—even if it was utter nonsense.

"You're an original, Magestro, I've always said that," he muttered. "Where does Doc hide the typing paper?"

2

It had seemed a mere lark five distant years earlier. Even Sal, Nate remembered, hadn't taken The Pact all that seriously. When Sal shared it with Luckovich, Tyler Briggs and Doc Flanagan for the first time—digging it out of his wallet while half-crocked at a Labor Day cookout in Doc's backyard just two weeks after typing it up—he joked about how he couldn't wait to die, just so he could witness the look of incredulity on Nate's face after he intercepted Nate's tee shot in midflight and deposited it in the hole.

"Just make sure Z brings an extra pair of boxers along," he'd bellowed.

Still, as amusing and irrelevant as The Pact may have seemed back in August 1999—especially to their golf partners, none of whom was particularly religious—Nate now felt strangely obligated to honor the document. If nothing else, he owed it to Sal Magestro, his closest friend since kindergarten.

Not that Nate had any choice in the matter. His golf brethren—Luckovich, Tyler and Doc—had been needling him to the point of obsession about The Pact and its potential ramifications ever since Nate had reminded them of the document the morning of Sal's funeral.

But now, as he stood on the No. 3 tee at Turtle Creek Golf Club almost four months later, on the first semi-decent spring day of the year, all Nate could think about was how badly he wanted this moment to be over.

Maybe that explained why he'd taken a snowman—a quadruple bogey 8—on the second hole, three-putting with trembling hands from less than 10 feet.

"Yeah, but just think how impressive your hole-in-one will look now," chortled Doc, a balding, droopy-eyed, sports blogger/columnist for *The Capital Times*, Madison's afternoon daily—the same paper where Nate, who was 55, had toiled for three years as a general assignment reporter before returning to college to get his master's degree in mass communications. (It all paid off in 1985 when he landed his dream job as an English teacher and student newspaper advisor at Madison's Frank Lloyd Wright High School.)

Doc had been up the previous night until 2:30 filing a story plus a blog on a Brewers-Cubs game in Milwaukee. But, he'd insisted, there was never any question about his making the 9:06 tee time.

"What? And miss the most spectacular golf shot since (Gene) Sarazen's double eagle in the 1935 Masters?" he cracked upon greeting his buddies on the putting green.

Nate, however, had no illusions.

Though he'd been the starting second baseman on Madison North High School's baseball team in 1967—despite his then-scrawny 5-foot-6 physique—and was now a top swimmer on the West YMCA's senior men's team, he'd experienced little but aggravation in golf. That was partly because his swing was too wristy—or so he'd been told—a flaw he attributed to his baseball days.

But an even bigger factor, Luckovich insisted, was that Nate was "the world's most pathetic head case." He had convinced himself long ago, Luckovich maintained, that golf wasn't his game. And so, whenever faced with a difficult shot or a critical putt, he invariably would choke.

Nate didn't disagree. And yet, he'd surmised over the last few weeks, if there was one hole that offered him even a remote chance at an ace—thus affirming Sal Magestro's unwavering belief in a hereafter—it was the 172-yard third hole at Turtle Creek Golf Club, the hole he and Sal had chosen to honor The Pact.

That's because Nate's most accurate club—or, as his golf partners liked to point out, his *only* accurate club—was his hybrid 4-metal. On most days, if he happened to hit it well, his 4-metal shots traveled 170 to 180 yards, depending on the wind and/or whether he'd struck the ball firmly.

15

Since the green on the 172-yard third hole at Turtle Creek was perched at the top of a rather steep hill—meaning there would be little roll after the ball landed—Nate figured the hybrid-4 was the ideal club. Particularly on this morning, with a slight, cool breeze in their faces.

Unfortunately, it also meant that he and his partners wouldn't be able to see the ball if it actually rolled in the cup. But Nate figured that was a minor tradeoff.

Besides, Doc mused, "it'll just heighten the suspense."

So did the fact that Nate was teeing off last, thanks to his quadruple bogey.

Tyler, who regularly broke 80 and possessed a silky, Ben Hogan-like swing, was the first to hit—as he almost always was.

"Hey Nate, what happens if I get the ace?" the retired high school basketball coach said with a devilish grin while searching the still dewy tee box for a spot to stick his tee. "It would be just like Sal to do something like that, you know."

Nate, who was standing with arms folded just a few feet away, didn't so much as blink. His mind was elsewhere. And he displayed little emotion as his barrel-chested 58-year-old friend took his usual effortless swing, then watched with frustration as the ball faded at the last instant and appeared to land on the far right side of the green, maybe 40 feet from the flagstick.

"Didn't want to steal any of your thunder, Z," Tyler said while stretching down for his tee.

Luckovich and Doc Flanagan immediately followed.

A college dropout and self-employed plumber, Luckovich was relishing every moment of this outlandish scenario. Though he was a good 10 strokes better than Nate, he didn't even care about his own score on this occasion—which became obvious when he howled with laughter after taking a huge divot and watched his ball plop in the bratwurst-shaped bunker directly in front of the green.

"Must've been the wind," he quipped.

Now it was Doc's turn. And for reasons he couldn't explain, the bespectacled scribe felt almost as jittery as Nate as he teed up his ball and glanced at the fluttering blue flag at the top of the hill.

A sportswriter since his college days—it was his love of sports, he often maintained, that helped him survive his pothead phase while attending the University of Wisconsin-La Crosse—Doc enjoyed a good drama as much as anyone. But did he believe for a moment that Sal Magestro's soul might be hovering over them, eagerly waiting to snare Nate's tee shot in midflight and drop it in the hole—if nothing else, to win some childish, decades-old argument? No more than he believed that a one-legged chimpanzee would one day win the Boston Marathon.

In any case, Doc just wanted to get out of the way and let Nate take center stage. So he wasn't even mildly upset when, after a wild, loopy swing, his ball momentarily threatened a flock of geese flying overhead, then landed with a dull thump some 60 yards from the tee.

"OK, Z-man, the tee box is yours," he said with eager anticipation.

Only Nate wasn't sure he wanted it. He wasn't about to admit that, of course—not to these guys.

But he couldn't shake the jumble of nerves that was making it difficult even to stick his tee in the ground. He took a deep breath and tried to think of a clever one-liner to defuse the tension, but his brain wasn't functioning either.

What's more, his mouth was dry and his legs felt like linguini. He glanced at his friends and smiled, but he knew there was no camouflaging his emotions.

"Enough silliness, Nathan," he whispered to himself after taking two less than graceful practice swings. "Just keep your head down ... hit it flush ... and this whole stupid ordeal will be over."

"Just another golf hole, Z," Tyler assured him.

Nate nodded in appreciation. Then he let out a sigh, peered upward and muttered, "OK, Sal buddy, I'm ready if you are. Let's shake this little ol' world up a bit."

He flexed his knees, took one last peek at the flagstick and ... swoosh!

It was, Nate thought for a fleeting moment, an exquisite shot. But as he snapped his head up, he felt his heart sink as the ball took off toward the flagstick and then began drifting to the right—similar to Tyler's shot just a minute or two earlier.

"So much for miracles," Luckovich said.

"Right club, Nate. Wrong direction," Doc noted disappointedly.

Nate was about to respond when the ball smacked hard against the branch of a lone oak tree some 10 feet right of the green. Then, as the four men watched with mouths agape, it ricocheted back toward the green and disappeared from sight.

"Nooo!" Luckovich exclaimed as they all flashed weird looks at one another.

"I don't hear any fat ladies singing yet," Tyler said.

"Yeah, right," Nate said, stuffing his club in his golf bag and pretending not to be fazed by what he'd just witnessed. "Sal was sitting on the branch—didn't you see him? And he kicked the ball in the hole."

Nobody said another word as they scrambled up the hill toward the green.

Nate led the way, marching right past Doc's partly submerged ball in the thick, moist rough. Seconds later, he spotted Luckovich's ball, just a foot or so below the front sand trap's rear lip.

Then he glanced to the right and spotted what was obviously Tyler's ball at the far edge of the large, kidney-shaped green.

There was no other ball in sight—and as Nate paused briefly at the front of the green to assess the situation, he could feel goose bumps dancing up and down his spine.

Luckovich laid his bag down next to the trap, surveyed the green and then felt his own legs go weak. Tyler and Doc had stopped just behind Nate and scanned the entire landscape for a fourth small white sphere, but saw nothing.

"Could be in the woods, I suppose," Nate said, observing the dense foliage directly behind the left side of the green.

"Then again," Doc mused.

"C'mon, Z," Luckovich said, motioning toward the hole with his sand wedge. "The suspense is killing us."

Nate glanced at Tyler and Doc, who were both grinning madly now.

"Seriously, you don't think …"

"Only one way to find out," Tyler said, nervously biting his lip.

Nate shook his head, as if to suggest they'd all gone batty.

Then he dropped his bag and slowly walked toward the cup, continuing to scan the rough just behind the green for any signs of a ball.

In a matter of seconds, he was standing beside the flagstick.

He peered down, glanced at his buddies and looked down again.

Then he leaned over and gingerly lifted a white Nike golf ball from the hole—a white Nike 2 with a dark scuff mark from where it had struck the tree.

"Holy … shit," he uttered.

3

"Nate? Nathan, is that you?" Brigitte Zavoral asked bewilderedly. "And what's all that commotion in the background? I thought you were golfing today."

Nate pressed the cell phone to his ear, straining to hear his wife's voice amid the din in the clubhouse bar at Turtle Creek Golf Club.

"Yeah baby, it's me," he said, shooting a quick glance at the dozen or so men —most of them complete strangers—who were huddled around the u-shaped counter, merrily sucking down beers at his expense, which was the customary practice when any golfer achieved an ace.

"And yeah, I'm at Turtle Creek—in the bar actually."

"The bar? At three in the afternoon? OK, what's going on, Nate? You finally broke 100?"

Nate laughed and was silent for a few moments. How to explain this—this totally preposterous thing that had just occurred? He lifted his mug to his lips and took a long gulp of beer.

"Uh, better than that, honey—much, much better than that!" he clamored.

Better than breaking 100? Now Brigitte was really puzzled. What could be better for her husband the golf fanatic than breaking 100? Then she remembered—The Pact. Sure, of course. How could she have forgotten?

Nate had casually mentioned it—he was chuckling actually—over breakfast. This was the day he was going to honor his agreement with Sal Magestro, the day he'd find out if Sal would keep his promise and guide Nate's tee shot on the third hole at Turtle Creek Golf Club into the cup—thus proving once and for all that there was indeed a hereafter.

And now, for whatever reason, Nate was toying with her—much as he'd done in their younger years.

"Wait, let me guess, honey," she said, deciding to play along. "You got the hole-in-one. Sal Magestro floated down from heaven … and you actually watched him catch your ball and drop it in the hole. And now you're celebrating. Oh Nate, how exciting."

Then, turning serious, she asked, "Nate, do you really think you should be joking about this? I mean, it's been only what—four months since he died?"

Nate grinned, looked around the room and groaned under his breath.

22

"Honey, I know—I know it sounds crazy. But it actually happened. I did get a hole-in-one—on the third hole! I'm not joking.

"OK, so we didn't actually see Sal drop the ball in the hole. But my tee shot hit a tree branch near the green and then—yeah, that's right, a tree branch. And then—what I can say? It caromed onto the green and rolled in the cup."

Now it was Brigitte who laughed. She knew when her husband—a legendary prankster in his college days—was joshing.

"Yeah, right, Nate. Like I really believe you," she said dryly. She was taking a break from her job duties—she was a receptionist at a busy chiropractor's office—but this being a Saturday, she was one of just two employees at the front desk and would have to return to her desk soon.

"Seriously, Nate, what's this all about? I've gotta get back to work—it's been harried ever since I got in today."

Nate knew the moment he'd borrowed Doc's cell phone—a virtual Luddite, Nate had no interest in owning one himself—and called his wife that this wasn't going to be easy to explain. Hell, he still wasn't sure he believed it himself.

And now he was stumped.

"Look, honey, hold on just a second, OK?" he said, sliding a hand through his thinning salt and pepper hair. He cleared his throat, set the phone down on the bar and frantically waved at Luckovich, who, between gulps of beer, was joyously describing the miracle he'd just witnessed to the frumpy female bartender, Gladys, and assorted others on the opposite side of the room.

Within seconds, Luckovich was at Nate's side.

"It's Brigitte," Nate whispered with a pained expression, handing the phone to his friend, who was already slightly tipsy. "She thinks I'm yanking her chain. Just tell her what happened, OK? C'mon, you're good at this sort of thing."

Luckovich grabbed the phone from Nate and pressed it to his ear.

"He did it, Brigitte!" Luckovich exclaimed. "Your husband is the great Messiah! I saw it with my own eyes. So did Tyler and Doc. His shot hit a tree branch and, just as Sal had prophesized ... What? I *am* being serious."

Luckovich flashed a grin at Nate, then shouted at Gladys to pour him another brew. "Brigitte," he continued, trying to stifle a giggle, "I swear I am not making this up ..."

Just then Nate felt a tug at his arm. It was Wilbur "Bookie" Finch, the crusty, silver-haired Turtle Creek pro.

"Here, I found this in the storage room," he said, presenting Nate a dusty but imposing two-foot-high trophy: A large, gold numeral one set atop a square wood base, with enough room for an inscription commemorating the momentous feat. There was even a space inside the numeral for Nate to insert his scuffed but now sacred Nike golf ball.

"But I gotta tell ya," the old pro groused, "that's the wildest Goddamn tale I've heard in the three decades I've been running this place.

"Oh, and by the way, you owe me big-time, pal. Somebody just asked what your score was and I told 'em I had no idea. I'm assuming you'd rather not publicize the fact that you shot a 112—even with the ace."

"One fifteen!" Doc shouted from across the room.

"That is," Doc said, "if you count his three whiffs on the hole immediately following the hole-in-one. Check his card. I don't believe he marked 'em down."

Nate recoiled. In all his euphoria over his 800,000 to 1 ace—an estimate agreed upon by his golf partners, but which Bookie Finch thought was conservative—he'd forgotten that he'd finished the round with an abysmal 112, which was about seven strokes higher than he normally shot at Turtle Creek. Or was it really 115?

He joggled his brain. Everything was a blur now. Then he remembered. Doc was right. He actually had taken three futile swipes at the ball after it landed in some gnarly rough on No. 4; and yes, he'd contemplated heading for the clubhouse, until Tyler pointed out that his ace wouldn't be valid under such circumstances.

Now it was Luckovich tugging at his arm.

"Your wife wants to talk to you again," he said with a grin, clearly enthralled by the whole idiotic scenario. "She says the whole thing is kind of creepy—assuming that it actually happened."

Nate took another drink of beer, then pushed the phone against his right ear and tried to explain again—this time in a slow, deliberate tone—that, yes, he honestly and truly had gotten a hole-in-one on the third hole. And yes, the ball had struck the branch of a tree and bounced onto the green before rolling in the hole.

25

Hell, the ball—a Nike 2—has a dark scuff mark from the collision, he told her. What better proof than that?

"Look, baby cakes," he assured her. "Nobody's more flabbergasted by this whole thing than I am."

And yes, he added, the whole thing *was* a bit creepy. But no, he didn't think for a moment that what had transpired on this chilly spring day had anything to do with The Pact. The very thought was absolutely ludicrous, he maintained.

"Isn't it?"

Brigitte was momentarily speechless.

She could feel all sorts of strange emotions bubbling up inside her—including, oddly enough, elation. She knew how over-the-top crazy her husband was about golf, and how long he'd fantasized of getting a hole-in-one. But this—this was beyond weird.

Then she gasped.

"Oh my God, Nate. What about Sal's mom?"

"Sophie? What about her?"

"Think about it, Nate. She still doesn't know about The Pact, remember? You said at the funeral that as far as you knew, Sal had never told her about it. He thought it would upset her, that she'd think it was sacrilegious. And you agreed that it wasn't something she needed to know about.

"And with Sal dead, you were afraid she'd become obsessed with it—that she wouldn't be able to sleep until you hit your golf shot."

Nate's stomach began churning again.

He didn't want to deal with this—not now. It had been a long emotional day. But he knew Brigitte was right. If Sophie Magestro heard about all this second-hand, she'd be deeply offended—probably outraged as well.

Doc had already served notice that the shot and the bizarre circumstances surrounding it would be the lead item on his blog on *The Capital Times'* website the next morning. Nate wasn't thrilled by the idea, but he understood. It was a quirky human interest story. Not only that, but Sal Magestro had been one of the city's best known characters, particularly in the close-knit Italian-American community.

Nate groaned and took another swig of his beer. He was having trouble focusing amid all the ruckus, but he knew he had to come up with some sort of damage-control scheme to avoid an adverse reaction from Sophie Magestro.

"Look, hon," he said after a long silence. "Do me a favor. The guys are treating me to a lobster dinner at The Shipwreck. They're insisting that we celebrate this—this *Twilight Zone* episode, as Luckovich calls it.

"Could you call Sophie and tell her I'll be stopping by after dinner—around 8 or so? Tell her I've got a goofy little story to share with her and that it involves Sal.

"But don't scare her. I mean, I sure as hell don't want her to panic. Just tell her—oh, I don't know. Tell her I was golfing today and that the heavens shined on me. And that somewhere, high above, her son is probably having a good laugh."

"And gloating," Brigitte interjected, finally appreciating just how goofy her husband's story was.

"He'd be gloating, Nate."

"Oh, I'm sure," Nate said, snickering at his wife's attempt at gallows humor. "But Sophie doesn't need to hear that."

―――――――

Darkness had descended on the upper-crust Fernwood Estates neighborhood, a sterile, virtually treeless new subdivision on Madison's far west side, by the time Nate pulled into the driveway of Sophie Magestro's exotic, white stucco, ranch-style condo. He squinted at his watch. It was exactly 8:15. He was still a bit shaky, but at least he was no longer feeling the effects of the three beers he'd downed in the Turtle Creek bar. And a part of him was still rejoicing over the hole-in-one— regardless of the bizarre circumstances.

Hell, he'd been dreaming about this for what—44 years? Ever since his dad had presented him some second-hand, Slammin' Sammy Snead-model wood-shafted clubs for his 11th birthday and then let him tag along at bucolic Evansville Golf Club, just south of Madison. And so what if he'd shot something like 85 for nine holes and was arm-weary when it was over—he was, from that day on, hooked.

He sat motionless for a half-minute or so in the cramped seat of his Austin Healey, gathering his emotions. Then he repeated the ritual he always went through when confronted with a pressure situation.

"Perspective," he reminded himself. If John Kennedy could coolly stare down Nikita Khrushchev back in October 1962, essentially telling the bellicose Soviet leader that unless he immediately ordered the removal of all Soviet missiles from Cuba, his country would be reduced to powder, then certainly Nate Zavoral could explain to octogenarian Sophie Magestro the silly five-year-old agreement that he'd had with her son Sal.

And how, much to Nate's astonishment —not to mention that of his golf partners, Freddie Luckovich, Doc Flanagan and Tyler Briggs—it had all played out earlier today much as Sal had predicted it would.

But please don't read too much into this, he would tell her. It was a good yarn, an amusing story—which is why Doc was going to mention it in his blog tomorrow on *The Capital Times'* website.

But it was undoubtedly just a wild coincidence. Think about it, Sophie, Nate would tell her. If God wanted us to know beyond all doubt that there was a hereafter, would he convey that message through a couple of ordinary stiffs like Sal Magestro and Nate Zavoral—one of whom happened to be an agnostic? And on a golf course no less?

Yeah, that might work, Nate decided. Still, he wasn't looking forward to this moment. While he'd always been fond of Sophie—he found her to be witty, upbeat, gracious; almost the exact opposite of her gruff, condescending late-husband Jimmy—he knew she was highly emotional, the kind of woman who could get teary-eyed over a shoe sale at Macy's.

And, in Nate's view, she was even more of a religious wacko than Sal. It was Sophie, Nate recalled, who'd insisted that Sal and his younger brother went to confession at least twice a month—as adults,

29

mind you—lest they be left out of the will. She'd even called the church pastor, Father Ryan, to verify that they'd followed through.

She did have one vice—though only one, as far as Nate knew. She gambled. Blackjack, the slots, gin rummy, church bingo or any other two-bit game of chance that involved money, Sophie always had her purse out.

But while it was well known that Sophie had the fever, Nate respected the fact that she knew her limits. Or claimed to, anyway. She liked to boast, for instance, that she rarely lost more than $100 on her many trips to the Ho-Chunk Casino, about 40 miles north of Madison. And she insisted that she won far more than she lost—which, Sal often noted, was the big reason Jimmy had turned a blind eye to his wife's addiction.

Then again, Jimmy had been so preoccupied running his liquor store—which he co-owned with his brother Frank—that he was delighted his wife had found a hobby that kept her out of his hair. Just as long as Sophie made sure the store's books were in order at the end of each week, he really didn't give a hoot what she did with her free time.

"Nate! How wonderful to see you," Sophie said with a tender embrace as she ushered her son's longtime friend into the entrance-way of her cheerful, if somewhat oddly arranged, home. "So what's this all about? Brigitte mentioned something about a weird thing that happened to you today—something that made you think of Sal?"

Nate smiled awkwardly but did not answer.

She led him into her spacious living room, which was decorated in bold, luminous colors and was dominated by a massive, framed oil-painting of The Last Supper that hung over a rust-colored sofa. She motioned for him to sit down.

"Something to drink? A glass of wine maybe?" Sophie inquired. A vivacious woman in her late 70s, with thick glasses and puffy, caramel-tinted hair, she was clad in a silk, paisley robe with matching slippers and plunked down directly across from him in a small beige recliner. And, as was often the case, she was clutching a rosary.

"Thanks, but I'd better not," Nate said, pointing out that he'd had a couple beers at Turtle Creek Golf Club earlier in the day. He inquired about her health and that of her Wheaton Terrier, Monty, who—to Nate's relief—was napping peacefully at the end of the sofa and had not so much as squirmed when Nate entered the room.

"Oh, you know, my hips ache and I've got bursitis in my neck, like most people my age," she said. "And hardly a day passes, of course, when I don't think of Sal—although knowing he's in a better place is comforting. But all in all, I'm OK.

"But I still worry about the girl—Connie Frataro. I'm sure she's still traumatized by the whole thing. But, you know, they weren't having sex. Your friend Doc Flanagan told me he knew for a fact that their relationship was strictly platonic."

Nate looked at her blankly.

"Well, I'm sure doc's right," he said meekly.

31

As he settled into the sofa, Nate studied Sophie's eyes, trying to gauge her mood. Obviously she was still grieving—but was she too fragile to hear this entirely preposterous story? Plus, it had been just a little over three years since the death of her husband.

On the other hand, Nate knew that Sophie possessed great inner strength and that her faith in God and the teachings of the Catholic Church had never wavered. He remembered how steady and resolute she remained after Jimmy was shot in the leg and hospitalized for about 10 days after the liquor store was robbed by two teenage punks back in 1971. (It was Nate, who worked summers at the store to help pay his college tuition, who found Jimmy sprawled on the floor, blood oozing from his right thigh, after returning from a delivery.)

Nate took a breath and leaned forward, his hands clasped on his knees.

"Look, Sophie, I know it's getting late, so I'll try to make this quick," he said, measuring his words carefully.

He then provided her with a condensed version of his extraordinary tale: the many spirited debates he and Sal had had over whether there actually was a hereafter; their fishing trip to Big Pike Lake in 1999 and the typing up of The Pact—though neither of them, Nate emphasized, actually took it seriously.

In brief—and this was Sal's idea, Nate made clear—The Pact decreed that whoever died first would send a signal to the one still alive. The survivor would drive to Turtle Creek Golf Club, he explained, and meet with their three closest friends, who would act as witnesses. When he got to his favorite par-3 hole—where the green is reachable with just one shot—he would hit the ball, and the deceased would descend from the heavens, catch it in midflight and magically steer it into the cup for a hole-in-one, "the rarest and most treasured shot in all of golf."

Nate paused and looked across at Sophie to assess her reaction. To his amazement, she was totally still and displayed no emotion—though she did dab at her eyes once with a tissue.

He then explained how he typed up The Pact at Doc's cabin and printed out a copy for Sal once they got home. But after sharing it with their wives and several golf buddies at a party a week or two later, he told her, he'd stashed the agreement in his wallet and never so much as peeked at it until suddenly remembering it the morning of Sal's funeral.

Nate apologized for not showing it to Sophie at that time, but explained that he'd figured it would just upset her and that she'd already gone through enough. Besides, even Sal never really believed—well, Nate didn't think so anyway, although he couldn't say for sure—that a dead person's soul could communicate with people down on Earth.

"Not directly anyway," he said, "you know what I mean?"

Sophie wrinkled her brow, completely mystified by what she'd heard so far. She knew Nate still hadn't fully recovered from Sal's death; could the poor guy be hallucinating?

"So—go on," she said in a calm, but puzzled voice.

At that moment, Nate felt his mouth go dry, just as it had earlier that day as he addressed his tee shot on the third hole at Turtle Creek. He considered excusing himself for a moment to get a glass of water. But no, he decided, it was best to get it all out now and not prolong the anxiety that Sophie undoubtedly was experiencing.

Or was she? He'd been so nervous that he'd given Sophie only a few furtive glances as he told his story—and, to his surprise, she'd remained almost stoic. Did she find it too ridiculous to take seriously, Nate wondered, his mind racing. Had she anticipated what was coming and maybe had gone into shock?

Heck, maybe she was about to keel over, plopping face first on the living room floor. How would he explain that to Tony and other family members—or the media, for that matter?

Nate could hear his stomach gurgling, but proceeded with his story. He explained how he'd waited for the first semi-pleasant spring day to honor The Pact, which happened to be today, April 24. And how, after watching his partners—Doc, Tyler and Luckovich—hit their shots, he stepped onto the tee and struck his own tee shot. And how he watched with disappointment as the ball tailed off to the right—and then, to everyone's disbelief, collided with the branch of a lone oak tree and ricocheted back to the green.

And how, moments later—incredulous as it might sound—Nate marched across the green and found the ball at the bottom of the cup.

Sophie stared at him goggle-eyed and let out a gasp.

"Well ... for heaven's sake," she said. Then she sank back in her chair with a befuddled look on her face and remained silent for a good 10 seconds.

"Sophie—are you OK?" Nate asked worriedly, slowing rising from the sofa.

"Oh honey, of course, don't worry," she replied finally, gesturing for him to sit down.

"Seriously, I'm fine. I was just thinking, well, you know, this could be an actual miracle—you realize that, of course. I mean, how else could you explain it, Nate?

"And if Sal really is up there and has the power to alter my life and your life and ..."

She paused to let the thought sink in, then gazed at Nate and flashed an ear-to-ear grin, her hazel eyes twinkling.

"I mean, I'm going up to Ho-Chunk Casino on Friday. You don't think ..."

4

Five minutes, she had promised him.

"Seriously, I do two or three of these quick-hitters every week," Naomi Winston cooed. "Just a couple of simple questions and you'll be on your way."

But as Nate Zavoral leaned against the towering, now hallowed oak tree to the right of the kidney-shaped third green at Turtle Creek Golf Club, he was getting antsy. He'd already been waiting nearly 10 minutes while the leggy, butter-blond Channel 9 reporter checked her notepad and twice pulled out a tiny mirror from her lavender, faux-leather purse to make sure her eyeliner wasn't smudged. Meanwhile, her sweaty, melon-shaped cameraman was quietly pacing back and forth in front of the tree and peeking back at the fast-sinking sun, trying to figure out the best camera angle on this unusually balmy late-April afternoon.

"Holy Christ," Nate growled as he glanced at his watch. He tried not to notice the foursome of college-age golfers who'd arrived at the green and were ogling the newscaster's gams and, Nate surmised, wondering why she'd be interviewing this nondescript, over-the-hill codger in the middle of a golf course on a Monday afternoon: Were they filming a commercial for erectile dysfunction, perhaps? Or a new ointment for hemorrhoids?

Maybe this interview wasn't such a brilliant idea after all, Nate thought. But in fairness to himself, it was only at the urging of Brigitte— who, in just a matter of hours, had done a complete flip-flop and encouraged him to make the most of this freaky, once-in-a-lifetime accomplishment—that he'd agreed to meet the Channel 9 reporter for an interview shortly after teaching his last class that day at Frank Lloyd Wright High School.

And while it was Nate who'd suggested the interview take place alongside the third green at Turtle Creek Golf Club—might as well let everyone see just how implausible the whole thing was, he reasoned— he'd also made it clear to Ms. Long Legs that it would have to be brief, because he needed to pick up Anna, his 15-year-old daughter, from track practice.

He glanced at his watch again and groaned out loud. It was almost 4:15.

"Uh, Miss Winston," he said irritably, "I really do need to be somewhere ..."

"Gosh, I'm sorry," she replied, sneaking a last glimpse in her mirror and gliding a wide-toothed, black comb through her shoulder-length blond locks. "It's just that the wind keeps messing up my hair."

Nate checked the flag on the third green, which was hanging limply, then turned his gaze to the oak tree and couldn't see a single branch moving. He rolled his eyes and cursed under his breath.

But then, wasn't this just like a TV reporter? he mused. OK, so maybe he was stereotyping and maybe he was biased, but Nate had long felt that TV reporters were a vastly different breed than their print counterparts. Hatched from a different shell, if you will.

Most TV reporters, he'd concluded long ago, were more interested in the glamour aspect of the news business—and getting their toothy-grinned mugs on TV—than they were in the stories they covered. While there certainly were exceptions, particularly at the national level—the esteemed investigative team at "*60 Minutes*" being the most obvious example—Nate still believed it was a hard, cold truth, and one that was based on his own experiences.

Before becoming a high school English teacher, Nate had bounced around for nine years in the newspaper business: first as a sportswriter for a small daily in Bradenton, Fla., followed by a five-year stint as a reporter/night editor at the Madison bureau of *United Press International*—back in *UPI's* hey-day, when it was the *Associated Press's* chief competitor—and concluding with his three reasonably satisfying years as a general assignment reporter for *The Capital Times.*

While he'd certainly encountered his share of prima-donnas in the print media, he realized early on that most print journalists weren't in it primarily for fame but, by and large, to educate and inform the masses, to help stimulate debate about vital public issues, to give voice to the underdogs and to expose injustices. And most print journalists—unlike their well-coiffed TV counterparts—weren't into sensationalism or trying to scare the bejabbers out of their audiences.

In fact, outside of Stacy Scharmach, the fair-skinned, strawberry-blond tease who'd joined *UPI* right out of Princeton and shared a computer with Nate at *UPI's* downtown Madison bureau, Nate couldn't name a single print journalist he'd known who could win a beauty contest.

Where would the country be—hell, the entire planet, for that matter—without the *New York Times* or *The Washington Post*? Nate liked to argue. And there were multitudes of smaller dailies that—even in the age of the Internet—were producing first-rate, compelling journalism and winning Pulitzer prizes.

Which he felt was in sharp contrast to the insipid, vacuous reporting found at most local TV stations throughout the land. But there were exceptions there as well, Nate would tell his staffers on *The Oracle*, the school paper at Frank Lloyd Wright High, and he'd long felt that Channel 9's Naomi Winston was one of them.

Though he didn't know her personally, he felt she not only came across in her interviews as sincere and knowledgeable, but that she usually did her homework and sometimes even asked challenging, insightful questions. If a family's home had just been leveled by a killer tornado and their Golden Retriever had been last seen spinning toward Chicago, she had more sense than to stick a mike under a family member's nose and dizzily inquire, "So tell us, what are you feeling right now?"

Furthermore, Nate realized that his hole-in-one—wildly improbable as it was—wasn't exactly the Normandy invasion. On the other hand, as Brigitte pointed out, the story did have a certain Capraesque appeal to it. So when Naomi Winston had called the night before and proposed doing an interview—after reading about Nate's feat on Doc Flanagan's blog—Nate hesitated only briefly.

And, of course, it didn't hurt—as Brigitte had aptly noted—that she looked like she belonged in a Victoria's Secret catalogue.

"Uh, Mr. Zavoral? I'm ready if you are."

Slightly startled, Nate forced a smile and took a step toward the newscaster, who had the mike poised under her chin and was peering at her cameraman, wholly oblivious to the four young men who were still watching with puzzled expressions as they trudged off the No. 3 green.

Then, before Nate knew it, the words were tumbling out of her ruby red lips: how, more than a decade ago, Nate and his friend, the late Sal Magestro, a local restaurant owner, had concocted this seemingly ludicrous scheme, which would decide once and for all if there is life after death. Whoever died first, she explained, would send a signal from the great beyond to the one left on Earth.

"So after Sal Magestro suffered a fatal heart attack last Christmas, while vacationing with his young girlfriend at his mountainside condominium in Colorado ..."

Nate's feet left the ground, as if somebody had dropped a firecracker in his shorts.

"Whoa, whoa, whoa," he exclaimed, frantically making a timeout signal over his head.

"There's a problem?" Ms. Winston said in a perturbed voice.

"Uh, yeah, a slight problem. Correct me if I'm wrong, Ms. Winston, but this was supposed to be about my hole-in-one, wasn't it? Not an expose on my friend's private life."

He paused briefly after noticing the hurt and surprise in the reporter's eyes, but proceeded anyway.

"I mean, can't we just say—oh, I don't know, that he recently died of a heart attack and leave it at that? Look, I'm an ex-newspaper reporter. I know what's acceptable and what isn't."

Her mouth agape, the young woman was too stunned to reply.

"As for Connie Frataro being Sal's girlfriend," Nate went on, "you apparently know a lot more than I do. Maybe she was, maybe she wasn't.

"But you know what? He was divorced. She's an adult. So as eager as you apparently are to cast aspersions on him, please keep in mind there was nothing the least bit illegal about their relationship.

"Furthermore, you apparently aren't aware that Connie's father, Benito 'The Bull' Frataro, is a former Teamsters' official from Chicago.

41

So I don't mean to be sarcastic, but if you value those pretty kneecaps of yours, I'd suggest that we stick with the hole-in-one angle. I mean, I don't need the grief and I'm sure you don't either."

The reporter turned to her cameraman and, for a fleeting moment, contemplated just stalking off and saying to hell with it. She was insulted and infuriated at the same time.

"Look, Miss Winston, I'm not trying to tell you how to do your job—seriously, I'm not," Nate said, backtracking slightly. "And maybe it's my fault for not asking what angle you were taking. I mean, to my way of thinking, this is just a light-hearted human interest story—and, yes, a rather weird one at that.

"But if you see it as something more sinister, well …"

The young woman pursed her lips and again peered at her sidekick, who was nervously staring back at her and not knowing whether to intervene or not. She wasn't one to lose her composure—or her temper—but she had to battle the urge to let this condescending middle-aged shlump know how much she resented his remarks. And to let him know that she wasn't just another pretty face with a mike in her hand—that she'd been in the business for five years now and had broken her share of big stories. Like her report just a year ago that Brenda McIntosh, the fleet-footed young woman who won the female division of the Mad-City Triathlon two years in a row—setting records both times— had undergone a sex change operation prior to moving to Madison in 2000, and that for the first 24 years of her life she'd gone by Brandon. It's all people were talking about for weeks, and the woman—a nurse at

University of Wisconsin Hospital—hastily left town and was rumored to be living in Key West, Fla.

On the other hand, having attended Frank Lloyd Wright High School a decade earlier, she knew that Nate Zavoral was a respected English teacher and journalism advisor at the school since, well, forever. And that he'd once been a crackerjack reporter for *UPI* and *The Capital Times*.

She also knew he'd raised a valid point. Police had ruled out foul play in the death of Sal Magestro, so there probably wasn't any justification in mentioning that he'd been sharing a hot tub with a 20-year-old waitress from his restaurant—nauseating as that fact may be. And, well, if she was being honest, the absurd circumstances surrounding Nate Zavoral's ace was a better news angle anyway.

So, after a clumsy few moments, Ms. Winston swallowed her pride, flashed an ear-to-ear grin and issued a curt apology to Nate—"for trying to make this sound like something out of *The Sopranos*."

She then quietly inhaled, nodded at her cameraman and lifted the mike toward Nate's chin. And once again the words tumbled out—only this time in a sprightly voice completely void of innuendo.

To Nate's astonishment, she related the entire story—accurately, no less—in about 45 seconds, even pointing out at the end that the hole-in-one was the high school teacher's first in the 44 years he'd been playing golf.

Nate smiled broadly. This was even better than he had hoped, the tension all at once retreating from his neck and shoulder muscles.

43

"So tell us," the reporter continued, shifting her attention to Nate and thrusting the mike to within an inch of his chin, "What's your take on this? Do you truly believe Sal Magestro guided your ball into the hole? And is it possible you've found the answer to the question that humans have been asking since the beginning of time—that there is, in fact, a hereafter?"

Nate cleared his throat and tried to counter with something cool, something profound, but no words would come out. He realized he'd have to answer a question or two, but he assumed they'd be the sort of creampuff questions that local TV reporters live and die by—like, say, whether he and his wife had celebrated after the shot. Or whether his feet had returned to earth yet. He didn't expect to be blindsided by a question that not even Stephen Hawking could answer, even if it was partly in jest.

Nate smiled at the reporter but remained mute for a long moment. He'd been so shocked and caught up in the excitement of his astounding feat that he had yet to ponder the larger questions associated with it—more specifically, the possibility that Sal actually *was* responsible and, as such, had provided bona fide proof that there truly is life after death.

"Well, uh, frankly, I'm not sure what it all means, Miss Winston," Nate said after an eternity, sliding a hand across his chin.

"There are people out there a lot smarter than I am, and I guess I'll let them debate whether this was divine intervention or not. If I'm grateful to anyone, I guess it's to Ernest R. Pettinger. He's the guy who designed this course back in the 1920s, and I'm told this oak tree was part of the original design."

Nate grinned and glanced up at the fading blue sky.

"So if Ernie happens to be watching right now," he said, waving his left fist in the air, "much obliged, my good man. Much obliged."

5

A little before 7:30 the next morning, Nate—still groggy after a restless night—and Brigitte traipsed through the front door of Lefty's Diner, the neighborhood gathering spot, and were instantly reminded of TV's still powerful and widespread impact.

It had been roughly 15 hours since his awkward and surprisingly strained interview with Channel 9's Naomi Winston—which had aired at both 6 and 10 p.m.—and Nate had assumed that, in today's frenetic, speed-of-light Internet world, it was already old news.

No such luck.

"Hey, Hollywood, when's the movie version coming out?" chided Vinny Colavito, the one-armed Vietnam vet who managed the Ace Hardware store that anchored one end of the newly renovated mini-mall and was clutching a mug of coffee while seated at the counter.

"Nice interview, Nate," said Dolores Townsend, a retired middle-school music teacher who, long as Nate could remember, had the most spectacular rose garden in the Willow Grove neighborhood.

"But, my," she added, "I guess I hadn't realized how gray you've gotten."

And, of course, there was no avoiding Louis "Lefty" Kelliher, the ornery but lovable oaf who not only owned and managed the place, but—as the sign in his front window clearly stated—made the "best bleeping pancakes in Dane County."

("Just let me know," Nate liked to grouse, "if you ever learn to make a decent pot of coffee.")

Almost as if on cue, Lefty poked his head out of the kitchen just as Nate and Brigitte were making their way to a corner booth in the L-shaped establishment.

He immediately dropped to one knee and made the sign of the cross as they walked by—evoking a chorus of laughter from the dozen or so regulars who were scattered throughout the diner, a neighborhood staple since the 1980s.

Nate grunted under his breath but said nothing as he quietly slipped into the booth.

But if her husband was embarrassed, Brigitte clearly was relishing the utterly absurd situation they now found themselves in. Just seconds before leaving the house, she'd gotten an e-mail from her brother Denny, a city sanitation worker in *Des Moines, Iowa,* who expressed shock at seeing a blurb about Nate's shot on, of all places, the

Des Moines Register's website that morning, tucked among the Midwest news briefs.

Nate, too, was shocked and more than a bit bewildered when Brigitte informed him that his story had now gone nationwide. Then it hit him. Yes, of course. Somebody at the *Associated Press's* Madison bureau had spotted the item in Doc Flanagan's widely-read Sunday blog—just as Naomi Winston had—and included it in the wire service's state news roundup. At least that's how *UPI* disseminated stories in its hey-day. Then an editor on the AP's national news desk in New York probably noticed it and, since Sundays are slow news days, added it to their national package; and then the *Des Moines Register*—and, in all likelihood, numerous other newspapers, radio and TV stations who subscribe to the AP news service, not to mention the dozens of Internet news "aggregators" that had emerged in recent years—ran the story on its own website because of the peculiar circumstances surrounding the shot.

Welcome to the insatiable 24-hour news cycle, where even trivial stories are transmitted and regurgitated across the country at the speed of light—and the kookier the better.

Nate chortled over the zaniness of it all as a waitress, a former student of his named Lana Hebl, suddenly appeared at their booth to take their orders. He wondered how much longer this ludicrous little tale was going to stay alive.

"The usual, Lana—and coffee, of course," he said, briefly looking up as she scribbled "tofu scrambler" and "oven-roasted potatoes" on her notepad. Brigitte complimented the young woman on her new ultra-short hairdo, then ordered her usual fare as well: two whole wheat pancakes smothered with blueberries, a glass of orange juice and a cup of decaf.

As Nate peeled off his gray hoodie, his wife leaned over the table and grinned.

"I know this will surprise you, honey" she said, "but I'm pretty much over my initial fears. I mean, when you think about how absurd the whole thing is, it's really kind of funny."

Before her husband could reply, she added, "But I also have to admit … it's a little, well, scary, too. Don't you think?"

Nate peered at his wife and scowled half-kiddingly as the waitress returned to fill their cups with coffee. He stayed mum as he poured some cream into his cup and then added two packets of sugar.

"Seriously, Nate," Brigitte continued. "Just between us, do you think it's even remotely possible that Sal had anything to do with your ball ending up in the hole? I just want to know what you're thinking."

"And so does your daughter, by the way," she said. "I don't know if she mentioned it to you, but she told me she was really weirded out after reading Doc's blog. So apparently were a lot of her friends."

Nate groaned quietly and took a sip of his coffee. Then he sat back and rested his right arm on the top of the frayed, brown leather booth. He turned his head and stared out the window at the two mop-haired kids performing skateboard tricks in the mini-mall's parking lot—but his mind was still groping with the chaos of the last few days.

Irritated as he was, Nate wasn't at all surprised by his daughter's reaction. He'd e-mailed their 22-year-old son, Sean, about his mind-blowing golf shot on Sunday—attaching Doc's blog for full effect—and expected a similar response once the message reached him. However, since Sean was a public health educator for the nonprofit Oxfam International and based in a remote village in eastern Mozambique, where Internet service was spotty at best—and making phone contact was even more problematic—that could be today or two weeks from today. Or, depending on the circumstances, he may not receive it at all.

Nate had actually gotten ahold of his son and informed him of Sal's fatal heart attack just hours after getting the news from Tony Magestro back in December. But he was almost certain he'd never told Sean about The Pact. Now he would know everything.

"Frankly, sweetheart, I don't know what to think," Nate said after a half-minute or so. "And, to be honest, I haven't given it much thought. Not yet, anyway. I don't know, maybe—maybe it does scare me a little. I mean, you know me. You know what I think about this God obsession most people have, and my feelings about organized religion in general.

"And I swear if I hear one more person talk about how there's this grand plan for all of us— excluding, apparently, the people who've seen nothing but war in their lifetimes or the billion people on this planet who are malnourished or starving—I'm going to puke."

He paused as the waitress set down their orders, then resumed his line of thought the moment she left.

"I mean, why can't people just accept the fact that we—the lucky ones anyway—have maybe 75 or 80 years down here and then it's over? That it's not a dress rehearsal but a one-shot deal? What's so difficult about that?"

He let out a sigh, then sat up straight and peered into his wife's dancing blue eyes, his hands folded neatly on the table.

"On the other hand, every once in a while …" He stopped in midsentence and laughed.

He took a bite of his tofu and washed it down with some coffee.

"I don't know if I ever even told you this," he said, "but remember that August night a few years back when your grandma in Milwaukee was in so much pain from lung cancer, even with all the morphine they were giving her? Well, I prayed that entire night and pleaded with God—if He or She truly existed—to put an end to her suffering. And remember how we got a call early the next morning that she'd died peacefully in her sleep—at least according to your mother?

"Or how about the time we took Brandy to the vet when she couldn't keep anything down and was diagnosed with a cancerous tumor in her abdomen? Remember that? The kids were just devastated. Well, I prayed then, too—and remember how flabbergasted we were when we took her back to the vet about a month later and the vet couldn't believe it, but somehow the tumor had disappeared?

"Well, I can't explain that stuff either. Which brings up a whole other point: Is praying supposed to work for ailing animals, too? Are those things ever addressed in the Bible? And if the answer's yes, does it just apply to pets? I mean, how about snails, for instance? Or cockroaches? I mean, those are God's creatures, too, aren't they?"

He paused and stuck a fork in his potatoes.

"So I guess that's where I'm at. The logical part of me says my hole-in-one was just a wild coincidence. But the idealistic side of me— the starry-eyed, adolescent side, I guess—says, well, who's to say for sure?"

He glanced up and realized the waitress was patiently waiting for him to complete his thought so she could inquire if their meals were satisfactory.

"And what does your idealistic side say about your tofu scrambler today, Mr. Z?"

"Well, if Lefty wants to know, tell him that for once I can't taste the E. coli," Nate said, drawing faint laughter from an older couple in the next booth.

As the waitress retreated to the kitchen, Nate leaned back and again stretched his right arm along the top of the booth.

"Is that it?" Brigitte inquired.

"Well, yeah, for now anyway," he said. "I really don't feel any different than I did four days ago. I certainly don't feel more spiritual or anything like that.

"But I will tell you this much," he said, staring directly into his wife's eyes again.

"The last I heard Tiger Woods has 19 holes in one, and I believe Jack Nicklaus has something like 14 or 15. And Tyler Briggs has three. And now Nate Zavoral has one of his own.

"Now granted, it wasn't the prettiest hole-in-one ever made. But it's still a hole-in-one. And I don't know if the fact that it struck a tree branch first suggests that Sal Magestro orchestrated the whole thing or if I'm the 'Chosen One' or what. But you know something? I really don't care. Not right now anyway. Not this very moment.

"All I know is that I finally got my ace—and it's probably never going to happen again. And a month from now, everyone around here—except maybe my golf buddies and a few religious freaks—are going to have forgotten it ever happened.

"So I'm going to savor it, baby cakes, while it's still fresh in my mind. I'm going to savor it as long as I possibly can."

She nodded and wiped her mouth with a napkin. She understood perfectly. End of conversation.

Wildly implausible or not, it was an achievement worthy of celebration.

6

By the end of the week, the hoopla had subsided, just as Brigitte had predicted.

The seemingly endless barrage of dinner-interrupting phone calls finally ceased. The stream of annoying e-mails from friends and relatives Nate and his wife hadn't heard from in years slowed to a trickle. And Nate no longer had to endure incessant razzing from his colleagues at Frank Lloyd Wright High.

Even Luckovich stopped inquiring if Nate had heard from St. Salvatore lately—though he persisted in referring to his golf partner as "the great Messiah."

The only ones who couldn't let it go were Nate's students, who remained awestruck by the fact that their teacher had actually been the subject of a TV interview—and all because of some idiotic golf shot. Too bad, they lamented, he'd come off looking so geeky.

"Did it ever occur to you, Mr. Z, to comb your hair before the cameras started rolling?" chided Lisa Hausfeldt, a self-assured sophomore who delighted in taking shots at her teacher's hopelessly outdated wardrobe—especially his "clownish" white bucks.

Josh Greenthal, the junior class's reigning smart-ass, was even more insufferable, insisting the morning after Nate's TV interview that his stumbling responses were a definite indication he'd been high on something—probably meth or heroin, he speculated out loud to his classmates.

"Sorry to disappoint you, Mr. Greenthal," Nate countered after the student's biting remarks evoked raucous laughter from his classmates. "But I was never into the drug scene. And just for the record, my generation preferred pot—or LSD."

Still, if Nate's golf shot was no longer the hot topic in bars, coffee shops and gym locker rooms around town, he couldn't help but notice the peculiar way some people were now behaving in his presence.

At first, he thought he was imagining it. But no, something clearly had changed. It was as if they had developed an odd sort of respect—almost a reverence—for him that most definitely had not existed before.

The first sign of it occurred early Wednesday morning, two days after his encounter with Naomi Winston. Nate had just finished shaving when he heard a knock on his front door, around 6:30. Puzzled and still clad in his pajamas, he stood at his bathroom sink and waited for Brigitte to answer it, then remembered that she'd gotten out of bed shortly after six to work out on the treadmill in their basement rec room.

His mind still a fog—he could barely function till he'd had that first cup of coffee—Nate stumbled toward the front door and, after creaking it open slightly, was surprised to see a tall, plain-faced woman in a knee-length wool coat smiling at him. She was clutching a large, white paper bag and looked faintly familiar.

As he struggled to attach a name to the face, the woman—whose silver SUV was idling in the driveway—apologized for showing up unannounced and at such an early hour, but noted that she'd hoped to catch Nate before he and his family had sat down for breakfast.

She handed him the bag, which she explained was filled with fresh bagels from Ovens of Brittany, the west side's premier bakery-restaurant. Without pausing for a breath, she apologized a second time, then stammered that she needed to talk to him about something that had been bothering her for almost a year: publicly berating Nate for giving her daughter Melanie a failing grade the previous June.

"Melanie?" Nate muttered quizzically. Then it clicked. Of course, how could he forget? The woman standing on his doorstep was the mother of Melanie Swenson, a willowy, scatter-brained former student who, Nate recalled, not only had scored something like a 52 on the multiple choice part of her final exam, but had stated in her essay that it was Benjamin Franklin who'd been forced to resign the presidency in disgrace after the Watergate scandal.

But why would Melanie's mother—was it Becky?—feel the need to apology now? He gawked at her, not knowing what to say.

"Look, Mr. Zavoral, I just wanted you to know I never really considered you a dimwit, or whatever it was I called you," she said. Still confused, Nate assured her that an apology wasn't necessary—especially for something that was said in frustration almost a year ago. (Nate vaguely remembered the woman confronting him in a school hallway shortly before the summer break in 2003. She had a distinctive nasally voice, and Nate later found out she was slightly off-kilter and a Jesus freak to boot.)

Visibly relieved, the woman thanked him for not holding a grudge, then abruptly changed subjects and congratulated him for his "super-miraculous" golf shot. She'd witnessed his TV interview, she excitedly explained, and was fascinated about the so-called pact he'd made with his friend Sal Magestro—promptly adding that, like everyone else, she was still saddened by Mr. Magestro's tragic heart attack.

"He was a good guy," she said. "And just so you know, I never bought all those Mafia rumors—you know, when Mr. Magestro ran for the county board? I mean, we used to go to his restaurant all the time. Still do, in fact—although, frankly, I don't think the pizza's nearly as good now that his brother's running the place."

She paused for an uneasy moment, then laughed nervously. "Next time he contacts you," she said with a half-smile, "please tell him I mentioned that."

Later that day, Nate met Tyler Briggs for coffee at Lefty's Diner, just minutes after his last class. Most days their conversations were light-hearted sparring matches over the burning issues of the day—they were on opposite ends of the political spectrum, Nate being an unabashed liberal and Tyler still worshipping at the altar of Reagan—or about Tyler's tumultuous love life. (Thrice divorced and an incurable romantic, the former coach was currently dating a yoga instructor and, he liked to gripe, had not received so much as a good-night kiss in the four months they'd been together.)

But this particular afternoon Tyler had far more urgent things on his mind. Was Nate aware, he asked as they slid into a booth, that his golf shot had touched off a heated debate on WTDY-AM, the local talk radio show, that morning?

No, he wasn't aware, Nate confessed. The very thought left him dumbfounded.

"They were discussing my golf shot—on talk radio? What am I missing here?" he asked bewilderedly.

"Well, it happened, my friend—they must have had a dozen calls in 10 minutes," Tyler said. "And I'll tell ya, Z, a lot of people—and not just the wackos—refuse to believe this was just a coincidence. Judging from the calls I heard, most people think it's a bit spooky."

Nate snorted and tried not to laugh. Then Tyler reached in his shirt pocket and nonchalantly slapped a $20 bill down next to Nate's mug.

"I know you'll probably think I've flipped," he said. "But as I was cleaning my golf shoes last night, it occurred to me that I'd never paid back the $20 you lent me on our golf trip to Myrtle Beach last fall.

"Remember that night we were bored silly and decided to drive around looking for Vanna White's childhood home? And how I nearly ran out of gas—so you lent me twenty bucks?"

Nate cast his friend a cockeyed look and tried figure out what had inspired this irrational gesture. Then he reached down and slid the bill back across the table.

"Tyler, my good man, how much money do you think I've lent you—oh, let's just say in the last two years? A conservative estimate would be fine."

Slightly offended, Tyler looked at his friend curiously. He was at a loss for words.

"I'd say a couple hundred dollars would be a reasonably accurate figure," Nate said. "And how many times have you offered to pay back any of it?

"That's right zero," Nate said, not waiting for a response. "So why on earth would you offer to pay me back a measly $20 that I gave you on a golf trip just six months ago?"

"Oh, I don't know," Tyler replied sheepishly. "Maybe because my dad, bless his soul, would've said it's the right thing to do? And maybe because it recently occurred to me that he might be watching me 24/7?

"Like I said, man, this whole thing's a little spooky."

Even Nate's boss, Milt Wilcox, the Frank Lloyd Wright High School principal, couldn't stop pondering the potentially disturbing ramifications of Nate's shot—especially after learning of the crazy and eerie pact that Nate had struck with Sal Magestro some five years earlier. And he was downright incredulous after learning that Nate's ball had ricocheted off a tree branch and rolled some 80 feet across the green before banging into the flagstick.

So on Friday morning, four days after Nate's TV interview, the principal had left a note on Nate's desk requesting that he stop by his office for a "casual chat"—a request Nate found baffling in light of the fact that he hadn't had a one-on-one talk with Milt in at least five years. And that one had occurred at Milt's annual winter solstice party—not in his office.

What could this possibly be about? Nate wondered. Was Nate displeased about the front page commentary in *The Oracle* that had taken the boys' track coach, Bernie Ferguson, to task for chastising one of his athletes in front of about 1,000 spectators at a six-school invitational meet a week earlier?

That must be it, Nate figured. Milt always sided with the coaching staff—what else would you expect from a former star forward at Pendleton State College, an all-black school in Mississippi that was a perennial small-college basketball power? And while Nate hardly welcomed the confrontations—at 6-foot-5 and close to 300 pounds, Milt was one intimidating guy—this certainly wouldn't be the first disagreement they'd had since Nate took over as the school's newspaper advisor in the early 1990s. It came with the territory, Nate often rationalized.

"So," Wilcox inquired, unloosening his tie and propping his size 15 wingtips on his shiny mahogany desk after Nate showed up at his office promptly at 3:30 and settled into a straight-back chair directly across from him. "How's Brigitte? And how's that old Austin Healey holding up? Let me guess—it's in the repair shop, right?"

Nate clasped his hands on his lap and responded with a half-smile.

"Brigitte is great, thank you," he said. "And I hate to disappoint you, Milt, but the Austin Healey seems to get better with age—like fine wine. I did put in a new starter last fall, but other than that …"

"And how about your, uh, friend Sal Magestro—heard from him lately?" The principal cackled, peering over his bifocals.

Nate was taken aback but decided to play along with his boss. He sank back in his chair, folding his hands behind his head.

"No Milt, nothing lately," he said. "But, you know, he always used to say that heaven was probably just a giant version of Pebble Beach—you know, where they sometimes hold the U.S. Open? So it could be he's lining up an 18-footer right this moment, under a magnificent blue sky, the waves crashing again the rocks, angels fluttering around him …"

"So you—you do think he's up there!" the principal exclaimed. "I mean, you don't buy this b.s. that your ace was a coincidence, is that what you're sayin'?"

Nate stared at his boss for a long moment and sighed.

"I was kidding, Milt. It was a stab at humor—a very weak stab, I guess."

The principal forced a smile as he shifted uneasily in his chair.

"Yeah, OK. But you have to admit, this *is* pretty wild stuff," he noted, trying his best not to sound like one of those religious yahoos who'd been dominating the debate about Nate's shot on local talk radio. "Now, if you'll excuse my boldness, do you think there's any chance—any chance at all—that you've stumbled onto something extraordinary here? You know, like that TV bimbo insinuated the other night—that maybe Sal Magestro *did* somehow guide your ball into the hole? And that maybe—maybe our loved ones who pass away *do* possess some control over our lives, just as people have presumed for ages?"

Nate's mouth dropped, and he was momentarily tongue-tied. He had trouble believing that one preposterous golf shot could have this kind of effect on so many people—and not just the dimwits.

Milt Wilcox had graduated near the top of his class at Pendleton State College. He'd served briefly on President Clinton's educational task force in the mid-1990s. He'd sat on numerous boards and state education committees and had penned a highly praised teaching primer. And now here he was, squirming nervously in his chair in his office and openly speculating—and obviously distressed by—the possibility that Nate's ace was, in fact, proof that there was such a thing as a hereafter.

Nate wasn't just astounded but slightly shaken by the mushrooming impact his golf shot was having.

"Look, the reason I ask," Wilcox said, wiping his brow with a handkerchief he'd pulled from his coat pocket, "is because, well, Evelyn's been dead going on five years now. And as you may have heard, I'm dating her best friend, Gloria Sherrod. I mean, half the school seems to be aware of it, so I'm sure you are, too."

He dropped back in his chair, turned his head and peered out his second-floor window. He clearly was straining to put his feelings in the proper context.

"OK, to be perfectly blunt," the principal said with a wide smile, "it scares the bejabbers out of me to think that Evelyn—my beloved Evelyn—might actually be watching me and Gloria, you know what I'm sayin'?

"I mean, you remember Gloria, right? An absolute knockout, if I do say so. Former dancer. Now runs marathons. Seriously Nate, this is one fine lady.

"And how do you think"—Milt shuddered at the thought—"how do you think Evelyn would react if she saw Gloria and me messin' around in the same bed that she and I shared for 17 years? I mean, Jesus Christ, Nate, just the thought of it … "

———

Slightly puzzled and more than a bit dismayed, Nate scanned the entire classroom for a student who might have the answer, but didn't spot a single hand in the air.

"Nobody?" he asked disappointedly. "Not one person in this room thinks the media went a little overboard? You all think the nonstop coverage for almost an entire week—you think it was justified?"

It was a little after 10 the following Monday and, as always, Nate was wading among his students, challenging them on the topic of the day, toying with their impressionable young minds and trying to provoke a rational but impassioned discussion. On this day he was failing, even though the topic—the media's fixation with Janet Jackson's so-called 'wardrobe malfunction' and the exposing of her left breast during the halftime show of the 2004 Super Bowl game just three months earlier—was still evoking harsh criticism from old-school journalists who felt the media's unrelenting coverage epitomized how just shallow and debased our celebrity-obsessed society had become.

He was so engrossed that he'd failed to notice the school secretary, Marge Mahoney, waving at him in the doorway.

"I'm terribly sorry for the interruption, Mr. Z," she said, after finally gaining his attention. "But you have a phone call from a Mr. Steinberg in Burbank, Calif. And he says it's rather urgent."

A Mr.Steinberg? In Burbank, Calif.? Nate knew of no such person—not that he could recall anyway.

He ordered his students to delve into their next day's assignment—"Remember, your final's in just three weeks," he reminded them—and left the room to take the call.

"Mr. Steinberg?" he mumbled to himself as he followed the secretary down the hall to Milt Wilcox's office. An irate parent, perhaps?

He wondered. That was always a possibility, of course. But why would the parent be calling from California? Or maybe it was just some slick telemarketer who had the audacity to contact him at work.

As Nate ambled into the principal's office, the secretary gestured toward the principal's small corner office and suggested he take the call there.

"Milt had an eye appointment this morning," she said.

Nate thanked her, then stepped into the darkened room, flipped on the light switch and plopped into his boss's king-size black vinyl swivel chair. He picked up the phone and pressed the flashing red button. He identified himself and then listened curiously as a man with a rich, baritone voice explained why he was calling—and why it was urgent.

"First, let me apologize for interrupting your class, Mr. Zavoral," the man said. "My wife teaches seventh-grade at a charter school in Santa Monica. So I'm well aware of how precious your time is.

"Anyway," he continued, "my name is Michael Steinberg, and I'm executive vice president of programming for *The Tonight Show* with Jay Leno. I take it you're familiar with the show?"

Nate's mind momentarily went blank. Then he chuckled.

Luckovich. Had to be. It didn't sound like Luckovich, but who else would even contemplate such a stunt?

Heck, it was just two years ago, Nate remembered, that Luckovich was so appalled upon hearing that Sal had spent nearly $300 for a pair of handcrafted golf shoes made in Sicily that he nailed them to the ceiling in the Turtle Creek men's locker room while Sal was taking a

65

shower. When Sal finally discovered them, he was so incensed that he retaliated by hiring a flabby, middle-aged hooker to crash a birthday party Luckovich's wife had thrown for him a week later.

"Jay Leno?" Nate replied in a voice laced with sarcasm. "You mean that second-rate, fat-assed hippo who couldn't hold Johnny Carson's jockstrap? Of course, I know who Jay Leno is. Where would the world's 200 million insomniacs be without him?"

He smiled smugly and waited for the response, but there was only silence.

"Hey, nice try, Luckovich," Nate said. "And I'm glad to hear things are so good in the plumbing world that you've got time to play practical jokes on a Monday morning. But I really do need to get back to my class. Exams start in three weeks, and I've got tons of stuff to review with my students, OK?"

After another long silence, the voice on the other end broke into laughter.

"Look, Mr. Zavoral," the man said. "I don't know who this ... Luckovich character is. But I can assure you this is no joke. And I can assure you that what we had in mind won't disrupt your job in any way—at least it shouldn't. We were just hoping you could fly out to Burbank so you could appear on our show Friday night. Assuming, of course, that you don't already have plans.

"I realize that's short notice. But Mr. Leno happened to hear about your rather strange hole-in-one—actually, one of our staffers read about it on some Internet site—and, well, he's not just amused but rather curious about the whole thing. So he decided we should try to get you on the show as soon possible to chat about it. He thinks it would be great fun ... and who knows what this could lead to, Mr. Zavoral. I mean, 4.4 million people tune into Mr. Leno's show every night."

Nate exhaled and laughed out loud.

"You're a *real* piece of work, Luckovich," he said stridently. "And I love the setup—did you write this all down before you called? Anyway, great prank. You had me going there for a second or two. But seriously, I really need to get back ..."

"Mr. Zavoral," the man interrupted. "I've been associated with Mr. Leno's show for almost seven years now, so believe me, I'm used to this kind of reaction. It's not often that your average Joe Shmoe gets invited to appear on *The Tonight Show.*

"So I'll tell you what. Your secretary was kind enough to give me your school's fax number. I'll send you an invitation on our official stationary—including all the information on where you'd be staying, the time of the show, the types of questions Mr. Leno will probably be asking you and so on.

"And after you look it over, you can just call me back later today and let me know if you're interested. Does that work?"

The voice sounded believable, and Nate suddenly felt confused.

"Uh, yeah, that would work," he said with growing uncertainty.

"And keep in mind," the man added, "there's absolutely no pressure here. I mean, most people would die for an opportunity like this, but we do occasionally run into people who shun the spotlight and turn us down, and that's fine with us.

"Also, I don't want to mislead you. While we do plan to fly you and your significant other out here for the entire weekend, there's always a chance you may not actually appear on the show. Every so often, our guests do get bumped when we run out of time.

"Oh, and just for the record Mr. Leno has lost about 20 pounds since New Year's day, so I'm not sure the fat-ass label applies—not that it ever did. In any event, have a wonderful day. And I really do look forward to meeting you."

Nate sat flummoxed as the line went dead.

The Tonight Show? Jay Leno? Nah, can't be. No way, he thought. Would Jay Leno really want to interview some obscure high school English teacher from Madison, Wis., who happened to get some ridiculous hole-in-one? Even if there was an outside chance—an infinitesimal chance—that it meant ...

No, the very thought was absurd.

"Had to be Luckovich," Nate groaned under his breath as he briskly shuffled through the outer office—totally ignoring Marge Mahoney and another female staffer, both of whom were anxiously waiting for some sort of explanation—and headed straight down the hall to his classroom.

"Who else could be that smooth, that conniving, that ... deranged?" he said.

Then he halted in mid-step.

Hadn't Luckovich left town two days earlier for a Caribbean cruise with his wife, Lillian? Nate was almost certain of that. He remembered Luckovich mentioning that the cruise ship was stopping at Barbados and two other islands—all of which had casinos. It's the only way Lillian could convince him to go.

Was it possible, Nate thought, to call Madison from a cell phone in the middle of the Caribbean? Not likely, he surmised.

But if it wasn't Luckovich, then who? Nate felt slightly disoriented and stopped in the hallway to take a deep breath. This is getting goofier by the moment, he told himself.

He took another deep breath, then slowly turned around and tramped briskly down the hall to the principal's office.

He scurried through the door just as the fax machine was spitting out a two-page memo from Michael Steinberg—a memo that had been printed on official *The Tonight Show* stationary.

Naturally, Marge Mahoney had absorbed every word by the time Nate got to the machine.

"Oh, my God, Mr. Z!" she shrieked. "You're going to be famous!"

7

"Go, get out there! You're on!" an associate producer shouted at Nate from the dark corridor just behind him. Nate felt a gentle shove on his upper back, then stumbled through the yellow silk curtain and onto the brightly-lit stage, his wife trailing close behind him.

He hadn't even heard the introduction, and as he reached back to grab Brigitte's hand—as much for moral support as anything else—a part of him wanted to bolt for the nearest exit and lose himself on the streets of Burbank. But there was no time for second-guessing now.

Nearly blinded by the klieg lights, he and Brigitte nervously turned to the right, just as they'd been instructed to do by Darcy Shaw, an NBC staffer, and clumsily made their way across *The Tonight Show* stage amid deafening applause.

Seconds earlier, as he and Brigitte waited in the shadows for this queer, surreal moment, Nate feared for a moment that he was actually going to throw up. But the moment passed, and he was now on too much of an adrenalin-high to be sick.

Thankfully, after just a few unsteady steps, he spotted the lantern-jawed host, who was beaming as he strutted toward Nate and Brigitte in a snappy blue suit and gray tie, then enthusiastically extended his right hand. He seemed smaller in person than he did on TV—smaller and beefier, despite Steinberg's claim that he had shed 20 pounds in recent months.

Nate shook the host's hand firmly, then stepped aside as Leno warmly embraced Brigitte—who, Nate thought, looked radiant in a form-fitting white lace dress that stopped just above her tanned, muscular calves—and whispered something in her ear that caused her to blush. He then ushered them to the familiar-looking camel-suede chair and sofa where thousands of celebrities and other assorted guests had bantered with the popular NBC host over nearly two decades.

The celebrity guest on this night was the rock musician Sting, who sprung to his feet as Brigitte approached and, in one fluid motion, leaned over, pulled her right hand toward his lips and gently kissed the top of it before sliding over and making room for her on the sofa. Nate, meanwhile, deposited himself in the chair just to the right of Leno's desk, as directed during a brief pre-show meeting with Marty Hankwitz, the show's producer.

To Nate's surprise, the crowd was still hooting and applauding wildly, leading Nate to wonder just what Leno had said in his introduction.

When the applause finally died down, the host didn't waste any time.

"So, Mr. Zavoral, let me see if I got this right," he said, glancing down at his notes.

"Back in 1999, you and your friend Sal Magestro—the late Sal Magestro, I should say—came up with this scheme to prove, once and for all, that life doesn't end when we die, that there really is such a thing as a hereafter. Is that correct?"

He looked up and winked at the camera, then flashed a grin at Nate and his wife, both of whom were smiling uneasily as they gazed out at the audience, which was hidden behind a sea of brilliant, grapefruit-size lights hanging over the stage.

Nate merely nodded, not sure if the host wanted a more definitive response or not.

"So then—oops, I guess I'm supposed to hold this up," Leno said, pausing to lift the now faded document known as The Pact, which Nate had given him during their brief pre-show meeting two hours earlier. He dangled it in front of his face for several seconds as the camera zoomed in for a close-up.

"What this is, ladies and gentlemen—well, it's basically just a two-paragraph statement that Mr. Zavoral and his friend Mr. Magestro typed up during a fishing trip to Big Pike Lake in Wisconsin in 1999."

He wrinkled his brow in befuddlement. "Wow—you were actually still using a typewriter in 1999?"

72

"Well," Nate said haltingly, realizing that all eyes were now focused on him, "it belongs to an old colleague—the guy who let us use the cabin. He's actually a journalist, but he's a technophobe—much like me—and believes computers should be banned from the north woods."

"Sounds like my kind of guy," the host said, nodding approvingly. "Just as long as they don't ban BlackBerrys up there, I think I'd do fine."

"Anyway, the agreement says—well, why don't you explain it?" Leno said, turning toward Nate and passing him the small, slightly frayed piece of paper.

The request caught Nate off-guard. He smiled at the host but his mind was still a haze and he again felt on the verge of panic. He'd been hoping that Leno would provide all the pertinent details and that he would merely respond—in as few words as possible—to any questions the host might have.

He struggled to compose himself and glanced at Brigitte, who was smiling back at him but whose eyes had tears welling in the corners, a sure sign that she was struggling to hold it together. Nate then noticed that her left leg was trembling, as it often did whenever their daughter Anna, a gymnast, performed on the 4-inch wide balance beam for her high school team.

And again, Nate tried to envision John Kennedy, his childhood hero, and how the steely-nerved 35th president would've handled this situation. And, as always, it had an immediate calming effect.

73

As Leno looked on with an impish grin, Nate leaned forward in his chair and provided a brief synopsis of how it had all happened. He noted that he'd been an agnostic since his teen years and that Sal Magestro was a devout Catholic who—unlike Nate, who'd also been raised Catholic—not only never questioned the church's teachings but could quote specific passages from the Bible.

"Not that there's anything wrong with that," Nate asserted, having heard several guffaws in the audience when he mentioned being an agnostic. "I guess you could say he drank the Kool-Aid, as the saying goes, and I didn't. I don't know how else to put it."

Leno offered a plastic half-smile, not about to become embroiled in what he well knew was a volatile issue where there was no middle ground.

After an awkward second or two, Nate continued, noting that, from the time he and Sal were teenagers, they argued incessantly about whether there really was a God—or, for that matter, whether a dead person's soul ended up in heaven or hell.

"Assuming," Nate promptly added, "that those places actually exist."

That comment triggered a murmur in the audience, and Leno—amused—jumped right in.

"Well—and let's be honest here. Most religious people get annoyed when someone suggests that things like heaven and hell and guardian angels are just fables that have been passed down through the ages and have no basis in fact. It makes them uncomfortable."

He thought about that for an instant, then backpedaled slightly.

"Actually, people love to talk about what heaven will be like—because, of course, that's where *they're* going to end up. It's that other place they don't like talking about."

The audience roared—greatly reducing the anxiety Nate was experiencing.

Suddenly imbued with confidence, Nate went on to explain how, on a sultry summer night in 1999, he and Sal had yet another contentious argument about the meaning of life; and how that argument inspired The Pact. Which,they agreed in their inebriated state, would decide the matter once and for all.

"We decided—well, it was Sal's idea—that whoever died first would send a signal to the one still alive," he said.

After typing up the two documents, Nate said—one for each of them—he stuffed his own copy in his wallet and had pretty much forgotten about it until Sal died unexpectedly last December, the day after Christmas.

"Of a heart attack, right?" the host interrupted.

"Right," Nate replied tersely, hoping to leave it at that.

And Leno was content with the one-word response, fully aware that Nate had worked out an agreement with Marty Hankwitz beforehand not to explore the circumstances surrounding Sal's death—Hankwitz having rationalized that since there'd been no hint of foul play, there really was no need to delve into Sal's relationship with a 20-year-old waitress. This was, after all, *The Tonight Show,* Hankwitz reasoned, not *Jerry Springer.*

"OK, let's talk about the signal—this is my favorite part," the host chortled. "The way I heard it, you're both lousy golfers. So you agreed that if the one still alive got a hole-in-one the first time he stepped on a course after the other guy's death, the odds were pretty good that the deceased—in this case, Sal—guided the ball into the hole. Does that sum it up, more or less?"

"It does," Nate replied somewhat bashfully.

And, of course, that's exactly what happened, Nate noted. On Saturday, April 24, he got a hole-in-one on the third hole at Turtle Creek Golf Club in Madison—a feat that was witnessed by three other men in his group.

"But it's not just that the ball ended up in the hole that people find so shocking," Nate acknowledged. "It's that the ball first struck a tree branch and then rebounded across the green—probably 80 feet or so—before rolling in the cup."

There were several loud gasps in the audience, followed by scattered bursts of laughter. Leno was laughing too, as were most members of *The Tonight Show* band, including its laid-back director, Kevin Eubanks.

"A tree branch, Uh-huh," Leno said, rolling his eyes. "And where was this—this tree?"

"Oh, maybe 10 feet to the right of the green," Nate said, relieved that Leno and the audience seemed enthralled by the story, just as so many others had.

The host raised his brow in mock astonishment—and again the audience exploded with laughter.

"So let's see" Leno continued, peeking down at his notes. "Your golf partners, the way I understand it, are convinced your buddy Sal was perched on a cloud somewhere, watching this whole thing unfold—probably munching on a slice of pepperoni pizza—then floated down, intercepted the ball after it banged off the tree and somehow maneuvered it into the cup. Thus proving that he was right all along and you were wrong. Which could mean, I suppose, that *you're* going to end up in that other place."

Again, the audience burst into laughter, lifting Nate's spirits. But he waited until it was relatively quiet before responding, eager to make clear that he personally felt it probably was just a fluke—that he just couldn't accept that Sal was responsible for what had happened. It was too absurd to even contemplate.

Before he could express his true feelings, however, Leno took command again.

"Now, regular viewers of this show know that we rarely invite our guest's spouses to appear on stage with them," he said, shooting a fast glance at Brigitte. "But I made an exception tonight, because I just had to ask Brigitte Zavoral what she thought when her husband called her from the clubhouse that day and claimed he'd gotten a hole-in-one—

just like Sal Magestro had prophesized. I mean, I'm guessing you figured he was pulling your chain, right?"

Nate turned to look at his wife and for a brief moment feared she was going to have a stroke—or, only slightly less worrisome, that her mouth would open but no words would come out.

To his surprise, however, she replied almost impulsively.

"Oh yeah, for sure—I just assumed he was teasing," she said anxiously. "And to be honest, there are times even now when I think if he's going to come home one day and say, 'Honey, guess what? It was all a joke.' At which point"—she glanced at her husband and laughed—"I'll probably reach for a butcher knife."

Tickled with the response, Leno beamed at Brigitte, then turned toward the camera and broke for a commercial.

"Hey, you're doing terrific," he muttered to the couple while exuberantly patting Nate on the shoulder. "We've still got about five minutes left, so keep your responses as brief as possible."

Amazed at how relaxed he felt, Nate shot a darting glance at Brigitte and realized she was counting the seconds until this truly mortifying experience was over.

"Did you want to say anything else?" he whispered to her, gingerly placing a hand on her trembling left leg. She smiled and shook her head while reaching down for a drink of water.

"OK, in case you just joined us," Leno announced suddenly, his head jerking up just as the camera zoomed in again. "We're here with Nate Zavoral, a high school English teacher and admitted duffer whose recent hole-in-one at a golf course in Madison, Wis., may have proven once and for all that there is life after death. Or so some people say."

Twisting toward Nate, he continued, "Now, in all seriousness, what is your own slant on this whole thing? All kidding aside. should I be concerned that, say, my beloved Aunt Agnes is up there somewhere, knitting away, and is aware of all the awful things I've done since she passed on?

"And does this mean when I get up there—assuming I *do* get up there—she'll be waiting for me with a billy club? Or maybe an ax? I mean, c'mon, we've all done things we aren't proud of. So the implications of this thing are pretty serious."

Nate was eager to respond to the myriad of questions the host had posed. But as soon as the audience's laughter ebbed, Leno—realizing he was on a roll—took command again.

"Now, somebody back stage, one of our researchers, told me that Harry Houdini, the famous escape artist—who, by the way, was also from Wisconsin—had a similar agreement with his wife Beatrice, back in the 1920s."

Leno asked Nate if he'd heard of their agreement, and Nate admitted he hadn't.

Leno explained that shortly before he died, Houdini had promised to send Beatrice a message from the great unknown. "But apparently 10 years after holding séances every year on the date of his death—which, by the way, was Halloween—she finally gave up and concluded it was all a bunch of hooey."

79

Nate, who was staring straight ahead intently and absorbing every word, clearly was intrigued. Then he slowly turned his head and realized the host was waiting for a response.

"Interesting," Nate said after a slight hesitation. "Maybe she should have held the séances on a golf course."

Leno chuckled and nodded appreciatively.

"Now you realize, of course, you've probably started a trend here," the host suggested. "I'm guessing that once people hear about your story, they're going to come up with similar agreements with their spouses or a favorite family member—and then we'll have thousands of people arguing about whether they actually made a connection or not.

"But hey, what do you care, right?" Leno said with a shrug. "You'll always be remembered as the first to accomplish this. I mean, we all know that Edmund Hillary was the first guy to scale Mount Everest. Nobody ever remembers the rum-dums that followed."

Again, the audience erupted in laughter.

"Look, we're running out of time," the host said, turning back to Nate, "but I've got one last question. Do people treat you differently now? Do they look at you kind of strangely, as if you possess some sort of super-natural power? Because some people *do* get freaked out by these sorts of things.

"I mean, it reminds me a little of *"Field of Dreams"*—or *"The Shining."*

Again, Nate waited for the laughter to subside before answering. He wanted to say something clever, something insightful, but the truth was he was still skeptical about Sal's involvement and had yet to sort it all out. And he certainly didn't want to deceive anyone.

"To be honest, Jay," he said after a short lull, "some people do look at me differently, and it is somewhat unsettling. I don't know if it will last, or what to tell those people.

"But do I believe my hole-in-one was an actual signal from my friend Sal Magestro? The common sense part of me says, 'C'mon, you've got to be kidding.' But when you think of the odds of something like this happening … it does make you wonder."

Leno grinned and flashed a bug-eyed look at the camera.

"Uh, I'd say more than wonder. Frankly, it makes me sweat a little."

He cast a look at Kevin Eubanks, who was visibly enthralled by the story and had been chuckling quietly from the moment the interview started.

"Does it make you sweat a little, Kevin?" Leno asked.

"Oh yeah, it definitely makes me sweat a little," Eubanks said with a wide grin.

"On that note," Leno said, shifting back to the camera, "I want to thank tonight's guests for being here—rock musician Sting, economist Garrett Ambrose, whose book, *The Impending Housing Meltdown,* will be in book stores next week, and the great Messiah, Nate Zavoral, and his wife Brigitte, from Madison, Wisconsin.

"On Monday night," he said with an exaggerated wink, "our guests will include Clarence, the guardian angel from the Christmas classic, *It's a Wonderful Life* ...

The audience howled, and the Zavorals did as well.

Much to Nate's surprise, he'd somehow pulled off his appearance on national TV.

It was his second electrifying, mind-numbing thrill in three weeks. But he couldn't wait to return home and be just an ordinary schmuck again.

8

"Welcome back the Great Messiah—and Mom!" proclaimed the red and white banner that stretched across the top of the Zavorals' garage.

Though emotionally drained and still somewhat miffed over an unexpected six-hour layover in Denver, Nate couldn't help but laugh when he observed the banner as he and Brigitte pulled into the driveway in their gray Saturn Ion.

It was almost 8 o'clock on an unusually warm and humid spring night, and as he paused to admire his daughter's handiwork, it dawned on him how rewarding it was to be back in civilized Madison, Wis. And what an enormous relief it would be to kick back with a glass of red wine on the sun porch of their modest three-bedroom ranch home with its leaky roof and crumbling front sidewalk but which Nate concluded long ago fit like a comfortable old shoe.

As he and Brigitte climbed out of the car, their daughter came bounding out the front door and greeted them both with affectionate hugs—the kind of hugs one doesn't normally expect from a detached 15-year-old high school freshman who—like teenagers everywhere—spent a large chunk of her waking hours on either her lap-top or her cell phone.

"How'd you like the poster?" she asked proudly. Then, in the next breath, "Oh my God, am I happy to see you guys!"

Nate and Brigitte cast apprehensive looks at one another. This was, after all, the same daughter who'd all but performed cartwheels down the hall when she'd learned that her parents would be spending four days in southern California. Had she hosted a drinking party in their absence, perhaps, and was now feeling contrite?

As they braced for what awaited them, Anna hurriedly led them through the front door and into the living room, then pointed to two large stacks of mail bound by rubber bands on the sofa.

"Both of those arrived today," she said. "And dad, most of it's addressed to you."

"And when I got home from school today," she continued breathlessly, "there were about a dozen messages on the answering machine. And wait till you hear some of them—they are soooo cuckoo."

"There was even one from a guy claiming to be Sal Magestro. He said something about how incredible you were on the Jay Leno show and that heaven's even nicer than he thought it would be.

"I think it was your friend Luckovich."

Nate dropped his suitcase on the floor and grimaced. "I can guarantee you it was Luckovich."

But he was deeply perplexed. A dozen phone messages? The Zavorals had an unlisted phone number. And the two stacks of letters didn't make sense either. How did people discover their address?

Even more perplexing, their appearance on *The Tonight Show* was Friday night. This was Monday evening—just three days later.

Nate ran a hand through his hair. He was truly confused and didn't like the implications.

"By the way, dad," Anna said, "you really *were* awesome on the Leno show. You too, mom. I watched it at Tina's, with her parents."

Nate didn't acknowledge the compliment. His mind was swirling. He walked warily to the sofa, reached down and slipped the rubber band off the first stack of mail. He tossed aside the pieces of junk mail, then sifted through the 20 or so letters, trying to determine if he recognized any of the return addresses—the few that had them anyway.

Brigitte, meanwhile, strolled into the kitchen, lifted the receiver from the wall phone and listened to the messages on the answering machine. She laughed upon hearing Luckovich's daffy remarks, but grimaced at some of the others.

"Ouch," she moaned several times. She retrieved a pen and a sheet of paper from a drawer and began jotting down notes. After about five minutes, she hung up the receiver and marched back into the living room.

"OK, are you ready?" she asked.

"I can hardly wait," her husband moaned, having already skimmed the contents of two letters from religious kooks—one condemning his interview on *The Tonight Show* the other applauding it.

There was a sweet message from Dolores Townsend, Brigitte reported. "She said we both looked fantastic and mentioned how cool it was to have a celebrity living on the same block.

"I think she means you."

There was the message from Luckovich and two from staffers at Frank Lloyd Wright High School—Andy Mertz and Jake McCormick—both of whom had equally positive things to say, Brigitte noted.

Marcus Taylor, Nate's old college roommate, had called from Nashville.

"You'll have to listen to his message—it's pretty funny.

"And Milt Wilcox inquired if you're returning to work tomorrow. He said something about how you owed him big-time for giving you two days off this late in the semester. And he reminded you that exams start on May 24.

"As for the others ..." Brigitte drew in a breath and shook her head. "Whoa!"

"One guy—I didn't recognize the voice—said your story was blasphemous and said he hopes you rot in hell." And the sooner the better, she added.

"Kind of scary, Nate. The guy sounded demented."

She checked her notes again. "What else, let's see. There was a woman claiming to be a psychic who said she had some sort of business proposition for you. And a local Baptist minister who wondered if you'd be interested in speaking at his church this Sunday. Gee, your ultimate dream, Nate.

"And I'm sure this won't surprise you," she said, peering down at her scribbling. "The TV critic for the *Milwaukee Journal-Sentinel* wants to do a phone interview on what it was like to be on *The Tonight Show*.

Nate stared glumly at the table. Nobody had to tell him what he'd gotten himself into. He was a former newspaper reporter, for cripes sake, and his school's journalism advisor. He had agreed to appear on *The Tonight Show* against his better judgment. And now he was suffering the consequences and about to pulverized by a merciless, unrelenting media blitzkrieg—his pact with Sal Magestro and his implausible hole-in-one being dissected and ridiculed by countless talking heads, bloggers and noxious cable TV pundits. The floodgates had been opened, and who knew what the future might bring?

"Is that it?" Nate asked hesitantly.

"Actually, there's one more—I saved the best for last," Brigitte said in a tone that suggested she was both amused and appalled. "You'll be thrilled to know that Susie McCall—who now goes by Susie McCall Hutchinson and lives in Milwaukee—also left a message. She said you looked amazing—gee, how about that?—and wanted to know if you'd like to get together for coffee the next time you're in town. Ooh, la, la!

"And, interestingly, she didn't even mention me."

Nate grunted and rolled his eyes.

"Who's Susie McCall Hutchinson?" asked Anna, who was stretching her hamstrings on an arm of the sofa.

"An old friend," Nate said, flashing a pleading look at his wife to please leave it at that. But Brigitte wasn't about to let this pass.

"A very cute blond your dad took to homecoming in his senior year," she said. "At least, she was cute 30 years ago. I believe she was captain of the cheerleading squad, isn't that right, Nathan?"

Nate tried not to overreact, but he was exasperated—not just about Susie McCall, but by all the other calls and the two stacks of mail. He didn't even want to think about how many e-mails were awaiting him on his laptop.

"So, where do we go from here, Nate?" Brigitte asked despondently. "I mean, what if this is just the beginning? "

Nate peered out the living room window. His spirits were sagging. He felt overwhelmed, deflated.

"Then we're in for an exciting couple weeks, I guess," he said.

He stretched his left arm over the sofa and pulled the cord on the blinds and closed them half-way, so that the neighbors couldn't see in. "Dad, what are you doing?" Anna said with a laugh. "People will know you're home—your car's in the driveway."

Brigitte's spirits were sagging now, too. She felt guilty. After all, she was the one who'd persuaded Nate to do the TV interview with Channel 9's Naomi Winston, which had ignited the growing firestorm.

She was the one who convinced him to accept the invitation to appear on *The Tonight Show,* rationalizing that they'd have some laughs, dine at some chic restaurants, check out some celebrity mansions along Malibu Beach and then return home to their unremarkable but generally pleasurable lives.

Now her husband was under siege and seriously stressed. He didn't come right out and admit it, but Brigitte could tell he regretted telling anyone but his immediate family and his close circle of friends about his hole-in-one. She knew how much he valued his privacy, and now—thanks in no small part to her—he was in danger of losing the thing he treasured above all else. At least for the next few weeks.

"Tell you what," Nate said, heading toward the front door. "I'm going to take a little walk. I need some fresh air and to figure a few things out."

As his wife and daughter flashed worried looks at one another, Nate shoved open the door and, without another word, proceeded down the driveway. He was so preoccupied that he nearly bumped into Anna's boyfriend, Carlos, who was headed in the opposite direction and seemed surprised that Nate had already returned home.

"Uh, welcome back, Mr. Z," Carlos said. "How was Los Angeles?"

"Los Angeles was … Los Angeles," Nate replied tersely, barely pausing to acknowledge the young man as they passed each other in the driveway.

A second or two later, the youth came to a halt and spun around.

"Oh, Mr. Z—I saw you on *The Tonight Show*" he blurted out. "My whole family did. You were awesome!"

"My dad said you'll probably write a book about your golf shot and make millions of dollars."

Nate glanced back and frowned without breaking stride.

"Tell your dad," he shouted as he turned and headed up the sidewalk, "he should audition at The Comedy Club!"

9

Tyler Briggs was never one to disguise his feelings or pull punches. If you sought his opinion, he gave it to you straight up. It was the one thing above all else Nate respected about him.

"Sorry, Nate, but I just don't get it," the former art teacher-turned-wood sculptor said while refining his latest masterpiece—a life-size replica of an adult harp seal—in the small workshop attached to the back of his home, just two blocks from where Nate and his family resided.

He stepped back to study the piece, which he'd carved out of a substantial slab of myrtle wood that he'd hauled back from the northern California coast in his pickup truck last fall.

"Could you grab me that chisel just behind you?" he asked, gesturing at the long, rectangular tool bench directly behind Nate. "The small one with the black handle."

Nate obliged then leaned back against a thick wooden beam. He took a sip of the red wine he'd poured himself from an open bottle next to Tyler's tool box the moment he rambled through the side door, which Tyler had kept open, hoping to catch an occasional breeze.

"I mean, seriously, what do you have against making a little extra dough?" Tyler asked, his eyes focused squarely on his artwork. "This life after death stuff is a hot subject, my friend. Especially with us Boomer types. Why do you think the Leno folks were so elated to have you on? People eat this stuff up. Even skeptics like you and me.

"And much as I hate to admit this, I thought you did quite well. You didn't even seem that nervous—although I did notice Brigitte's leg trembling at one point. But all in all, not bad, my friend. Not bad at all."

He dug the chisel into the large block of wood, chipping off several small pieces, then stepped back again and tilted his head to examine it from a different angle. Pleased, he resumed his conversation without so much as a glance at his former teaching colleague and longtime chum.

"So I say, seize the moment. Set up some more interviews. Write a book. Become a spiritual consultant. Make some serious dough. I know you're not the promotional type, but c'mon, this isn't that difficult a decision—not in my mind, anyway."

Nate merely smiled and took another sip of wine. He knew that if Tyler were in his position he'd do exactly that—temporarily put his life on hold to pursue the potential riches that might await him if he played his cards right. Then again, Tyler was a natural born showman: he'd craved the spotlight during his 14 years as boys basketball coach at Frank Lloyd Wright High School, especially in 1995 when his team was runner-up in the state high school Class A tournament—losing in the final seconds to Milwaukee Lincoln—and he was voted Class A coach of the year by the Wisconsin AP Sportswriters Association.

Tyler paused and laid down his chisel. He peeled off his gloves and set them on the table. Then he lifted his own glass of wine off the shelf just behind him, took a sip and gave his friend a knowing smile.

"Heck, if you play this thing right," he mused, "you and Brigitte could retire to Panama in just a few years. Kiss the rat-race goodbye, forever. I mean, c'mon, that's the dream, right?"

Nate grinned and momentarily let his mind drift. A few years earlier, while visiting his brother Paul—a Vietnam vet who'd relocated to the alluring Central American country in the early 1990s, just months after the maniacal dictator Manuel Noriega had been removed from power by U.S. military forces—he and Brigitte had discovered their own version of paradise: the town of Boquete, a little-known artists' and writers' haven nestled beside a lush rain forest in northern Panama; a virtual Eden where the temperature rarely rose above 80 or dipped below 50, and the cost of living was about half that of the United States.

The only downside was that it had recently been discovered by wealthy U.S. and European retirees, who were relocating to Boquete in droves and were doing what well-heeled retirees usually do when they discover a tropical nirvana: sparking local resentment by building lavish gated communities so that they didn't have to fully integrate with the locals and their culture.

Still, as troubled as they were by that development, Nate and Brigitte, upon returning to Madison, had openly rhapsodized about one day retiring to Boquete, where Nate could spend his golden years churning out best-selling novels while snacking on fresh papaya and guava, and sipping countless cups of locally-produced java—arguably the richest and purest coffee grown on the planet.

It was a lofty, ambitious dream and a comforting one but, Nate eventually came to realize, not a very practical one—although, frankly, it seemed a lot more practical at this moment. In fact, for the first time in his adult life, Nate felt trapped, conflicted.

And he suspected Tyler was right. If Nate was shrewd enough and willing to subject himself—and his family—to the media meat-grinder for a few weeks or months, he probably could make some serious money by publicizing his story.

But that's not who Nate Zavoral was. His life was not about glitz or self-promotion—hell, he'd started out as a newspaper reporter and was now a public school teacher. It wasn't exactly a vow of poverty, but it was pretty damn close. And while there were days when he arrived home demoralized after dealing with unruly students—or, worse yet, their parents—he was, by and large, content with the path he'd taken.

So, from his perspective, the thought of deviating from that path and offering himself on a platter to the media vultures—even temporarily—hardly seemed worth it.

It was almost 9:30, and Nate was already feeling better just being in Tyler's workshop and engaging in small talk with his multi-talented friend, a soothing classical music CD barely audible in the background. He knew he'd find Tyler here, of course, because this is where Tyler spent most nights since his rocky divorce from wife No. 3, Julie, almost a decade ago.

For all his flaws—most notably, his tightwad tendencies and a demeanor that bordered on arrogance—Tyler was a man of principle, which was another reason Nate admired him. He'd demonstrated that many times over the years, most recently in 2002—Nate still remembered the exact date, Feb. 18, 2002—when Tyler announced out of the blue that he was resigning as Frank Lloyd Wright's boys basketball coach.

Even more startling, he'd informed Milt Wilcox the very same day that he also was resigning from the teaching staff once the spring semester ended.

Less than 24 hours earlier, the normally even-keeled coach had gotten into a shoving match with a belligerent parent moments after his team's season-ending defeat to arch-rival Madison La Follette—a shoving match that was witnessed by several dozen alarmed spectators.

The parent—like many parents of high school athletes these days—felt his kid wasn't getting enough playing time. And while no blows were exchanged, the man sprayed spittle in Tyler's face during their intense exchange, and Tyler decided as he drove home that night that it just wasn't worth it anymore.

And it wasn't just the pressure from overbearing parents that pushed him over the edge, he later confided to Nate. He was 56 at the time and very much aware that his best years were slipping away. What better time, he concluded, to pursue his own longtime dream of becoming a sculptor?

"After 60, we're all dangling by a string—that's just reality," he'd casually noted. "I want to try this while my hands still work. And my brain."

Now, two years later, it was Nate who was in a fix. And the biggest question he was wrestling with had nothing to do with the potential for financial gain: it was whether he believed in his heart that Sal Magestro had been responsible for his ace—and, if so, whether to publicly acknowledge as much; or whether to listen to the little voice in his head that kept insisting it was just a highly-improbable coincidence— and acknowledge that as well?

"I mean, c'mon, Ty," he said, as they stood side-by-side in his friend's garage. "This idea that Sal was watching the whole time and somehow willed the ball into the hole. I mean, it's ludicrous, right? Seriously."

Tyler glanced at Nate and smiled faintly. He slipped his gloves back on and grabbed his chisel, and turned his attention to his sculpture.

Once an avowed atheist, Tyler's own views on religion had evolved in recent years. Though he too believed that organized religions exploited people's fear of the unknown and, by and large, did more harm than good, he'd grown more spectral as he aged and was now open to some of the beliefs promoted by Hinduism; more specifically, samsara—the belief that after people die they are reincarnated again and again. Until they get it right, as he put it.

"What I think really isn't important, Z," Tyler said after a long silence, pausing to pull a handkerchief out of his pants pocket and wipe the sweat beads off his forehead.

Nate looked at him quizzically.

"What's important," Tyler maintained, "is what *you* think happened. And it sounds to me like you need more proof—maybe another signal? I mean, isn't that what you're really suggesting here, buddy? That in order for you to totally accept that Sal was behind all this, you need to hear from him again?"

Nate puckered his lips and gazed soulfully out the large window directly behind Tyler at the pitch-black, moonless sky.

Almost instantly, he could feel his spirits rising again.

"By God, Mr. Briggs, I think you're right," he said. "That's exactly what I need—another signal. Hell, if I'm going to turn my life into a giant burlesque show, I sure as heck better believe with absolute certainty that Sal was communicating with me.

"I mean, if he really possesses this power, what's to prevent him from signaling me again?"

The more he contemplated the idea, the giddier Nate became. It was entirely rational, he mumbled under his breath.

He broke into laughter, then lifted his wine glass toward the ceiling fan, which was spinning quietly high above Tyler's masterpiece.

"If you're listening Sal, old pal," Nate said cheerily, "I need another sign. I don't know how, or what, or when. But if you want me to move forward with this thing—if you want me to honor The Pact—we need to connect again.

"C'mon, you can do this. Just one more time. And then ..."

He paused to look at Tyler, who had stopped carving and was watching with a droll smile.

"And then," Nate continued, gazing upward, "I'll let the whole world know.

"With Tyler as my witness, Salvatore, I give you my word."

10

Bookie Finch could appreciate what his friend was going through.

In the long, rich history of Turtle Creek Golf Club—whose 18-hole layout was carved out of rolling farmland on Madison's western fringe in 1921 (it was dubbed "Billy Goat Hill" in its early days)—there had been 13 recorded aces on the 172-yard third hole. But none, the portly, diminutive 67-year-old head pro had to admit, that had caused any near the hysteria as Nate Zavoral's implausible, mind-boggling feat of April 24. Good golly, it's all anyone at the course wanted to talk about since the day it happened.

There'd even been a retired couple from Rhode Island who'd shown up recently and asked to have their photo taken next to the now famous oak tree next to the No. 3 green. More absurd yet, after Zavoral's appearance on *The Tonight Show,* the Turtle Creek Men's Association was considering posting a bronze plaque near the third tee commemorating the shot.

The crusty, silver-haired pro had missed Nate's interview with Channel 9's Naomi Winston. But he—and, it seemed, everyone else in the city—had managed to catch his amusing and admittedly thought-provoking interview with Jay Leno. Indeed, Finch couldn't stop thinking about it while driving to work the next morning, and how it provided further proof of what a loony, unpredictable world we live in.

In his nearly 30 years as the course's head pro, Finch had met—and, in some cases, taught—dozens of talented golfers whose smooth, efficient swings had produced many notable achievements. How about Bobby McLaughlin, who'd competed in two Greater Milwaukee Opens and even had a brief stint on the PGA tour before becoming a successful life insurance salesman? Or Derek Gengler, who was still a pretty good stick in his mid-50s after having set the Turtle Creek course record with a 10-under-par 61 back in '72?

On the distaff side, there was Erin Donker, the supremely confident 14-year-old string bean who'd stunned even Finch by finishing second in the State Women's Open last summer.

And if you're talking about momentous holes-in-one, how about the ace that Hank Klingbauer got in 2002 on the 224-yard 17th hole—the first ace at No. 17 since the course opened in 1921. And Jesus, Finch muttered to himself while easing his black pickup truck into his private parking stall, Klingbauer is 71 and blind in one eye. Poor guy had to ask his playing partners what all their shouting was about.

But whose story is trumpeted worldwide on the Internet and then—more outrageous yet—gets flaunted on *The Tonight Show,* before millions of people? Who will be forever immortalized and linked with Turtle Creek Golf Club? And who's put himself in position to capitalize on what was obviously a ridiculous fluke and—if he's smart—might never have to work another day the rest of his life? Nate Zavoral, a 20-plus handicapper who slices his tee shot off some giant oak that's practically in the next county, and whose goddamn ball ricochets onto the green and slams into the flagstick.

And why does anyone besides his wife—and a couple of harebrained sidekicks—care about this? Because of some screwball bet he'd made with the owner of a pizzeria who suffered a massive coronary a few months earlier while fornicating with some young tart at his mountain condo in Colorado.

And yet, a part of Finch was delighted for Nate Zavoral. Yes, he was a typical Madison lefty whose Pollyannaish, let's-save-the-whole-bleeping-world views often made the conservative Finch want to vomit. And yes, Nate hung out with Doc Flanagan, the glib, acid-tongued sportswriter for *The Capital Times*, who—word had it—had been a pothead and Grateful Dead disciple during his younger years.

Nonetheless, Finch had heard that Nate was a top-notch teacher—a number of his former students were regulars at Turtle Creek—and he knew from his own experience that he was a good egg. Indeed, each spring for the last decade or so, Nate had discreetly presented Finch with a $100 check to be used for the club's First Tee program for under-privileged kids.

So when Nate showed up in his pro shop on a slow Thursday evening, saying he wanted to play a "quick nine" and asking if his wife Brigitte could tag along—even though she wouldn't be playing—Bookie was happy to accommodate him.

"But the sun's sinking fast," the pro noted as Nate slipped him his debit card. "I doubt you'll be able to get in an entire nine. The last group—a twosome—teed off about 15 minutes ago."

Nate shrugged as Bookie handed him back his card, which he stuffed in a back pocket.

"No big deal," he said. "If I finish, I finish. I just want to work on my swing a bit." He took a quick glance around the pro shop to make sure no one was within earshot. Then he looked at the pro and smiled.

"Don't know if you heard, but Fensin's Golfland wants to use me in one of their TV ads."

Bookie arched his white, billowy eyebrows, waiting for the punch line. When he realized Nate wasn't joking, he gasped in befuddlement.

"No, I hadn't heard that. Whoa boy," he groaned. "Must be an ad for their miniature golf course, right? And don't tell me—you get to dress up in a bear costume."

"You got it," Nate said as he turned and hurried toward the door. "Thanks for the vote of confidence."

To be sure, Nate had no intention of playing a full nine. But he didn't dare risk further ridicule by revealing the real reason he'd returned to Turtle Creek Golf Club this particular evening: to see if he could duplicate his feat of April 24—with Sal's assistance, naturally.

The idea had flashed in his Nate's head within seconds after leaving Tyler Briggs' workshop the previous night. Tyler, as was often the case, had made a legitimate point, Nate had concluded. If Nate was going to promote the belief that his friend had contacted him from the dead, he had to be convinced in his own mind that that's precisely what had happened.

And he knew the only thing that would convince him of that was if Sal somehow provided him with further evidence—in the form of another sign. A sign that proved beyond any reasonable doubt that Sal had accomplished exactly what he'd promised to.

The problem, however, was that he and Sal had never talked about a second signal. So Nate would have to improvise. What kind of signal would it be? And how would he communicate that to Sal—assuming, of course, that Sal had indeed become an ethereal presence in Nate's everyday life?

The answer came to him as he was strolling down the sidewalk. He would conduct a simple, straightforward and, at the same time, brilliant test of sorts. He would return to the third hole at Turtle Creek, with Brigitte as his witness, tee up another ball and attempt to get another ace.

Imagine, he mused, the odds of him succeeding a second time if, in fact, Sal wasn't involved. He recalled reading once that the odds of getting struck twice by lightning were one in nine million. Considering the circumstances, this would be even be rarer than that.

But if Sal *was* responsible for the first ace, what would prevent him from doing it again? If he really wanted to demonstrate his super-natural powers—and, in the process, provide proof that there is, in fact, a hereafter—why wouldn't he relish a second opportunity to do just that?

Just as important, Nate reasoned, if his attempt to repeat his feat of April 24 ended in failure, only he and Brigitte would know about it. Which not only would save him from embarrassment but would pretty much verify that his ace really was pure happenstance—implausible as that seemed, too.

Nate stepped outside the clubhouse, picked up his golf bag, which he'd propped against a tree, and slung it over his shoulder. He smiled at his wife and pointed in the direction of the third tee, which was a good 20-minute-walk away.

"Bookie's working alone tonight, and he bought it completely— he thinks I'm trying to squeeze in a quick nine," Nate said elatedly. "I told him I was perfectly aware that we'd never finish before darkness, but that I needed to work on my swing. He didn't bat an eye."

Nate and his wife never broke stride as they clomped past the first tee, which was already shrouded in shadows.

"I think we'll have at least a half-hour of sunlight once we get there," Nate said as they marched briskly down the No. 1 fairway.

Brigitte, who'd kicked off her sandals so she could feel the cool carpet of grass beneath her bare feet, wasn't sure what to think of her husband's latest brainstorm. She was amused when he first mentioned it over breakfast that morning—and a little surprised, too. Knowing his aversion to being in the public eye, she'd just assumed he would wait for the controversy to peter out—even if it took a month or two—and then resume life as usual.

On the other hand, she also understood Nate's need to honor The Pact—or attempt to anyway—despite his lingering doubts.

Of course, the notion that Sal was actually behind it seemed preposterous to Brigitte as well. Then again, she didn't completely rule it out. After all, even the wisest, most astute minds in the world really don't have a clue about what happens after we exit this life, she deduced. It's all just one big, bewildering—and, to some, terrifying—mystery.

So perhaps, she decided, her husband's idea to return to the No. 3 tee and try again wasn't as boneheaded as she had first thought. Maybe Nate was right. If Sal had actually orchestrated Nate's hole-in-one on April 24, why wouldn't he be willing to do it again—this time with Brigitte as a witness?

Moreover, truth be known, she was almost as caught up in the rapidly-evolving drama as Nate was. She wanted to satisfy her own doubts—although she knew she'd absolutely freak if she actually witnessed Nate's tee shot rolling into the hole.

In any event, she was relieved that there wasn't a single person in sight as she and Nate reached the No. 3 tee. Though not much of a golfer herself—she preferred more physically demanding sports, like running and tennis—she'd played at Turtle Creek a number of times and didn't particularly care for the third hole despite its panoramic setting, the green perched at the top of a hill, with the thick, intimidating forest as a backdrop.

Even though the women's tee was halfway up the hill, a mere 115 yards from the green, her tee shots almost always ended up short—in the wide, yawning bunker guarding the front of the green. And she absolutely abhorred sand shots; it was a big reason she'd stopped playing competitive golf and dropped out of the Turtle Creek women's association several years earlier.

As Brigitte stood beside the slightly-elevated tee box and peered up at the green—which was partially cloaked in darkness from the lengthening shadows of the trees left of the green—Nate unzipped a pouch at the bottom of his bag and pulled out a shiny new ball and an extra-long white tee.

After studying the tee box for several moments, searching for the best angle, he strolled over to the right side and stuck the tee in the ground. Then he pulled his hybrid-4 from his bag and, while gripping it at each end, lifted it high over his head to stretch his upper torso before finally addressing the ball.

As he went through his routine, Nate immediately began to second-guess himself. Was he asking too much—of himself *and* of Sal? he wondered. He pondered the thought for several moments, then walked over to his bag and dumped the remaining balls out of its side pouch. There were seven, plus the one already on the tee.

"You know, I'll tell you what," he said to his wife. "I'm trying to be fair here. I've got eight balls. And eight's my lucky number—even Sal knew that.

"It's going to take a couple swings just to warm up. So I think I'll hit all eight of these, and if any one of them ends up in the hole, I'm moving forward—I'll honor The Pact. I mean, the odds of even that happening would be rather astronomical, don't you think?"

"Uh, yeah, I'd say so," Brigitte concurred.

"Well, then, what are we waiting for?" Nate said, content that his new plan was more realistic. "Why don't you head up to the green and stand next to the flagstick? That way you'll actually witness the ball falling in the hole."

"Uh-huh, right," his wife said with a smirk.

Nate continued to limber up as Brigitte trotted up the hill. But as he waited for her to reach the top, he couldn't believe how shaky his entire body felt again.

Maybe that was good, he rationalized. Maybe it was a sign that he and Sal were in the process of making another powerful, cosmic connection.

He squinted in the direction of the green and watched patiently as Brigitte positioned herself next to the flagstick, which was on the far right back of the green—almost directly opposite from where it had been on April 24.

She waved at her husband to alert him that she was ready. He waved back, relieved that there was still enough sunlight to make out her image against the darkening backdrop. He had a tougher time spotting the blue flag, but that wasn't important: he could at least take aim at the general vicinity.

Nate calmly bent over and placed his first ball on the tee. He took a quick look around to make sure there were no other witnesses to this utterly bizarre scene. Satisfied that there weren't, he cast his eyes upward and stated his case in a loud voice, so there would be no confusion about what he was trying to accomplish.

"OK, Sal, this is it, my friend," he said. "I know this wasn't part of the original deal, but I need your help. Just do your thing and direct one of these balls into the cup, just like you did three weeks ago. That's all I'm asking.

"I know you did it once—or, at least, I think you did. But I need more evidence if I'm going to put my life on the line. Just once more and I'll tell every soul on the planet about our discovery. So it's in your hands now. Make me a believer, pal!"

After a final glance around, Nate inhaled audibly. Then he slowly took the club back and made a smooth, fluid swing. His head shot up the moment he made contact, and he cringed as the ball curled far to the right—similar to his shot on April 24. But this one missed the oak tree by the length of a bus and skittered harmlessly down the slope toward the No. 4 tee.

Nate grunted under his breath and immediately placed another ball on the tee. This time he swung even harder, but the result was painfully similar—a banana slice that he lost sight of as it disappeared some 20 yards right of the tree.

His irritation growing, he leaned over and placed a third ball on the tee. He took another mighty swipe, then watched dejectedly as it landed in the sand trap in front of the green.

He tried not to notice Brigitte, who was standing beside the flagstick with her hands on her hips and appeared to be glaring down at him, as if to say, "You're kidding, right?"

He moseyed over to his bag, squatted down and yanked out a sport drink that he'd stashed in a side pouch. He took several gulps and remained in that position for about half-a-minute, gathering his emotions. Then he stepped back in the tee box and set another ball on the tee.

"Slow down. Concentrate," he reminded himself while checking his posture before addressing the ball.

The next swing was much better, and as he jerked his head up, he felt a surge of excitement as the ball soared straight as an arrow, directly at the flagstick.

He screamed "Fore!" at the top of his lungs, causing Brigitte to duck and throw her arms up in front of her as the ball bounded hard on the front of the green and appeared to skip past her.

Brigitte turned to watch it, then peered down the hill at her husband and applauded.

But Nate was hardly ecstatic. Close was not good enough. He needed an ace; and it didn't matter if the ball landed in the hole on a fly or a single hop or if it rattled off a half-dozen tree limbs and caromed off a porcupine's behind before rolling in the hole. Anything less than an ace and his quest was over. And he was down to his last four balls.

He reached down and took another gulp of his sport drink.

His next shot was a repeat of the first two, a wicked slice that never had a chance. And the one after that—ball No. 6—was a rare duck hook that bounced once in the rough before jumping into the woods halfway up the hill.

Again, Nate dropped his head and waited a half-minute or so until regaining his composure.

Then he teed up ball No. 7, took a quiet, deliberate swing and watched with frustration as it curved at the last moment and dropped harmlessly on the far left side of the green, perhaps 25 feet from where Brigitte was standing.

Emotionally spent, his burgundy polo shirt drenched with sweat, Nate leaned over and placed his final ball on the tee. He stepped back and peered once more at the heavens. Then he carefully positioned himself over the ball—making sure it was lined up with his left heel—took yet another sharp breath and unleashed a wild, furious swing.

The instant his club struck the ground, a massive piece of sod splattered in his face, momentarily blinding him, and he knew immediately that he'd stone-cold chunked it, the ball coming to rest no more than 20 yards from the tee.

"Choke artist!" he howled, angrily pounding his club into the ground.

Then, with his hybrid-4 in one hand and his golf bag in the other, Nate lumbered up the hill to the green. He paused along the way to scoop up the last ball he'd hit and another that had landed in the greenside bunker. By the time he arrived at the crest, Brigitte had retrieved several other balls, but had purposely not touched the two that had ended up on the putting surface, so that her husband could see for himself what his efforts had wrought.

"The closest one is 23 feet from the pin—I walked it off," Brigitte dutifully reported.

"Twenty-three feet," Nate said bleakly.

He dropped his club on the neatly-manicured grass and glared upward. Then he opened his arms wide, so that there was no mistaking his bewilderment—and exasperation.

He didn't say a word, but Brigitte knew what he was thinking.

"Thanks a lot, pal. Now what?"

11

Nate touched his car brakes gently, allowing two startled doe to scamper across the desolate two-lane road.

He glanced in his rear-view mirror and, upon seeing nothing but empty blacktop buffeted on both sides by dense forests of white birch and evergreen trees, stifled a yawn and took another sip from his coffee mug.   Then he peered through the windshield into the distance and spotted a long sliver of dazzling blue water peeking at him just over the horizon, perhaps a half-hour's drive away.

Lake Superior. The sight gave him goose bumps.

Gosh, how he loved it up here in Michigan's sparsely populated Upper Peninsula. He pressed down on the accelerator and flicked on the cruise control again.

Even in the height of summer—still a month away—the place was never overrun with humanity, largely because it was so far removed from any big city. Indeed, its saving grace, Nate long felt, was that it was a good seven-hour drive from Chicago and five hours from the Twin Cities. And considering there wasn't a single water-theme park or even a fast-food joint within 50 miles, most big city-folk wouldn't find it appealing anyway, he often surmised.

Granted, it was also home to millions of tiny, nasty black flies, which would be hatching shortly—earlier each year it seemed, thanks to global warming—and stick around until the first frost in September. However, much as he relished this vast, largely unspoiled chunk of wilderness, Nate shuddered at the thought of the UP's grim, six-month-long winters and its 300 or more inches of annual snowfall.

But for his purposes on this particular visit, it was ideal.

He checked his watch. It was a little after noon. He would arrive at Porcupine Mountains Wilderness State Park no later than 1 p.m. He would stop at the ranger's office and pick up a key for the austere, one-room cabin he'd reserved by phone just two days earlier, benefitting from a cancellation, the ranger informed him, that had occurred less than 10 minutes before he called. Then he would drive to a remote parking lot in the heart of the 60,000-acre park, strap on his 10-pound backpack and tramp slightly more than a mile through heavy forest to a primitive two-bunk cottage overlooking the Little Carp River—just as he and Brigitte had been doing on their anniversary every September for more than a decade.

113

There would be no trucks rumbling by, no train whistles, no eardrum-shattering jets streaking overhead. And, seeing as how there were only 16 cabins and a smattering of campsites in the entire park, he didn't have to concern himself with human magpies blabbering mindlessly on cell phones or twentysomethings carousing till daybreak—or human activity of any kind, save for the occasional backpacker traipsing through on nearby trails.

For the next two and a half days, it would be Nate Zavoral all by his lonesome in the eerily isolated yet exhilarating solitude of the north woods. And he couldn't wait.

It was the ideal spot, he mused, to slow things down and try to make sense of the chaotic last few weeks.

More important, it was an excellent place to have a private conversation with Sal Magestro, if in fact Sal was now a permanent, hovering presence—albeit, an invisible one—in Nate's life.

He'd felt so strongly about coming up here that he'd called in sick shortly after rolling out of bed at 6 a.m.—only the second time he'd used a sick day in his 19 years at the school.

The plan was simple: he would take long, energizing hikes during the day and unwind by the campfire at night, all the while attempting to make some sort of metaphysical connection with his late friend. And, as part of that effort, he would verbally request—plead, if necessary—that Sal send another signal that would erase the doubts Nate still had about what had transpired on April 24.

Of course, he'd made a similar plea the night before his attempt to get a second ace at Turtle Creek Golf Club a week ago—and had failed miserably. However, he wondered in retrospect if asking Brigitte to tag along had been a mistake. Again, maybe this *was* a faith thing, and maybe now this was just between him and Sal—their private, sacred little deal.

Even then, Nate realized he wasn't being fair—that he was violating at least the spirit of his pact with Sal Magestro. And he could understand why, if Sal was in the vicinity and observing all this, he might be irked—since, after all, he'd kept his vow.

"Hey pal, what's going on, pal," Nate could visualize Sal saying. "I mean, who's kidding whom? Your tee shot might have ended up in Pittsburgh if I hadn't intervened."

But, unfair or not, Nate needed confirmation.

As it was, the trip didn't sit well with Brigitte—one of only four people (the others being Doc, Tyler and Luckovich) who knew about it. She appreciated Nate's need to seek additional proof, but questioned whether he'd even know it if he saw it, seeing as how he and Sal had never talked about a second signal.

And to drive 260 miles and expect to make yet another ghostly connection in the secluded, gnat-infested woods of the Upper Peninsula bordered on folly, Brigitte had intimated.

She'd also questioned the wisdom of spending three days alone in the wilderness. What would he do, for instance, if he began having a heart attack? Nate agreed it was a legitimate question—particularly since heart disease ran in his family. But, as he'd pointed out, he'd just had a physical and, outside of a few minor concerns, was found to be in excellent health overall—a fact he attributed to still being a competitive swimmer and his strict adherence to the Mediterranean diet.

Heck, he still had a 32-inch waist: how many 55-year-olds could attest to that?

Nonetheless, Nate was still troubled by his wife's ambivalence about the trip. He wished he didn't always need her unconditional support, but he did. That's just the way it was.

As he neared the end of Highway 64, he slowed down and observed the stands of white birch and towering pines on the left side of the road, searching for the entrance to the park. He spotted the Last Chance Bar and realized he still had several miles to go. He pressed down on the accelerator again and, almost immediately, his mind returned to the question that had haunted him from the moment he'd slipped behind the wheel: How *would* he know?

The signal needn't be anything farfetched, mind you, he'd concluded—like, say, returning from a late afternoon hike and happening upon a 300-pound black bear cooking spaghetti and meat balls over the fire pit. Or a red-tailed hawk landing on the branch of a pine tree, a golf ball wedged in its beak; which, frankly, were the sorts of things one might expect from Sal.

On the other hand, it needed to be highly unusual—and at least slightly queer, so it would stand out. Then again, maybe just seeing a black bear would suffice, seeing as how he and Brigitte had never seen so much as a fresh bear print in the 12 years they'd been visiting the park, even though the rangers claimed there were hundreds of them in the area.

Whatever form it took, Nate just felt he'd know—somehow.

As he contemplated the possibilities, his thoughts turned to Sal and how he still had difficulty accepting that his longtime friend was actually dead. It seemed odd not having him around. They'd practically been joined at the hip since childhood even though—as their friends often pointed out—they were polar opposites in how they viewed the world and went about their own lives.

Sal was extroverted—to a fault, Nate sometimes felt—and a community activist since his college days, part of which was spent working alongside Nate on evenings and weekends at his parents' liquor store. Despite his humble, blue-collar upbringing, he lived in an ostentatious mini-palace in one of the city's most exclusive neighborhoods, loved fancy cars—his trademark once his pizzeria became established was a jet black Mercedes convertible, which he traded in for a new model every two years—was known for his lavish parties and was a fixture at social functions hosted by the city's mucky-mucks.

Nate, meanwhile, kept a low-profile, preferred the company of a few close, liberal friends, lived in an unpretentious home in a solidly middle-class neighborhood and, for the most part, abhorred the kind of people Sal routinely rubbed shoulders with. (Sal, who often could be found toiling in his restaurant's kitchen in a neatly-pressed white shirt

117

and tie, once confessed to Nate that he had more than 40 sport coats in his bedroom closet; Nate owned but two—one for winter and one for the other eight months of the year.

And unlike Sal, who spent a large part of each day texting madly on his BlackBerry, Nate was an unashamed technophobe who still preferred books and newspapers to TV and the Internet; in fact, he took great pride in not owning a cell phone. He fully embraced solitude and couldn't fathom why people would choose mindless blather over peaceful contemplation while ensconced in their vehicles—especially while cruising along serene, country roads.

And yet, their bond was a tight one; a bond that was forged out of mutual respect and the kind of ironclad trust that's exclusive to lifelong relationships. Indeed, they'd often joked that they really had just three things in common: a weakness for pretty women, an obsession with golf and a sincere love of kids.

But whereas Nate was fortunate to have two loving and healthy children of his own, Sal's contentment came mainly from the countless hours he devoted to the kids who frequented the Boys and Girls Club in his old neighborhood on Madison's south side. However, as fulfilling as Sal found it, Nate knew his friend was still reeling from the horrifying death of his 3-year-old son, Gabe, who'd pushed through a screen in his second-floor bedroom window and plummeted to the concrete patio at the Magestro's home in 1996.

So distraught were Sal and his wife Tammy over the tragedy that they'd vowed to never have any more children—which meant that on many days and nights their massive four-bedroom, 6,000-square-foot home was as lifeless as a mausoleum. And, perhaps not surprisingly, their marriage eventually collapsed—though they did manage to keep it together for another seven years, until finally divorcing in the summer of 2003, which was one of the saddest days of Nate's life.

But that was ancient history now. In less than an hour, Nate would be back in the north woods, and he knew it would be therapeutic. He was absolutely sure of that. Just seeing the glistening body of dark blue water beyond his windshield lifted his spirits, and for the first time in weeks he was encouraged.

He spotted the blacktop road off to his left that led to the ranger's office and turned his car in that direction. A few minutes later, he pulled into a gravel lot, which was empty save for a lone white Jeep and a red pickup truck jam-packed with broken tree branches and other debris.

He pushed open the door of his car and was immediately greeted by the soothing aroma of pine needles. It smelled the same every year and elevated his spirits even more. Then, as he lifted his orange backpack out of the trunk, he noticed a bald eagle circling majestically overhead.

There was no golf ball in its beak. Nate smiled and pulled the backpack over his shoulders, then yanked the straps tight. This was definitely the right decision, he declared out loud.

———

By late Sunday morning, Nate had had it.

Almost 48 hours after arriving at Porcupine Mountains State Park in radiant sunlight, the arthritis in his lower back ached and his attitude had soured from relentless rains that had pummeled the park and its inhabitants since Friday evening—just a couple hours after Nate had arrived at his stark one-room cabin, a 45-minute trek from the park's south parking lot.

Now, as he poked at the fire in the small stove in his cabin, he cursed loudly. He had managed to burn breakfast—scrambled eggs with cheese and fingerling potatoes—for the second consecutive day.

What's more, in his haste to get out of Madison, he'd neglected to pack any rain gear. Hence, his nylon wind breaker, a new hooded sweatshirt, two pairs of jeans and his only pair of hiking boots were thoroughly drenched. So were his socks and all but one pair of underwear—the pair he'd slipped on just minutes earlier. He was famished and fatigued, even though he'd spent most of his time perched on the wooden foot-bridge over the stream that led to Greenstone Falls, observing the park's abundance of creatures, big and small, and patiently waiting for some sort of sign.

And what sights had he witnessed? A solitary, inquisitive deer—and then only fleetingly—staring at him from a nearby thicket as Nate scurried down to the fast-flowing river to fill a plastic jug of water for an evening meal. A mother raccoon and three babies scampering across the bridge in mid-afternoon. A large bullfrog springing across a moss-covered log before disappearing into a clump of tall, thick grass at the river's edge.

"Hot damn!" Nate exclaimed sarcastically the moment he saw it. "A bullfrog, smack dab in the middle of a vast forest. Who would've thought …"

He glared upward, making no attempt to camouflage his mounting aggravation.

"I think we can do better than that, Salvatore!"

The worst part was the black flies—more black flies than he thought could possibly exist. They were everywhere—even inside the cabin—and Nate had a dozen or more ugly little welts on his arms and neck to prove it. Even the oppressive rains hadn't slowed them down.

But he had not witnessed a single thing that could've been construed as a signal—save, perhaps, for the deer tick he had discovered on his inner left thigh, perilously close to his genitals, while slouched over a log, heeding nature's call—with only a soggy newspaper to shield himself from the rain—early that morning.

Could the tick—which he carefully removed with a tweezers—possibly have been a sign? Nate asked himself later. No, he reasoned. Even Sal wasn't that twisted.

The trip had been a total waste, Nate gloomily concluded while stuffing the last of his garbage into a large plastic bag as he prepared to vacate the cabin. He took a last look around, then stepped outside and laid the bag on the small porch. Ignoring the rain, he trotted down a muddy path leading to the stream and for several tranquil moments just stood and listened to the mesmerizing, fast-flowing water. He bent down, picked up a stone and skipped it across the brook. Then he turned and headed back to the cabin, his water-logged boots squishing as he went.

He snatched his orange backpack off the porch and slid it over his wet shoulders. Then he stepped onto the small porch, slipped the lock into the latch, clicked it shut and, his head drooping as the raindrops continued to pelt him, began the long trek back to the parking lot.

"OK, Mr. Genius," he said with disgust. "Any other brilliant ideas?"

Nothing came to mind. In fact, the harsh truth was, he'd driven all the way up here—a journey of nearly five hours—searching for answers and now had even more questions, and more nagging doubts, than when he'd arrived.

How, he wondered, could he possibly go back to Madison and tell people with a straight face that he truly believed that what had transpired at Turtle Creek Golf Club was a truly a miracle? How could he even suggest that it was all because of the pact he'd had with Sal Magestro—and not some ludicrous, one in a million fluke—when he really wasn't convinced himself?

He swatted at another black fly that was stinging his forehead, and moments later, tripped over a small jagged rock and fell to one knee on the muddy path and nearly toppled over with the backpack.

He uttered a slew of profanities as he picked himself up. He was completely demoralized now and, as a survival mechanism, tried thinking nothing but pleasant thoughts as he trudged on. Like soaking his aching bones in a steamy tub the moment he got home. Or taking Brigitte out for a candlelight dinner at their favorite Laotian restaurant, just the two of them, and then falling asleep spoon-style, as they always did when the stresses of the world were pressing in on them.

And who knows, he reasoned. Maybe by the time he got home the talking heads and the shrill voices in the blogosphere will have moved on to their next prey. Maybe the media storm will have subsided and, considering the short-attention span of most Americans today, the Nate Zavoral saga will be yesterday's news—even in Madison.

What an incredible relief that would be, Nate thought.

"Uh, excuse me," a voice called out, seemingly from nowhere.

Nate raised his head and stopped dead in his tracks. He'd been plodding along with his eyes down, trying to avoid the puddles and barely visible tree roots on the narrow, slippery trail, and was surprised to see a heavyset, moon-faced man in an olive-colored hat and matching slicker standing just a few feet away. Behind him was a small group of boys all clad in similar attire and carrying olive-colored umbrellas with the words "Troop 121" stamped in big red letters on each one.

The man inched closer and, while peering at Nate through the raindrops, held out his right hand.

"Rick Cunningham," he said, as the two men shook hands loosely. "I'm head master of Boy Scout Troop 121 out of Mukwonago, down near Milwaukee. Camped overnight about a mile from here and, I'm embarrassed to say, we've run out of dry matches.

"Wouldn't happen to have few extra, would ya?"

Nate smiled. "As a matter of fact ..."

123

He found a dry spot under a nearby pine tree, then laid his backpack down on a stump and kneeled down next to it.

"Crazy weather, isn't it? How long you here for?" Nate inquired, unzipping a side pouch.

"Well, originally we figured three nights," the man said. "But if this monsoon doesn't stop soon, we'll be heading back tomorrow. How 'bout you?"

"Been here since Friday—at a cabin near Greenstone Falls," Nate replied with a dour expression. "Not much fun, I'm afraid."

As the rain continued to pelt them, the scout leader noticed that Nate's clothes were drenched and caked with dirt.

"Uh, you're OK, right?" he asked. "I mean, you're not lost or anything, are you? Because I've camped here dozens of times and I know this park …"

"No, no," Nate said without looking up. "I'm fine. Just a little tired is all. And I can't wait to get to my dry car."

After several seconds of digging, Nate retrieved a small, cellophane bag that contained about 10 matches. He passed it to the man, who Nate guessed to be in his mid-40s, and wished him luck. Then he slipped on his backpack.

"Troop 121 thanks you, sir. You're a lifesaver," the man said gratefully, staring directly into Nate's eyes for several seconds. He was smiling at first, then seemed somewhat befuddled.

Feeling uncomfortable, Nate nodded, then swiftly started down the trail again. He'd taken no more than a few steps when he heard the man call out to him again.

Nate stopped, twisted around, and watched perplexed as the man approached him.

"Uh, this may sound silly, and I hope you don't mind me asking," the man said with a sheepish grin.

"But aren't you that hole-in-one guy who was on Jay Leno last week?"

12

His eyelids growing heavier by the minute, Nate hoisted his waterlogged backpack out of his car trunk in the late night darkness. It was good to be home, and he couldn't wait to shed his grungy, still damp clothes and start running the bath water.

The trip had been an absolute flop, but that was OK, Nate told himself as he slammed the trunk shut and tromped across the driveway to his front door. As he searched for his key, the door flew open without warning and his wife leaped out to greet him in a pink terrycloth robe. She squeezed him tight and gave him a long, sloppy kiss on his chapped lips.

"I missed you too, sweetie," he said softly as they stepped into the house and into the breezeway. He dumped the backpack on the tiled floor, then unzipped his hooded sweatshirt and removed his boots and tossed them in the closet. Then he wrapped his right arm around his wife's tiny waist, tugging her closer.

But he knew what was coming—the question he'd been dreading since departing from the Porkies.

"Well?" she asked excitedly. "Any luck?"

Nate gazed down at his feet, unable to hide his disappointment.

"Fraid not, babycakes."

"Nothing?"

He shook his head glumly as they made their way into the living room, then removed his arm from her waist and plopped his weary body in his favorite recliner.

"It was serene, relaxing, breathtakingly beautiful, as it always is—although it rained like heck the entire time I was there," he said in a soft voice so he wouldn't wake Anna, whose bedroom was just down the hall.

"But no, nothing out of the ordinary—certainly nothing that could be construed as a signal. Saw some bear tracks, but no bears. A couple of deer. A big raccoon that tried to steal my lunch one afternoon. A giant bullfrog hopping across a log just a few feet from the fire pit.

"Pretty exciting, huh?" he said, gliding a hand over his gray-flecked stubble. "Actually, there was one thing that did get my attention."

He looked at his wife, arched his eyebrows and laughed. "I found a deer tick yesterday just an inch or two from my testicles—thank goodness I packed a tweezers."

Brigitte cringed in horror. She'd always been paranoid of ticks, ever since one of her best friends, Sherri Larue , was bitten below an ear while camping at Devils Lake State Park and was hospitalized with Lyme Tick disease for three weeks back in the late 1980s. Two decades later, Sherri still wore scarves whenever out in public to hide the scars on the left side of her neck.

For an uneasy moment or two, Nate told his wife, he'd wondered if perhaps the tick itself was a signal. But he'd immediately dismissed the possibility.

"I sure hope so," Brigitte said, not certain if her husband was serious or not. "I mean, Sal joked around a lot but that would be—gosh, I don't know, depraved!"

When it became clear just how deflated her husband was, Brigitte had a tough time masking her own disillusionment. Nevertheless, she tried her best to appear upbeat as she pulled her robe tightly around her. Maybe it was ridiculously naïve, but she'd actually convinced herself that her husband and his former best friend *would* make another connection.

She realized now that wasn't very realistic—or fair, for that matter.

One could argue that Sal had already accomplished the seemingly impossible and sent a signal to her husband, just as he'd promised. So why would he need to do it again? If Nate refused to acknowledge the feat--after signing an oath stipulating that he would--

he'd probably find an excuse to dismiss a second signal as well. So why even try?

As Brigitte reconsidered her feelings, Nate had fallen silent. His head was throbbing from lack of sleep, and he was fighting to prevent his eyelids from shutting. He leaned forward and buried his face in his hands, and seemed not just exhausted, Brigitte thought, but crestfallen as well.

Then, all of a sudden, his head shot up and he smiled.

"I almost forgot," he said, stifling a yawn. "You'll get a kick out of this. I bumped into a group of Boy Scouts as I was leaving the cabin today in the rain.

"They were coming from the opposite direction, and the scout leader—a chubby guy, around 50—stopped me as we passed each other and asked if he could borrow some matches.

"So I dig through my backpack and give him the few I had left, and as I resume hiking, the guy shouts at me again. And as I turn around to face him, he blurts out that he recognized me from *The Tonight Show.* I mean, is that crazy or what?"

Nate chuckled and held up his hands in bewilderment, but Brigitte was too tired and disillusioned to find humor in anything at this point.

"Crazy," she replied somberly.

Then she stood up, grabbed her husband's hand and led him toward the kitchen. "Speaking of crazy," she said.

As they entered the room, Brigitte switched on the light and gestured to five stacks of letters on the table, each neatly bound with rubbers bands.

"I've already flipped through them—and, just like last week, they're all addressed to you," she said.

Nate stared at the piles in disbelief. "Welcome home," he sighed.

He knew he shouldn't be surprised, but he was—surprised and more than a little depressed, too. His life was tumbling madly out of control, and he didn't like it one bit. He was starting to feel helpless—as if he were shoveling back the tide, as Doc liked to say.

"I say just dump 'em," he said, motioning toward the pile. "I mean, obviously I'm not going to waste my time going through all of them."

"But what if this continues, Nate?" his wife asked in a panicky tone.

"I don't know, honey. I've got to think this through. Maybe I need to hire a secretary to handle all this crap for a month or two, until the whole thing blows over. I really don't know."

Brigitte crinkled her nose. There was more bad news.

"I know you don't want to hear this," she said, "but there are more phone messages, too. I stopped listening to them yesterday. A lot of weird stuff, just like before.

"Not all of them, of course," she added. "*The Capital Times* wants another interview. So does Channel 9. There's also another message from the TV critic for the *Milwaukee Journal-Sentinel.*

"And you'll like this—a reporter for *People* magazine wants you to call him. *People* magazine, Nate!"

Nate wasn't impressed. On the contrary, he wanted nothing to do with *People* magazine or any other devious, self-serving publication hoping to exploit his story.

"How in God's name are people getting our number?" he reiterated out loud.

"I have no idea hon, but they are," his wife said gloomily.

Nate slumped into a chair at the kitchen table.

"Any of them worth returning?"

"Well, there's one from Jim Gremminger," Brigitte said, her face brightening slightly. "He's living in Eau Claire now. Wants to know how you're holding up. He left his number."

The news brought a smile to Nate's face. He and Jim Gremminger had been teammates on Madison North High School's baseball team, and Gremminger had been best man at Nate and Brigitte's wedding. But they hadn't heard from him since he moved to Virginia to take over a beer distributorship nearly two decades ago.

"Is he still in the beer business?" Nate inquired.

"Didn't say. But you should call him. Really."

"Anything else?"

Actually, there was another call he'd probably want to return, Brigitte said, trying desperately to boost his spirits. Providing it was legitimate, of course.

"That guy from Fensin's Golfland called again," she said. "Mentioned that offer to appear in a TV commercial and asked if, at the very least, you'd just call him back.

"And I don't think it was a prank—I mean, it didn't sound like Lefty Kelliher or any of your golf buddies, which obviously was my first thought."

Nate smiled weakly. Of all the things that had happened in the last month, this was without question the strangest: Doing a TV commercial for Fensin's Golfland? With his swing? What's next, he wondered. An offer to perform live with Coldplay?

Brigitte strolled over to the cabinet, removed two wine glasses and without saying another word, poured each of them a glass of pinot noir.

"Please tell me there's nothing else," Nate pleaded as she handed him the glass.

Brigitte pursed her lips as sat down across from him.

"Well, there is one other thing," she said after a long pause. "I talked to Doc earlier tonight. And he said they actually talked about your hole-in-one on *The Larry King Show* tonight."

Nate set down his glass and looked across the table at his wife stupefied.

"I don't know all the details," Brigitte continued, "but I guess Bill Maher was the guest, and some caller asked if he'd heard about your shot and what he thought about it. And I guess—I guess he said the whole story was loony toons, or something like that. And then he made a couple of derogatory comments about you—apparently questioned if you truly were an agnostic.

"You'll have to ask Doc about it. But I think they only discussed it for a minute or two."

She peered worriedly across the table, concerned that her husband's brain was on overload.

He seemed dazed and completely deflated as he took a long sip of wine.

The Larry King Show," he muttered in befuddlement. "*The Larry ... King ... Show?*"

"I'm sure Doc wasn't the only one around here who watched it," Brigitte said. "But I took the phone off the hook after I talked to him and turned off my cell phone too. That was around 11. And I haven't had the courage to check my e-mails yet."

After what seemed an eternity, Brigitte looked at her husband intently and asked, "So what are you going to do, Nate?"

"Damned if I know. Take a bath, I guess. And then try to get a good night's sleep—well, a good three or four hours anyway. Other than that, I don't have the foggiest idea."

He leaned forward and pulled the closest stack of letters toward him. He slipped off the rubber band and quickly browsed through them, checking to see if he recognized any of the names above the return addresses. As he got to the bottom of the pile, one caught his eye: Mitch Crandall, the former Madison police chief.

Nate had met him in the 1980s and actually penned a profile of him for *The Capital Times.* He'd been one of the most revered police chiefs in the city's history—and one of the most progressive law enforcement officials in the country—and was one of the few public officials Nate had interviewed during his career whom he genuinely admired.

Indeed, Nate had often related the story about how shocked he was to walk into Crandall's office the first time and see large framed photos of Gandhi and Martin Luther King side-by-side on the wall behind his desk

Nate also remembered how astounded he and everyone else in town was when Crandall abruptly announced that he was stepping down as police chief in the late 1990s to enter the seminary and prepare for a new career as an Episcopalian priest.

But this was mystifying: Nate hadn't seen or spoken to Crandall in probably 20 years.

Nate tore open the envelope and read the letter with a perplexed look on his face. It contained just a single paragraph:

"Hey Nate,

A heartfelt congratulations on your "unusual" hole-in-one. (Sorry, I'm not sure how else to describe it.) Any chance we could meet for coffee one day soon? I realize your life has gotten rather insane the last few weeks. I think I can be of help. My cell number: 608-882-2421.

"Sincerely, the Rev. Mitch Crandall"

134

13

Amazing, Nate Zavoral marveled under his breath as the Rev. Mitch Crandall got up from a table to greet him.

It had been 22 years since they'd met at the same State Street coffee shop—back when Nate was a reporter for *The Capital Times* and Crandall, then in his 40s, had just been named Madison's police chief. And yet, despite the passage of time, the bespectacled Crandall looked much as he'd looked then.

There'd been subtle changes, of course. The lines in his craggy face were crevices now; his receding hairline had evolved into total baldness; and the close-cropped salt and pepper beard was mostly salt now. But he still had that lean, rugged, athletic look and the same disarming smile, along with a small but distinctive snake-like scar on his right-cheekbone from a bullet that had grazed him early in his career. Only this time he wasn't wearing a shiny gold badge or black police garb. He was clad in a gray polo shirt with a small red Bucky Badger logo—one of his sons had competed for the University of Wisconsin's men's rowing team—khakis and white running shoes.

"Mitch Crandall, what a pleasure—or, I guess I should say, the Rev. Mitch Crandall," Nate said, shaking the minister's hand.

"Mitch is fine," Crandall said as he cupped Nate's hand warmly.

They walked up to the counter and ordered two large coffees, then retreated to a table stuffed in a corner of the coffee shop, which at the moment had just two other customers—young college-age men, both fixated on their laptops.

"Still teaching Tae-Kwon-Do?" Nate asked while settling into his chair. "I mean, are ministers allowed to partake in such violent pastimes?"

"Yes they are," Crandall said with a smile, "and yes I am."

They exchanged the usual pleasantries, inquiring about each other's health, their families—Crandall's wife was still a Madison fire fighter, and they had four adult children, all adopted—and the fact that it had been more than two decades since they'd met for an interview at this exact spot, although it was a combined bakery-coffee shop back then.

"As I recall, that was some interview," Crandall said, gritting his teeth at the memory. Nate grinned, knowing full well what the minister was alluding to: Never one to mince words, Crandall had blasted the mayor for laying off 10 police officers during a severe budget crunch, and the ensuing controversy dominated the local news for days.

Crandall survived that brouhaha, and over the next 15 years hired a higher percentage of women and other minorities than any police chief in the country. But after putting his personal stamp on the department, the ultra-liberal police chief who as a college student had marched in a civil rights protest alongside the Rev. Martin Luther King Jr. in Alabama, then dropped his bombshell: He was stepping down at the height of his power to pursue a second career as a man of the cloth.

Nate confessed to Crandall how stunned he'd been by the announcement, but confided that he'd pretty much lost track of his whereabouts once he'd left office.

"Don't feel bad, I think most people have," Crandall said. "Except, of course, the 90 or so people in my parish. Which is fine with me."

Indeed, his law enforcement career was but a distant memory today, Crandall mused. He was now pastor of Lakeside Episcopalian Church, located in an archaic but still imposing red-brick building on Gaylord Nelson Boulevard, just a few blocks from the Capitol Square. And while his new calling presented its own set of problems—like the growing number of homeless people who camped out every night in the small park adjacent to the church's front steps and sometimes used the bushes as a latrine—he now had to answer to no one but Mitch Crandall and an eight-member parish advisory committee.

"And to the Man himself, of course," he asserted.

"So," the pastor said, promptly shifting directions, "I saw you on Jay Leno."

"You and everyone else in this city, I'm afraid," Nate moaned.

Crandall chuckled as he tested his coffee.

"I take it from your response that you're having trouble with your new celebrity status? Does that mean you regret having gone public with your story, with your—do I dare call it your miracle?"

Nate forced a smile and set down his mug.

"Call it want you want, Mitch. But yes, I suppose you could say I'm having some second thoughts. A lot of second-thoughts actually."

"And this so-called pact you had with your friend Magestro. Do you regret that now, too?"

"Oh, I don't know," Nate said, turning his head and gazing across the room, which had maybe 10 tables and several eye-catching reggae posters—including one of Bob Marley and Peter Tosh that dwarfed all the others—on its mustard-colored walls. "The Pact, as we called it, was just … I don't know how to explain it.

"I guess you'd have to understand our friendship to appreciate why we did it. I mean, we'd known each other since we were in diapers, practically. And for the last 20 years or so, we'd argue about the dumbest stuff—Would the great Jack Johnson have beaten Muhammad Ali? Are border collies smarter than gorillas?

"But the issues that really got us going usually had a religious context—did Jesus really walk the Earth? And if there is a God, is it a loving God? Would a loving God have allowed the Holocaust or the killing fields in Cambodia—or 9/11? I mean, pick your calamity. Would a loving God allow the mass starvation and suffering that still occurs daily on this planet?

"So yeah, we argued about these things—the kind of things religious scholars argue about all the time—although I should point out that we never considered ourselves religious scholars by any stretch of the imagination."

Nate grinned while making the admission.

"Sal claimed to have the read the Bible almost word-for-word back in his college days. But sometimes—especially when pressed—confessed that a lot of it didn't make sense to him. And I dropped out of catechism class when I was 14.

"On the other hand," Nate continued, "do you have to be a so-called expert to have an opinion about these things? To me, the answers aren't all that complicated."

Crandall listened earnestly without changing expression. He was clearly intrigued—even somewhat amused.

"Sal, like most staunch Catholics, had some very strong feelings about these issues." Nate said. "And I, being a recovering Catholic, enjoyed taking potshots at his beliefs, because in my mind they're—no offense, reverend—absolute hokum."

The reverend nodded, but seemed unfazed by the remark.

"So in your heart, you really don't think Sal Magestro—or, I should say, Sal Magestro's soul—had anything to do with your hole-in-one? You've completely ruled out the possibility?"

139

Nate looked at the reverend curiously. He wondered where the conversation was headed.

"Well, frankly, Mitch, I'm still trying to sort that one out," he said. "Naturally, the logical side of me says the notion that my deceased friend—or his spirit or whatever—somehow snatched my ball in midflight and magically guided it into the hole is laughable—pact or no pact.

"At the same time ..." He paused and took a quick glance around the room to make sure the other two patrons weren't eavesdropping. Satisfied that they weren't, he continued, "At the same time, I'm open-minded enough to admit that the odds of me getting an ace under those circumstances are, well, off the charts. So ... so I just don't know what to think."

There was, Nate added, another strange aspect to his story. Maybe he was just imagining it, he said, squeezing his mug tightly, but—as he'd admitted to Jay Leno—people seemed to be treating him a bit queerly since word of his hole-in-one had gotten out.

Not everyone, of course, he told the reverend.

"But all of a sudden some folks seem to be—well, almost in awe of me, as if I possess some super-natural power," he said. "I mean, they don't come right out and say that—it's more of a subtle thing. But it's there. I can see it in their eyes. I hear it in their voices. My neighbors, several of my co-workers. Even my golf buddies, for gosh sakes."

"Doesn't surprise me at all," Crandall said, taking a sip of his coffee.

"It doesn't?"

"Are you kidding?" the reverend said, his voice rising. "Life after death. Heaven and hell. Guardian angels. They may seem like hokey, simplistic notions to cynics like you, but deep inside everyone wonders about those things.

"I mean, what do we really know about our existence down here, Nate? Not a whole lot. We know that every day tens of thousands of babies are born all over the world. And as those kids grow up, they all learn at a very young age—certainly by the time they're six or seven— the stunning reality that every person who inhabits this planet eventually dies, themselves included.

"And if that weren't jarring enough, they discover around the same time that nobody really knows why we're down here or what happens after we pass on. We don't know if this is just some complex sort of test for what comes next, or whether our existence is due to some Big Bang in the universe, as most scientists claim, or what."

Nate smiled at the reverend's acknowledgement that life on Earth might just be a freak cosmic accident. He wished Sal were around to hear this.

"So, not knowing the answers, what does everyone do?" Crandall went on. "We cope—or try to anyway. And many people turn to religion, because at least it offers them a kernel of hope. Now, do some people use it as a crutch? Of course they do. But what's wrong with that? If it helps them deal with the uncertainty of life, I say all the better."

Just then, an elderly woman wearing a lavender shawl entered the coffee shop and shuffled up to the counter. Crandall stopped speaking when he noticed her, and watched stoically as she placed her order. After placing her order, the woman turned her head and, upon noticing the two men, broke into a smile and waved.

"Oh brother, here we go again," Nate said, dipping his head in embarrassment.

After waving back, Crandall laughed. "Uh, I hope this doesn't damage your ego, Nate," he said, "but I think she was waving at me, not you. Her name's Maggie Waldoch, and she's a member of my parish.

"You're not the only celebrity at this table, you know."

Chagrined, Nate offered a quiet apology, then turned his head and smiled sheepishly at the woman, who was still beaming at them.

Moments later, the woman tottered to the door clutching her soy latte. As soon as she was outside, Crandall shifted his attention to Nate and refocused.

"Let's see, where were we? Oh yeah, the reason we're down here," he said. "I guess the point I was trying to make is that most people who believe in God—and a hereafter—do so out of faith. Granted, to say as much isn't exactly new or profound. I'm just stating the facts.

"And the reason they rely on faith, obviously is because they have to—because there's never been any actual proof. Not in modern times, anyway."

The reverend put down his mug, then leaned over the table and stared laser-like into Nate's eyes.

"Until now," he said, flashing a wide smile.

"Outrageous as it may seem, Nate, a lot of people who saw you on Jay Leno—and not just the yahoos—think you may have stumbled upon the answer. I mean, you had this five-year-old pact with Sal Magestro—which you'd shared with your wife and a couple of your golf buddies, right?

"That pact stated that Sal would send you a signal when he died. And you know what? Some people—a lot of people—would argue that's exactly what he did."

Nate squirmed in his seat. It was the same point many others had made, but Nate didn't want to hear it—certainly not from someone for whom he had the utmost respect. He felt pressured and torn.

"So, if I can be so forward, what happens now?" Crandall asked.

"Well, to be honest, Mitch," Nate replied, "I'm still trying to make up my mind. As you can probably imagine, I've been under siege ever since I got back from Los Angeles. E-mails, letters, crank calls on my answering machine. Interview requests."

"Again, hardly surprising," Crandall said.

"I'm not a public person," Nate continued, "so a part of me says to lay low and it will all settle down in a couple of weeks. I mean, I used to be a reporter. I know that laying low and not making yourself available sometimes is the only way to defuse these things.

"However, Brigitte—my wife—thinks I should just continue to tell my story and let people make up their own minds about whether or not it was a signal. She thinks some good might actually come of it—that if people truly believed it was a signal, it might cause them to think twice whenever they're tempted to do bad things."

The reverend's eyes widened. This was precisely the larger point he was trying to make.

"But here's the thing, Mitch," Nate said. "If I'm going to do that—and allow my life to become a giant fish bowl and forever relinquish my privacy—I need to hear from Sal again. I need another sign."

"Another sign?" Crandall said, somewhat confused.

"That's right," Nate replied. "Some sort of signal that convinces me beyond all doubt that the hole-in-one wasn't just a fluke."

The reverend laughed as he tilted his chair back. "Wow, you really aren't big on faith, are you?"

"Fraid not," Nate admitted. "And here's the other thing. Even if I did get another signal and decided to promote my story, what good could it possibly do?

"I'm talking about lasting, meaningful good once the novelty of the whole thing wears off and the media switches its attention to the next bizarre, freaky incident, whatever and wherever it might be."

When that happens, Nate said assertively, the vast majority of people will forget that his so-called miracle golf shot ever happened.

"And I'll have abandoned my principles and turned my life completely upside down—and for what? A few minutes of fame? Well, I'm sorry, reverend. But to hell with fame."

Crandall studied Nate's face for a few seconds, then set down his mug.

"What good could it possibly do?" The reverend asked rhetorically. "That, Mr. Zavoral, is the $64,000 question, as far as I'm concerned. It's the reason I asked you to meet with me today. And here's my answer. Are you ready?

"We have, as you know, a serious morality crisis in this country. Runaway corporate greed. Corrupt government leaders. Wall Street millionaires who don't give a rip about anyone else. Rampant drug abuse. Blatant racism. Homeless people everywhere. Staggering violent crime rates in our inner cities—all of which our political leaders ignore.

"Oh, and lest I forget," he added, "the never-ending sex scandals in the Catholic Church."

Nate nodded firmly.

"Now, I know there's always been some of that," Crandall said. "But never, I would argue, on the scale that we're seeing today. And yet, the truth of the matter is, it could be worse—a lot worse. But you know why it isn't? Organized religion, and religious leaders like me.

"Skeptics like you might scoff at that, but it's true. No, religions aren't perfect. And, yes, there are extremists who exploit religion and use it to scare people—and, in too many cases, to justify killing other human beings and waging war."

But the reason things aren't worse, Crandall maintained, is because a fairly large percentage of people still go to church on a regular

145

basis and believe in a Supreme Being—and in things like good and evil, and heaven and hell.

"What I'm saying, Nate, is that one big benefit of religion is that it acts as a deterrent. It causes people—some people, anyway—to think twice before cheating on their spouse or embezzling money from their company. Or maybe even committing murder.

"Conversely, most religious people believe that if they live their lives honorably and treat their fellow beings with respect and exhibit some compassion, they'll be rewarded in the next life."

Nate listened while fidgeting with a napkin, but said nothing. He didn't disagree with any of it, just as he had rarely disagreed with anything Crandall had said or done as police chief. But he finally sensed where Crandall was heading, and it made him jittery.

"OK, so here's my final point," Crandall said, pausing briefly for effect. "Imagine if people actually had proof that there was a hereafter; that their loved ones who preceded them in death *were* hovering over them and helping protect them.

"Imagine if Nate Zavoral actively promoted what happened to him and let people decide for themselves if they think it's believable—as your wife suggested. And imagine if just a tiny fraction of those people changed their behavior as a result of your—your miracle.

"Do you realize the impact that could have? And not just here in Madison, but in Detroit and Newark and Los Angeles—and in countries across the globe. Heck, it might even shake up some of the sleazebags in

Congress—and in corporate boardrooms in New York. It might even prevent another Enron."

Nate returned Crandall's gaze, but remained mum. He found the clergyman's pitch compelling—even provocative—if not entirely persuasive.

Crandall sat back and sighed. "Look, I can appreciate your fears, Nate—I really can. But do you know why I went into the ministry?

"Because, as the cliché goes, I wanted to make a difference. And slapping handcuffs on thugs and tossing them in the slammer for a night or two didn't do it for me.

"But you know what? Nowadays I *am* making a difference. I am having a positive effect on the 90 members of my parish. But as rewarding as that is, I've gotta tell ya, Nate—I'd give anything to be in the position you're in right now. Anything! To have the potential to influence, I don't know, maybe millions?"

Nate stared at the reverend and frowned.

"This whole thing is so preposterous—I mean, just off-the-wall absurd," he said.

"You're right about that," Crandall said. "And I'm sure a lot of people will say it's utterly ridiculous to suggest that divine intervention—or whatever people want to call it—would occur on a golf course of all places."

Then again, the reverend posited, why not?

"Nate Zavoral is a decent guy—I think that's obvious to everyone. He's a teacher—just as Jesus was. Yes, he's also an agnostic.

But in a way, that makes perfect sense, too. I mean, what better way to win over the skeptics?"

Nate smiled wanly. Crandall had made valid points, but he felt a sudden need to step outside and get some fresh air.

"I know you're feeling a bit overwhelmed right now," the minister said in a gentle, reassuring tone. "But I think it would be an incredible mistake to let this opportunity pass."

14

"Where's J.D. Salinger when you need him?" Tyler Briggs cracked in the cramped three-season sun porch attached to the equally-as-cramped kitchen in the Zavorals' home.

"Or Woodward and Bernstein," countered Doc, who was seated at a round marble table on the right side of the room, directly across from Tyler.

Nate and Brigitte were seated together in a white wicker loveseat just a few feet away, but Nate was too fixated on the list of names he'd drawn up on his notepad to respond to his friends' jibes.

The late Saturday morning gathering had been Nate's idea. He had made his decision two days earlier, after an invigorating two-hour hike through the University of Wisconsin Arboretum following his

149

enlightening discussion with the Rev. Mitch Crandall. He'd informed Brigitte of his plan over dinner that evening.

Crandall was absolutely right, he told her. As distressed as Nate was by the prospect of his life becoming a public spectacle, he'd concluded that no reputable person who found themselves in the position he was in—with the potential to positively impact thousands if not millions of people—would let that opportunity pass, regardless of the reason.

Though he couldn't shake a few lingering doubts, he'd decided that henceforth he would publicly maintain that he believed that his hole-in-one was indeed a signal from Sal Magestro. And that, yes, in all likelihood it was a sign that human beings ascend to another life after this one ends—and, in so doing, acquire the ability to influence the lives of those they left behind.

Besides, he'd confided to his wife, he really didn't have much choice anymore. Around the same time that he'd been meeting with Crandall, another clergyman—the bombastic Rev. Jerry Falwell, the longtime, self-anointed spokesperson for the Religious Right—had noted at the duration of a wide-ranging interview on *CNN* that "this Nate Zavoral character in Madison, Wisconsin" who claimed on national TV that he'd communicated with his deceased friend was "obviously a publicity hound and a fraud." It was ludicrous to suggest, Falwell proclaimed, that God would send a message through "some guy on a golf course—and an atheist at that."

("But God didn't send the message—Sal did," Doc asserted after Tyler informed him of the reverend's mean-spirited diatribe prior to the meeting.)

In any event, Nate had assured his wife that he and no one else would dictate how and when and to whom he would make his extraordinary admission. He was determined not to allow the media to control the process. Or his life.

How would he do that? By granting a single in-depth interview to an esteemed, nationally known journalist and live with the consequences—whatever they might be. That way, he explained, he not only could resume his life with a clear conscience and, at the same time, fulfill his obligation to Sal—he'd be deferring to the Rev. Mitch Crandall as well.

What's more, he was fairly confident, he told Brigitte, that by taking that step, the volatile debate about his hole-in-one would eventually simmer down, and the wolves in the media would soon find another hapless soul to dig their fangs into.

But before he took that step, he explained to Brigitte and his two closest friends, he needed their advice. He'd pored over the nearly two-dozen names of journalists and news organizations that had requested interviews in the last two weeks and recently had made a critical decision: the interviewer would be a print journalist.

"Gotta be," he said, noting that he'd spent nine years as a news reporter—including five with a major wire service—prior to becoming a teacher and was still a print guy at heart. Internet be damned.

He'd fleetingly considered another TV interview, he pointed out, realizing it had the potential to it reach a considerably larger audience. That would be especially true, of course, if he accepted the jaw-dropping offer that had arrived in the mail just the day before: to appear on *The Oprah Winfrey Show*.

But as flattered—and dumbfounded—as Nate was by the invitation, being a guest on Oprah scared him. It was just too big a stage—although he knew that the potential benefits of such an appearance were incalculable. One of his former newspaper colleagues, Rhonda Green, had been one of the first authors to appear on Oprah's book club, and the icon's endorsement of her novel was a big reason the book catapulted to No. 1 on the *New York Times'* fiction best-seller list and stayed there for 16 weeks.

Even so, Oprah was out, Nate decided. And with the exception of the gifted reporting team at *60 Minutes*, Nate didn't trust the TV media—particularly the toxic pundits on cable. After all, their very existence was based on their ability to get under people's skin and make their blood boil, and it angered Nate that so many Americans failed to grasp that reality. The cable pundits, he was convinced, would find a way to distort and sensationalize what was already a captivating human interest story, and that's the last thing Nate needed.

And since *60 Minutes* wasn't among those who'd requested interviews, TV was not a consideration. Plus, he'd already given a TV interview to Ms. Long Legs at Channel 9 and appeared on *The Tonight Show,* Nate rationalized. That was enough.

Moreover, given all the classroom lectures he'd given about how TV journalists often opted for shock and titillation over actual substance—and, in so doing, pandered to viewers' basest instincts—his students would never forgive him if he went the TV route, he'd concluded.

That narrowed the list significantly. Nate had automatically eliminated the dozen or so reporters associated with tabloids—"Should I be offended that they're even interested?" he asked, only half in jest—and those with a strictly religious agenda.

That left just seven possibilities, Doc noted as he examined the list that Nate had provided him: Doc's employer, *The Capital Times,* where Nate had toiled for three years as a general assignment reporter. The *Milwaukee Journal-Sentinel. The Chicago Tribune.* A freelance writer whose name Nate didn't recognize who wanted to do a piece for *Esquire* magazine. And the *Deseret Morning News,* of Salt Lake City, a solid, no-nonsense daily that had won a Pulitzer back in the 1960s, but which Nate instantly rejected because it was owned by the Mormon Church.

And two national publications: *People* magazine and *USA Today.*

"*USA Today* doesn't grab you?" Doc asked quizzically.

"Yeah, you don't want to get *too* picky here," Tyler cautioned. "They may not have any reporters who look like Naomi What's-her-name. But you could do a lot worse, my friend."

In fact, Nate was both complimented and befuddled that a mainstream publication like *USA Today*—or *People* magazine, for that matter—would be even remotely interested in his story. But after pondering the idea for just a few moments, he glowered and shook his head.

"Nope, not a good fit," he said.

He was aware, of course, that *USA Today* was one of the best-read newspapers in the country and, since its inception in 1982, was one of the few that still had a nationwide audience. However, like many one-time print powerhouses, its circulation had plummeted in the Internet age, and its future was murky at best.

If that wasn't enough, there was also the fact that Nate had never been a fan of the publication. From the paper's much-ballyhooed beginning, Nate had deplored its emphasis on glitz and cartoonish, gaudy design over substance; and he'd long felt that the Gannett-owned paper was chiefly to blame for the industry's shift from impact journalism—whether in the form of compelling features or investigative pieces—to shorter, drier, less urbane stories, which he believed helped hasten the industry's decline.

So, no, *USA Today* was not in the running.

"Not even if Pete Lovejoy writes the story?" Doc inquired, peering at the concise interview request the newspaper had sent.

Nate's head shot up.

"Pete Lovejoy? They actually say Pete Lovejoy will do the story?" he stammered.

"Well, not really," Doc replied sheepishly, fully aware that he'd just uttered the magic words. "But who's to say you couldn't request Pete Lovejoy?"

"Request? Hell, demand," Tyler said. "Let's not forget who's the white-hot commodity here."

Nate leaned back and folded his hands behind his head, a big smile creasing his lips.

He'd forgotten that *USA Today* had achieved a journalistic coup several months earlier by hiring Pete Lovejoy to write an occasional thumb-sucker—the showcase centerpiece stories that anchored the newspaper's front page every day. Some news experts argued it was an act of desperation on *USA Today's* part—a strategy intended to enhance the paper's cache and, at the same time, to help stanch its hemorrhaging newsstand sales. *USA Today*, for its part, claimed Lovejoy's hiring demonstrated its desire to raise the bar for its entire reporting team and to expand its coverage of every-day Americans.

Whatever the case, Nate felt it was a masterful move that couldn't help but boost the newspaper's circulation—provided the paper was smart enough to aggressively promote Lovejoy's hiring.

He was *that* good.

Indeed, as a kid growing up on Madison's working-class north side, Nate had actually learned how to write by reading *Sports Illustrated* magazine, where Pete Lovejoy rose to fame in the 1960s and '70s.

An uncle had presented him with a subscription to the magazine at his 8th grade graduation party. And although he was a mediocre student who several years later would flunk Geometry II by getting a 19 on his final exam, he was immediately taken by the hard-hitting reporting and moving literary style practiced by the magazine's large stable of talented writers—over which Lovejoy, a Dartmouth grad who'd survived a brief stint in the Vietnam War, later presided. On many occasions, after his older brother Paul had nodded off on the upper bunk, Nate would—with flashlight in hand—slip under the covers and devour the magazine's entire contents before falling asleep well after midnight.

A suave, sophisticated Texan, Lovejoy had left the magazine in the 1980s to become an acclaimed nonfiction author —he was nominated for a Pulitzer in 2000 for his unauthorized biography of President Clinton—and, until *USA Today* signed him to a contract, divided his time between his novels and occasional news commentaries for *Newsweek* magazine and *National Public Radio*.

Lovejoy would be—well, beyond perfect, Nate concluded.

"I think we've hit the bulls-eye," he said, almost giddy at the prospect of meeting the venerable Pete Lovejoy face-to-face.

Everyone else in the room immediately agreed.

"It'd be pretty hard to top Pete Lovejoy," Brigitte conceded, knowing full well her husband's almost childlike adulation of the author.

"But you've got to promise not to wet your pants when you meet him—you'll have to control yourself," Tyler deadpanned.

"Now all we have to do is convince *USA Today* that Pete's the guy," Doc said. "And that, unfortunately, could be a tough sell."

Nate asked to see the letter and was surprised by its brevity. Just three paragraphs from an associate editor named Andrea Dwyer explaining that several of the newspaper's editors had witnessed Nate's appearance on Jay Leno and were charmed by his story and amazed by the buzz it had created. The newspaper, she wrote, was interested in pursuing a profile of Nate, focusing on who he was and how he was coping with his new celebrity status. But just seeing the word "celebrity" caused Nate to blanch.

The editor stressed *USA Today's* large and eclectic readership and its long commitment to fairness and accuracy. And she concluded by providing her cell phone number and saying she hoped to hear from him shortly, which indicated to Nate that while the newspaper was being cagey and didn't want to come across as too earnest, it was genuinely interested in landing an interview.

"It's a long shot, I suppose," Nate said, staring at the letter. "But just the possibility that Pete Lovejoy would conduct the interview … that *does* make me want to wet my pants."

He got up from the wicker chair and excused himself, saying he needed to take a walk around the block and gather his thoughts, and to make sure he'd considered the idea from every conceivable angle. He still had a ton of final exams to correct, but he realized that was of secondary concern this particular moment and that the decision he was about to make could have a profound effect on his long-term future. And, oddly enough, he no longer was alarmed by that prospect.

157

Some 20 minutes later, Nate returned from his walk and barged through the front door. He marched briskly into the sun porch and announced to the group that—assuming he didn't get cold feet at the last moment—he would call Andrea Dwyer first thing Monday and set up the interview. And he would make a fervent case that only Pete Lovejoy could do justice to his story.

"I mean, the worst that could happen is they reject the idea, right?" he said.

"Well, no—she could fall off her chair laughing and break an ankle," Doc replied dryly. "But I still think it's worth a try."

Tyler shrugged but didn't offer an opinion. Brigitte smiled faintly, then opened her hands and sighed loudly.

She was resigned to accept whatever decision her husband made at this point. But she knew that once he dialed Andrea Dwyer's number, their lives would never be the same.

15

After nudging his car into a narrow stall in the small parking lot squeezed between two student housing complexes behind Magestro's pizzeria, Nate turned off the engine and silently fretted for several moments before stepping outside.

He did not want to be here, could not see what good it would do. But he knew Brigitte would be upset if he did not take to heart her pointed suggestion the previous night that he meet face-to-face with Connie Frataro. He needed to do this, his wife had asserted—not only to find out how the young woman was faring emotionally but, just as important, to make sure she had no objections to Nate's decision to pursue an interview with a reporter from *USA Today* regarding his implausible golf shot.

Nate had stubbornly argued otherwise—though only briefly because it always tied his stomach in knots if he knew Brigitte was perturbed with him. There was no legitimate reason to meet with Connie, he'd protested, because he had no intention of expounding on Sal's relationship with the 20-year-old waitress; other than the fact she was present when he died—albeit, while they were both naked in the outdoor hot tub at his mountainside condo in Steamboat Springs, Colo.

He would set the rules before the interview—just as he had with Naomi Winston, and just as he had with Jay Leno—he affirmed to Brigitte. The question in everybody's mind—including his own, he pointed out—was whether his unlikely ace was a signal from his departed friend; not whether Sal was in the midst of an orgasm when his heart gave out.

Furthermore, Nate noted, he hardly knew Connie Frataro, having chatted with her briefly maybe two or three times since Sal introduced her to him shortly after she began waiting on tables at the pizzeria about a year ago. Granted, the mere sight of Connie in her clinging, white Magestro's t-shirt and denim mini-skirt always caused a stir in his lower anatomy—a reaction he presumed was fairly common for most male customers who observed her. But the simple fact was he knew little about her except that she was a student at Wingra College on Madison's near-west side, and that she was the daughter of Bendito "The Bull" Frataro, a well-known former Teamsters official from Chicago.

No matter, Brigitte had scolded. "You have to do this, Nate," she'd said sternly before turning off the lamp on their bed stand the night before. "You can make all the excuses in the world, but you know I'm right about this—don't you?" She poked him gently in the ribs, but he merely rolled over on his side, jerked the covers over him and ignored her the rest of the night. And he avoided the subject over breakfast as well, determined not to give her the satisfaction of a response because he knew from past experience the debate was over and that he needed to contact Connie Frataro and put the issue to rest.

He was irritated, of course, but also grateful that he'd married such a level-headed, principled woman. He wasn't about to admit it outwardly—he had too much pride for that—but Brigitte had always been the voice of reason in his life, even when they first started dating at Madison North High School. He vividly remembered the first time she'd admonished him, after he'd boasted to her one night about how he would sharpen his spikes before every varsity baseball game—just as the legendary Ty Cobb used to do. That way, any opposing player who attempted to tag him as he flew into a base feet-first risked having their forearms or ankles sliced open, like ripe tomatoes.

"Eww, that's sick—barbaric!" Brigitte had yelped in disgust after he'd made the disclosure during an intermission at the Starlight Drive-In Theatre. And when it occurred to him she was dead serious and not the least bit impressed by his bravado, he assured her that he was embellishing—and thereafter was never even tempted to sharpen his cleats again.

Now here he was in the parking lot of his late friend's pizzeria, trying to get himself in the proper frame of mind should he happen to bump into Connie while picking up a takeout order—a meatball sandwich on a whole wheat roll and a small Mediterranean salad—while on his lunch break from Frank Lloyd Wright High. Thinking she'd be pressed for time, his plan was to quickly re-introduce himself and slip her a note that he had tucked in his shirt pocket.

The pithy message, which Nate had rewritten four times during a free period that morning, inquired if she'd be interested in meeting for coffee or a beer sometime in the near future; that as Sal's closest friend, he'd been concerned about her welfare and wanted to know if he could assist her in any way. He'd signed it, "Sincerely, Nate," and added his e-mail address.

Finally satisfied that he could accomplish this small but nerve-wracking task, Nate sucked in a deep breath, then pushed open the car door and traipsed across the weathered asphalt parking lot. When he got to the corner of the weathered, gray brick building, he turned sharply to his right, then followed a middle-aged couple through the large glass door. As he stepped inside, he noticed that the trusty neighborhood establishment was already filling up with the lunch crowd even though it wasn't quite 11:30.

He immediately spotted Shelly Jackson, the restaurant's robust and seemingly ageless manager, who was standing behind the cash register and engaged in animated conversation with an elderly male customer leaning on a cane.

As soon as she noticed Nate, Shelly cut the exchange short and politely sent the man on his way. Then she rushed out from behind the counter and greeted Nate with a hearty grin and an exuberant bear hug.

"Good heavens, stranger, where've you been hiding?"

"Sorry. Guilty as charged. No excuses," he replied shyly. "But things *have* been hectic."

"Oh, that's right. You're a big TV star now! How could I forget?"

As they bantered, three more customers entered the restaurant, and one of Shelly's co-workers hustled over to replace her at the register.

"Look, I know you're busy," Nate said apologetically. "I'm just curious—how is Connie Frataro doing?"

Shelly's smile disappeared. She shrugged and waved her hands.

"Hard to say, you know? She came back to work about a month ago. She's working tonight, in fact.

"Obviously, she doesn't talk about what happened—at least not with anyone here that I'm aware of. On the surface, she seems, well, OK. But I'm sure she's damaged. This healing stuff takes time. You know that.

"All in all, though, I'd say she's doing surprisingly well. Tough kid."

Encouraged, but slightly embarrassed for posing the question, Nate averted making eye contact and instead gazed down at his feet. He hesitated, then reached in his shirt pocket, pulled out the note and handed it to his longtime friend.

163

"Look, I've got to pick up my order and get back to work," he said, touching her affectionately on the shoulder. "But could you do me a favor? Could you give this to Connie when she comes in? I'd really like to talk to her."

Shelly accepted the note and gave him a half-smile. She completely understood.

"Sure thing, Nate. Now, no more of this recluse stuff, OK? We've missed you!"

————

Perhaps it was an omen, Nate surmised, as he watched two adult giraffes nibble on newly sprouting leaves on a towering green-ash tree no more than 20 feet from where he was standing.

Much to his surprise, Connie Frataro had responded to his note late Friday night—just hours after he'd delivered it to Shelly Jackson—suggesting in an e-mail that they meet at Henry Vilas Zoo at 11 o'clock the following morning. She planned to take a 3-mile run in the University of Wisconsin Arboretum and would finish at the zoo entrance. She'd look for him at the giraffe enclosure, she wrote, and they could take a leisurely stroll while she cooled down from her workout.

As it turned out, Nate had a particular affection for giraffes, dating back to his youth. He'd always been awestruck by their graceful, distinctive beauty, and they impressed him as being unusually civil, peaceful and intelligent—as wild beasts go anyway. So perhaps, he thought, the young woman's suggestion to meet here was a promising sign that he had nothing to worry about, that she not only wouldn't be offended that he was consenting to another interview, but would appreciate why he was doing it.

After glancing at his watch, Nate swung to his left and saw a young woman in a canary yellow nylon jacket and black running tights walking briskly toward him. She was wearing a white headband that kept her long, auburn locks from blowing in her face, and white earplugs that were attached to a white i-Pod that she was clutching in her right fist.

They smiled upon seeing one another, and as Connie Frataro paused to remove the earplugs, Nate waltzed toward her and nervously proclaimed, "Great day for a run!" ignoring the fact that it was damp, breezy, and overcast, with the temperature in the mid-50s.

"Yeah, if it weren't for the frickin' wind," she replied sharply while shaking his hand, apologizing not only for her moist palms, but for the drops of sweat that were cascading down her face and neck. "But it's Wisconsin, right? At least it's not snowing."

Slightly taken aback, Nate peered at her and grinned. Then, spontaneously, they turned to their right and began to aimlessly stroll through the grounds, oblivious to the dozens of parents—many pushing baby strollers—and other zoo patrons who seemed delighted just to be outdoors after another relentlessly brutal Wisconsin winter.

Just seeing Connie Frataro in the flesh again gave Nate an appreciation for why his best friend had swooned. She was, as Nate's bachelor brother in Panama would say, a divina chiquita. Compact and lean, she was about two inches shorter than he was and had seductive brown eyes and a radiant smile that all but buckled Nate's knees. He was thankful that none of his female colleagues at Frank Lloyd Wright High looked anything like this. Who needed the temptation?

Still, her prickly response had given him a jolt. And before he began his carefully crafted little speech—which he'd rehearsed several times in front of his bathroom mirror the previous night—he recalled that on the few occasions that he'd exchanged small talk with Connie Frataro, she seemed to have a bit of an edge to her.

Nothing too caustic or off-putting, mind you. And there was no denying her brassy charm. But Nate remembered that she'd once uttered the F-word while describing a well-to-do, middle-aged businessman who dined at the restaurant several nights a week and never left more than a $1 tip. And he remembered his surprise the first time he noticed a small red and black tattoo on her left tricep of a demonic-looking clown with a cigar clenched in its teeth.

It wasn't the tattoo itself that caused him to do a double-take. He knew that a lot of men and most women under 40 had one somewhere. Indeed, he assumed that Connie also had a tattoo at the base of her spine, which seemed like a rite of passage for most females of her generation. But an evil clown puffing on a stogie?

Somehow it didn't fit. She was, after all, a student at Wingra College, a small, private Catholic school on the shores of weed-infested Lake Wingra. The long-held cliché was that nice girls attended Wingra and the wilder ones attended UW-Madison. But now he was dealing in stereotypes, he cautioned himself at the time—and besides, it was one lousy tattoo. Who cares?

"So, what would you like to know?" the young woman inquired after a long silence.

"Oh, I don't know. I guess … I guess I just wanted to make sure you're all right. I mean, not that it's my business. But being Sal's closest friend and seeing as how I'm the father of a 15-year-old girl, I just thought I'd check to see if there's anything I can do for you.

"I heard you dropped out of school, and I wasn't sure what that was about. But being a teacher, that concerned me a little—again, not that it's any of my business."

He shot a glance at her just as she was making a sour face and rolling her eyes.

"Look, Mr. Zavoral, I don't mean to be a bitch—seriously, I don't. But you're right. It's not your business. I get enough of this shit from my dad, OK? I mean, I appreciate your concern, but I'm fine. I just need some time to myself.

"But if it makes you feel any better, I'm returning to school next fall. In fact, I'm still living in my dorm."

Nate stopped and lifted his hands defensively. The fiery outburst caught him by surprise. But as he struggled to come up with an appropriate response, the young woman made another comment that froze him in his tracks.

"Just so you know, I did love him—and he loved me," she said without flinching as they shuffled along the asphalt path that wound around the sea lion compound.

"I've never shared that with anyone else, by the way. But it's true," she added, her eyes cast downward. "I'm not saying it would have lasted forever, OK? You know, because of the age difference and all that. But we dated for over a year, and I can tell you it wasn't just about sex—although the sex was pretty darn hot. I'm not about to deny that."

Nate winced and held up his hands again. She was now straying into territory that he did not care to explore.

However, he was stunned by her revelation that she and Sal had been seeing each other for over a year. That meant, among other things, they were dating while Sal was still married to Tammy. Nate was aware that the marriage had been unraveling for some time, but he was still taken aback, because Sal hadn't even hinted he was seeing someone else.

It made Nate wonder what else his lifelong friend had concealed from him over the years.

"So, I'm curious—what did you talk about?" Nate inquired, trying hard to mask his skepticism about her true-love assertion.

"Anything and everything—politics, sex, movies, relationships. Even the (Green Bay) Packers, if you can believe that," the young woman said without lifting her head. And while they had their share of "lively" debates, she acknowledged, there were just two subjects that caused them to argue. "So we tried to avoid both."

One was her taste in music—mostly her love of hip-hop. He absolutely despised it, she said with a half-smile. He claimed it wasn't really music and forbade her from playing it in his presence. Whereas, being Italian, she could at least tolerate his collection of Sinatra, Dean Martin and Bobby Darin CDs, she said.

The other subject that was taboo—"And I'm sure you can relate to this," Connie said—was religion.

"I'm like you. I was raised Catholic and think it's a bunch of crap," she said matter of factly. "Sal was horrified the first time I told him that, of course. And, naturally, he tried to convince me I was wrong. And that would really piss me off, so we finally just decided that the subject was off-limits.

"I mean, he'd get that look in his eyes whenever he talked about God and guardian angels and all that other bull—you know, that demented look that religious fanatics get? Absolutely gave me the creeps," she said with a shudder. "Uhh—I don't even like to think about it."

Nate, of course, knew exactly what she meant. There was no need to even comment.

"Again, just curious—did he even mention our pact?" Nate asked.

"Nope. Never came up. Not that I can recall anyway," she said.

The answer shocked Nate. They'd been dating for a year, he thought, and Sal never so much as mentioned it? But he pretended he was unfazed by the disclosure.

However, Connie hastily added, Sal did talk about how close he and Nate had been growing up and the many pranks they pulled—and the

169

belt lashings they'd both suffered at the hands of their fathers whenever they got caught.

One of Sal's favorite stories, she noted, was the time the two of them were spotted deflating the tires of dozens of cars that were parked at Immaculate Conception Catholic Church for a wedding.

"Sal said a nun grabbed the two of you by the hair and practically dragged you to see the pastor—was it Father Rick?"

Nate smiled and nodded.

"And Sal told me," she continued, "that for some reason Father Rick's wrath was directed mostly at you—that he was worried you'd lost your way or something like that, because you'd also been involved in a number of fights that year. Sal said he just stood there and didn't say a word, but the moment the two of you were dismissed and got outside, Sal fell to the ground laughing and didn't stop for about 10 minutes.

"And he told me that for years after that, whenever you got into trouble, he'd razz you and say that you'd lost your way and were going to end up in jail by the time you were 18."

Nate glanced at the young woman and broke into a grin. He'd forgotten that story. He'd even forgotten Father Rick, one of the few religious figures he'd ever respected and who, despite a gruff exterior, was actually a gentle soul who genuinely cared about the members of his parish. Even brash, smart-alecky kids like Nate.

As they strolled past the concession stand, Connie stopped abruptly and said she had to use the restroom. Nate told her to take her time and deposited himself on an empty brown bench directly across from the snack bar. He was still wounded that Sal had never mentioned their agreement to his feisty, young girlfriend—perhaps because he sensed what Connie's reaction would be—but pleased that at least Sal had shared with her some of the crazier tales of their childhood. Even though Nate was quite certain he'd exaggerated most of them.

As Nate reclined and rested his arms on the bench, he wondered what had become of Father Rick Cunningham. Then, as if struck by lightning, he bolted upright. Wait a minute, he thought, putting a hand to his mouth. Didn't the Boy Scout leader Nate had encountered in the Porkies—the guy who professed to be concerned about Nate's emotional well-being—say his name was Rick Cunningham? Nate was almost sure of it.

Wow, this gets loopier all the time, he muttered quietly. Then, in a flash, he reversed direction. OK, pal, don't get caught up in any mind games, like the kooks do, he admonished himself in a soft but firm voice. This wasn't karma or any other such nonsense. It was probably just an odd coincidence.

For that matter, was he 100 percent sure the scout leader's name was Rick Cunningham? Maybe he said Nick Cunningham. Or Mick.

As he attempted to make sense of it all, Nate looked up just as Connie was approaching him. Her face still flushed from her workout, she pointed to her watch as Nate got to his feet.

"Sorry to cut this short," she said, "but I didn't realize it's almost noon. I'm meeting a friend for lunch at 12:30 on Monroe Street, and I've still got to get back to my dorm and shower."

Nate had been hoping for another half-hour or so, but he didn't protest—especially since she'd agreed to meet with him on short notice. Instead, he offered to walk her to the entrance gate.

"Actually, I do have one other question—it's a big reason I wanted to meet with you," he said. "I've decided to give one last interview, to a reporter from *USA Today*, if you can believe that. And then that's it. I go back to being Nate Zavoral, high school English teacher."

"But I wanted to clear it with you first—to make sure you're OK with that."

The young woman came to a halt and flashed him a puzzled look.

"Why would I care? Just as long as you keep my name out of it. I mean, this is about your agreement with Sal, right?"

"Oh yeah, exactly," Nate assured her. "But, well, I'm sure the reporter will bring up Sal's heart attack, so it's quite possible your name could be mentioned—just as it was in my interview with Channel 9.

"But that would be it. I mean, I'll insist beforehand that the interview focuses on the pact Sal and I had—and, of course, on whether it's even remotely possible that Sal was responsible for my hole-in-one."

The young woman frowned, but continued to look straight ahead, ignoring Nate's apprehensive gaze.

"Whatever," she said. She trusted him.

Neither one uttered another word until they reached the tall steel gate at the zoo's entrance. As Nate gave it a shove, he turned his head and peered directly into the woman's doe-shaped brown eyes and posed one final question: If she were in his shoes, Nate asked, would she publicize what had happened?

She looked up at him somewhat confused—as if it were a loaded question.

Then she began to laugh.

"Look, Mr. Zavoral—Nate. If you honestly want to know what I think of the so-called pact you had with Sal, well, I don't mean to hurt your feelings, but I think it was really lame. I mean, just very, very strange. Especially the part about the golf shot being a signal of some kind. Seriously, were you guys on crack or what? Because that's the sort of thing I'd expect a couple of middle-schoolers to dream up."

She paused to gauge his reaction. He seemed collected, but it was obvious he was also anxious for her to complete the point she was trying to make.

"Now, having said that, you guys did have an agreement. And both of you promised to abide by it, right?

"So, if you really want my opinion, I absolutely believe you have an obligation to tell people what happened. I mean, if you guys were as close as you both claimed, there's no other alternative, as far I can see. So, yes, Nate, I think you have to keep telling your story, until people finally get tired of it—*if* they get tired of it.

"I mean, it's not even a question as far as I'm concerned. To just go on with your life and pretend it never happened …To me, that would be the ultimate betrayal."

16

"Lordy, lordy, now that's a body made for sinnin'," Pete Lovejoy chortled as a young waitress clad in a candy cane-striped blouse and white mini-skirt sashayed down the Edgewater Hotel pier with their drink order. "Ah, what I'd give to be 25 again."

"Oh, I don't know," Nate observed. "I'm guessing you still do pretty well with the ladies." For a guy well into his 60s anyway, Nate was tempted to add. And certainly for a guy who wore a black leather glove to conceal his prosthetic left hand—a permanent reminder, Lovejoy had freely noted a day earlier, of his Vietnam War days. (The device not only hadn't affected his career, the author had boasted, but he typed faster with the index finger of his healthy right hand than most reporters did with two hands.)

In fact, from everything Nate had heard, the famed author was still somewhat of a rogue, senior status or not. And now, seeing him up close, Nate could understand why. Though he squinted a lot and had prominent creases in his forehead, Pete Lovejoy was still a ruggedly handsome guy— tall, tanned and fit, his chiseled good looks accentuated by a neatly-trimmed mustache and a mane of slicked-back black hair that, save for a few streaks of silver, begged a comparison to Clark Gable's Rhett Butler in *Gone With the Wind*.

He was, Nate guessed, at least 6-foot-4—and he appeared even taller while striding down the street in his trademark designer alligator boots, which conveyed that he was an authentic Texan and, in an odd sort of way, were a perfect complement to his gray herringbone sport coat, white dress shirt and skinny jeans.

As they squeezed into green plastic chairs at a table at the far end of the long, white pier, which jutted out into serene Lake Mendota, they continued to trade small talk—mostly about the tragic decline of print journalism—and size each other up. It had been like this from the moment Nate had picked Lovejoy up at Dane County Regional Airport around 11 Friday morning—just a half-hour or so after passing out the last of his final exam grades to the approximately 100 juniors and seniors in his English and journalism classes—and treated him to a brief tour of Wisconsin's capital city and the solid Willow Grove neighborhood where he and his wife had lived for nearly three decades.

They'd met Brigitte and Anna for lunch at Lefty's and visited Turtle Creek Golf Club, where Nate introduced him to Bookie Finch. And then, with the head pro's permission, Nate escorted him on a motorized cart to the third hole, so Lovejoy could see for himself just how improbable Nate's ace was. They were joined there by Hank Meyer, a shy, beefy, somewhat disheveled photographer, probably in his mid-50s, who was based in Chicago and had been with *USA Today* since its highly publicized debut on the U.S. journalistic scene in the summer of '82.

On Saturday, their second day together, they began with a late breakfast at the historic Edgewater, where Lovejoy had booked a deluxe suite with a dazzling view of the sailboats dotting the waters. After that, they'd gone jogging down a pedestrian-bike trail and then visited Frank Lloyd Wright High School, where Nate introduced him to Milt Wilcox, who was working out in sweats in the school's weight room. (Lovejoy, it turned out, had interviewed Milt back in 1978, when he was a small college All-American and had helped lead unheralded Pendleton State to the NCAA Division II basketball semi-finals.)

That was followed by a four-course meal at Nadia's, one of the city's foremost Middle-Eastern restaurants, near the University of Wisconsin campus, where they were joined by Brigitte. And, despite Nate's protests—"If anyone at my school gets wind of this, I'm history," he pleaded fruitlessly as they entered the establishment—the two men capped off the day with more bantering and drinks at Visions, the city's lone nude dancing establishment.

The only real surprise for Nate was that the author, as far as Nate could tell, had taken out his notebook only once—and then just briefly—while conversing with Brigitte over dinner at Nadia's. Was he, Nate wondered, recording all this in his head? Hey, whatever works, Nate decided, knowing from personal experience that every reporter had their own methodology.

As Nate eased back in his chair, overjoyed by his good fortune—Nate Zavoral and the legendary Pete Lovejoy, sharing tales and basking in the late afternoon sun on the pier of Madison's finest hotel—the waitress returned with their drinks: a Scotch on the rocks for Lovejoy and a glass of pinot noir for Nate. At which point, the author lifted his glass and proposed a toast: "To Nate Zavoral's 16 million to one ace—and to miracles in general."

"May we all be so lucky," he added puckishly as they clinked their glasses together and paused for a long moment to gaze out at a cluster of sailboats sharing the still chilly waters with several rubber-suited kayakers.

As he soaked it all in and privately pondered how Lovejoy perceived him, Nate found himself marveling at how easily this slightly surreal meeting had fallen into place.

Just six days earlier—less than 24 hours after the lively discussion on his sun porch—he had called *USA Today's* headquarters in McLean, Va., and was put through to associate editor Andrea Dwyer, the same woman who'd signed the interview request he'd received in the mail.

USA Today's editors, she informed Nate, were delighted that Nate had accepted the newspaper's offer; and she seemed even more pleased when Nate disclosed that this was the only interview he would be granting and that, once the hubbub subsided, he was intent on resuming his rather ho-hum, middle-class lifestyle as if nothing had happened.

He did have one request, Nate said assertively. If at all possible, he preferred that Pete Lovejoy write the story. Dwyer chuckled out loud—then promptly apologized.

"I'm sure this won't surprise you," she replied, "but most of our subjects want Pete Lovejoy to write their profiles." Keep in mind, she said, *USA Today* has a large, highly-talented reporting staff—a good percentage, she sniffed, were Ivy League graduates—and "every single one would do a first-rate job of portraying you."

Just the same, Dwyer said, she would check with one of her bosses and get back to Nate within the hour. "Much obliged—I appreciate that," Nate said hopefully as he hung up.

No more than 10 minutes later she did get back to him—merrily informing Nate that not only had Lovejoy already been selected to handle the story, but that it would be one of his signature front-page profiles—not just a short feature buried in the back of the paper. However, her bosses had a request of their own, she related: that Lovejoy be allowed to spend an entire weekend with Nate in Madison; and not just any weekend, but the one coming up—just four days away.

Now, here they were, just the two of them, engaging in sprightly chitchat on a picture-perfect Sunday afternoon after spending nearly two entire days together, oblivious to the fact that Lovejoy would have to retreat to his hotel room in a matter of minutes and begin pounding out the piece in time for his rapidly-approaching mid-week deadline.

Nate chuckled at the absurdity of it all. Being a former newsman and having faced hundreds of stiff deadlines himself over his nine-year reporting career, he fully understood how the process worked. He also knew that Lovejoy had few equals when it came to turning out lucid, compelling prose under such rigid, nerve-wracking circumstances—and he felt honored just to be in the author's presence.

Then, ever so casually, Lovejoy dug inside his sport coat with his good hand and retrieved a micro-cassette tape recorder, laying it on the table next to a black, plastic ash-tray. Then he reached in his breast pocket and pulled out a long, thin cigar and, after that, a lighter. After lighting the stogie, he slumped back in his chair and began firing away.

He inquired about Nate's decades-long friendship with Sal Magestro and whether there was a particular moment or issue that caused Nate—and Brigitte, for that matter—to sour on the Catholic faith; and about Nate's disenchantment with organized religions in general.

Nate, who'd conducted a mock interview on Thursday night with Doc, wasn't the least bit fazed by any of it.

Actually, there *was* a specific moment when he began to question Catholicism, Nate acknowledged—or, at least, the extent to which the church would go to instill fear in its youngest, most vulnerable members. While attending catechism class one Sunday when he was about 12, his teacher—a nun, who like many nuns of that era, would swat

179

students on the hand with a ruler or an eraser if they were misbehaving—had shown Nate and his classmates a grainy black-and-white newsreel of a horrific fire that had engulfed an old Catholic elementary school in Chicago, killing 92 children and three nuns a year or two earlier.

Nate related that he and his young classmates were aghast at the images—particularly the sight of grim-faced fire fighters carrying limp young bodies from the carnage. This was in the early 1960s, mind you, he told the author, a time when most of them had never seen anything more gruesome than the Lone Ranger getting a chair busted over his head by some dastardly bank robber. And they were even more alarmed, he said, when the nun, after apologizing for making them view the newsreel, told Nate and his fellow students that the fire had been a warning from God. God was upset, she claimed, because of all the hatred and sinning on Earth; and she warned that unless humans started changing their behavior and treating each other with love and respect, there would be similar catastrophes in the future.

"When I told my parents about it after I got home," Nate told the author somberly, "my mother was so incensed she called the pastor and threatened to switch parishes.

"As for my dad—well, he just shook his head angrily and said to my mother, 'What about this surprises you?'"

Understand, this was standard operating procedure for the Catholic Church in the 1950s and '60s, Nate said. "The church's hierarchy ruled by intimidation. They still do, in my opinion—only they're a lot more subtle today."

Over the years, Nate said, he'd come to acknowledge that the Catholic Church and other religions do a tremendous amount of good, too—such as their work aiding the homeless, the disabled and other disenfranchised groups in their communities. And their heroic role in organizing and distributing humanitarian aid after natural disasters— even in places like Pakistan and Haiti.

But he also strongly felt they could be doing so much more.

"I mean, criminy, Pete," he said. "Last I read there were something like 900 *million* people on the planet who are either starving or seriously malnourished. How often do you hear religious leaders talk about that?

"Instead, the Catholic Church ..." he stopped in mid-sentence, staring out at the cobalt-blue water. "The Catholic Church essentially tells the people in Third World countries, 'Go ahead, keep having kids. God will take care of everything.'"

Realizing he'd struck a nerve, Lovejoy just sat back and took it all in. He was elated by the candid—if long-winded—response. He'd hit the jackpot. A juicy story had just gotten juicier.

"And here's another thing I just don't get," Nate continued. "I find it extremely ironic that so many supposedly religious people are racist at the core and consumed by hate—and how materialistic they are.

"I mean, I'm still not convinced there really was such a person as Jesus Christ. But if there was, I'm the first to admit he was an amazing role model—a guy who reached out to the poor and the frail, a guy who rejected the rich and the powerful and their lavish, self-indulgent lifestyles. And yet, a lot of these supposedly religious people go to church every Sunday and hear all the stories about this extraordinary individual and the example he set—and somehow it never sinks in. To me, it's absolutely mystifying—not to say hypocritical."

As the author leaned over and checked his recorder to make certain it was functioning properly, Nate was determined to make one final point. He told Lovejoy he yearned for the days when religion was considered a private matter, when most people—at least in the neighborhood where he grew up—respected the beliefs of others and weren't so quick to condemn.

Then he abruptly got off his soapbox and reached for his wine glass.

"I guess I'll leave it at that," he said contentedly, making clear that he was not a religious scholar and never claimed to be. Besides, he added, the last thing he needed was to be targeted by the fanatics who refused to tolerate any religious views but their own—let alone that of an agnostic.

The author took a drag of his cigar, his placid expression suggesting that he completey understood where Nate was coming from.

Then he sat up straight in his chair and asked pointedly, "So, you've had three weeks to think about it. Do you truly believe Sal Magestro was communicating with you on the third hole at Turtle Creek Golf Club? That he was, so to speak, honoring your—your so-called pact? Or was your ace just a mind-boggling coincidence?"

Nate didn't flinch. He knew Lovejoy would pose the question at some point during the interview.

"You're right—I have given that a lot of thought, obviously" he replied sincerely. "And I'd say right now I'm 99.99 percent sure that Sal was behind it."

The author tilted his head and looked at Nate curiously.

"Really? You're a believer now?" he said. "Because I'd heard you were more like 50-50. I mean, if you're 99.99 percent sure, why did you return to Turtle Creek the evening of May 13 to see if you could duplicate the ace? And why did you drive up to the U.P. a short time after that and spend three days, alone, in the wilderness, in a mini-monsoon?

"My sources say you did it because you still have major doubts—that you need a second signal before you'll wholeheartedly accept that Sal was, in fact, responsible for your hole-in-one. And I'm told you came up empty both times."

He took another drag of his cigar, then smugly exhaled, producing a small white circle of smoke that lingered over the table for a long, clumsy moment.

Nate was flabbergasted. He wriggled uneasily in his chair. How could Lovejoy possibly know about those things? Who squealed?

He must have talked to one of his golf partners—or perhaps all three, Nate thought. They were the only ones who possessed that information—outside of Brigitte, and Brigitte was iron-clad. Or was she?

Could Lovejoy possibly have coaxed that information out of her after her third or fourth cocktail at Nadia's?

But any feelings of anger Nate was experiencing were tempered by admiration as well.

"Wow, the guy's good," Nate thought, fully appreciative of the fact that—like any good reporter—Lovejoy had done his homework. But the one piece of information the author didn't possess—couldn't possibly possess—was Nate's meeting with the Rev. Mitch Crandall, Nate surmised. Because the only person who knew about that was Brigitte. And it was Brigitte who'd urged Nate to keep it a secret, pointing out that providing that information to others served no useful purpose and would only complicate matters.

"OK, Pete, you got me," Nate replied after a long silence. "I did return to the third hole at Turtle Creek, and I did spend three exasperating days in a monsoon at the Porkies—in both instances hoping to get another signal from Sal.

"It's also true that, as you put it, I came up empty both times."

He looked across the table at the author and remembered what Crandall had said about all the good he could accomplish, regardless of whether he actually believed Sal had orchestrated the hole-in-one or not.

"But I'll tell ya what, Pete," he said. "Something significant *did* happen during my three days in the wilderness. I guess you could call it a spiritual thing—even agnostics can be spiritual, you know—but I came to realize that Brigitte was correct all along, that in the end it really comes down to faith.

"So here's the thing. It may sound asinine or sophomoric, but Sal and I did have a pact, and we both promised to honor it. Sure, I thought it was just a lark back in 1999, the night we got smashed on Big Pike Lake. But it wasn't a lark to Sal."

"It sounds kind of creepy in retrospect, but Sal was such a believer in a hereafter that sometimes—well, sometimes it seemed he couldn't wait to kick the bucket to prove his case."

Nate turned his head and gazed out at the tranquil waters. He wanted to get this exactly right.

"So, the truth is," he said, in a measured, deliberate tone, "a week ago I was maybe 75-25. But today, right now, like I said, I'm just about 100 percent sure Sal kept his promise."

He smiled and returned his gaze to the author.

"But, you know," he added, "I'm not saying people don't have a right to be skeptical. I'm just explaining where I'm at. I'm not claiming that what happened at Turtle Creek was a miracle or divine intervention or whatever else the religious folks might call it. All I know is it happened—just as Sal insisted it would."

Lovejoy was glowing now. He stretched his right arm across the table and flicked his cigar over the ash-tray, then settled back again, his left leg crossed over the other.

"Which begs the obvious question—where do you go from here?" the author inquired. "I mean, you're aware, I'm sure, that some people—and not just the Rev. Jerry Falwell—claim you're a con man, that this was all a ruse, that you'll end up writing a book or signing a million-dollar deal for a made-for-TV movie. In other words, that you'll walk away from this—this *incident*—a very rich man."

Nate rolled his eyes and guffawed. "Yeah, right," he said sarcastically.

Just then the waitress appeared and asked if they'd like another drink.

"Just in time, sweetheart—another Scotch on the rocks would be super," Lovejoy said with a mischievous grin. He looked across at Nate, who motioned that he'd already reached his limit.

The author waited for the young woman to turn around—then studiously examined her swaying, peach-shaped behind till she reached the end of the pier.

"Look," Nate interrupted, "I can understand how some people might think I'm a fraud—especially these days. Which is why, as I told you earlier, this is the last interview I'll be giving for a long, long time. Maybe forever."

Nate explained that anyone who actually knew him understood that he valued his privacy and was the last person who'd seek fame and fortune from this incident. So no, there would be no book deals, no movies, no hiring of agents or p.r. firms or anything of the kind.

In fact, his first impulse after the initial barrage of letters and phone calls, he told Lovejoy, was to run off and hide. Much like Harper Lee, the famous author of *To Kill a Mockingbird*, did after fame began intruding on her life a half-century ago.

And he probably would have done just that, Nate said, had Brigitte not persuaded him that he did have an obligation here—to Sal.

"As for this being some sort of hoax," he continued, "my golf buddies all witnessed it. I mean, go talk to them."

"I have," the author said glibly as he pulled the ash-tray toward him and snuffed out his cigar. Figures, Nate thought.

"So where do I go from here?" Nate asked rhetorically "I honestly don't know. I guess I'll just wait and see what happens.

"My biggest hope, quite frankly, is that once this story is published and the great Pete Lovejoy explains who I am and what happened to me, that people will be content with that and eventually lose interest.

"And then I can go back to being Nate Zavoral—just an ordinary, deeply flawed human being. Just your average middle-aged guy with a bum knee and chronic heartburn and one of the worst golf swings on the planet—but a guy who, nevertheless, is reasonably happy with his lot in life.

"Just an ordinary guy and one-time agnostic?" the author teased.

Nate set down his glass and sighed wearily.

"Yeah, OK," he said firmly. "And one-time agnostic."

17

The newspaper landed with a thwack, just inches from Nate's ham and Swiss panini.

"Hot off the press!" Doc Flanagan announced gleefully, looking down at his friend with a rascally grin in the Turtle Creek Golf Club's dining area.

Nate stopped chewing and glared in disbelief at the paper's flashy front page. It was the latest edition of *USA Today*—and there, right before his eyes, just above the fold, was a two-column color photo of a beaming Nate Zavoral. He was clad in a black polo shirt and jeans, and was clutching his hybrid 4-metal and leaning against the fabled oak tree near Turtle Creek's No. 3 green.

Nate dropped his sandwich, scooped up the paper with both hands and opened it wide.

He was stunned and more than a bit confused. Today was Tuesday, June 8.

He'd been told the story would run on Friday, June 11, at the earliest. Lovejoy, he surmised, must have pulled an all-nighter on Sunday in order for the story to be published so quickly.

"I saw that studly mug staring out at me from a *USA Today* box as I was mailing a letter," Doc said while sliding into a chair at Nate's table. "Figured I'd buy a copy before all the hotties in town got wind of it and there wouldn't be any left."

Nate didn't hear a single word. His eyes were transfixed on the photo and the bold black headline just beneath it: "Miracle at Turtle Creek?"

And just below that, in smaller print, a subhead proclaimed: "Wisconsin Teacher's Bizarre Ace Ignites Divine Debate."

There was just one other story sharing the top of the page: "Thousands Say Farewell" read the headline, which was positioned over a photo of President Reagan's funeral procession in Simi Valley, Calif.

However, Nate's gaze was frozen on the humdrum, middle-aged golfer with the dorky smile whose image overshadowed even the Reagan story. He tried to express his astonishment, but was too stunned to say anything.

Although Pete Lovejoy had left a voice message the previous night alerting him that the paper's editors were eager to have the story published, Nate assumed that meant that Friday was a go. So he figured he had three days to prepare. And now, actually seeing his image beneath the masthead of one of the most established and widely-read newspapers in the country left him muddled and queasy—as if he'd been tossed around in a blender.

He did not even acknowledge Tyler Briggs as he arrived at the table with a cheeseburger platter and dropped into the chair directly across from him. Without so much as a word, Tyler reached over and ripped the paper out of Nate's hands, stared at it for several moments and unleashed a hoot.

"Whoa! Nate Zavoral on the cover of *USA Today*—so much for maintaining a low profile!" he exclaimed.

More than a bit agitated, Nate leaned over and snatched it back. He briskly glossed over the first few paragraphs of the story, then flipped to the jump page, where the remainder of the surprisingly lengthy piece was creatively laid out. The banner headline on that page declared: "The Shot Heard 'round the World." And underneath, a smaller headline teased: "Was It a Sixteen Million-to-One Fluke? Or a Signal from a Deceased Friend?"

There were two photos accompanying the jump: A black and white shot of Sal mugging in a chef's hat in the kitchen of his restaurant, which, Nate deduced, Tony Magestro must have provided to the author. And, to Nate's dismay, a small color shot of the Rev. Jerry Falwell railing about the "atheist schoolteacher" from Madison, Wis., and "his alleged pipeline to the Almighty" during a press conference in front of his church in Lynchburg, Va.

The Falwell photo wasn't exactly a shock, but as soon as he saw it, Nate began second-guessing himself again, wondering if his decision to grant the interview had been a colossal mistake.

Only moments earlier, Nate had completed a stress-free nine-hole round with Tyler and one of Tyler's former basketball players at Frank Lloyd Wright High. Now he was frantically examining the *USA Today* article for anything incriminating, oblivious to the mindless chatter at nearby tables and the unrelenting verbal potshots from his two companions.

Upon reaching the article's end, Nate slouched back, peered up at the ceiling and uttered an emphatic sigh of relief. At first glance anyway, it appeared to be a mostly positive—and accurate—account, he told his friends. What's more, Lovejoy had devoted just four paragraphs to Sal's death—as background, nothing else. There was no lurid speculation of what had transpired at Sal's mountain-side condo prior to his heart attack, and no snide judgments about Sal sneaking off to Colorado for the Christmas holidays with a 20-year-old employee of his restaurant.

There was, in fact, just a single line that made Nate squirm ever so slightly: the revelation of Sal's "involvement" with young Connie Frataro, Lovejoy wrote, "was almost as big a jolt to his friends and family as the coronary itself."

"I read the whole thing," Doc said, still waiting for Nate's reaction, "and you can relax. It's a fine piece of reporting—classic

Lovejoy. Not sure you noticed, but he even quotes Tyler and me—verbatim, by the way.

"Overall, he was quite charitable, in my opinion. Believe it or not, Z, you actually come across as a nice guy."

"So he doesn't mention the wife-beating, or the drug dealing?" Tyler snickered.

"Not a word," Doc said, not missing a beat. "But there's a wonderful line about Nate's golf swing—that it's got all the grace of a deranged farmer beheading a rooster."

The cocksure scribe chuckled as he watched Nate scour the article, both amused and fascinated by his friend's uncharacteristic nervousness, which bordered on paranoia. "But, you know," Doc continued, turning serious, "Lovejoy definitely was intrigued by the shot itself—and what it might mean. You get the impression he's a believer."

Nate remained tight-lipped, but the gratitude he was feeling toward the author was evident in his eyes and his body language. While driving Lovejoy to the airport three days earlier, he'd made just one request: That the scribe find a diplomatic way to describe Sal's relationship with Connie Frataro. Yes, she was only 20, Nate had acknowledged. And yes, they'd both been drinking heavily—and, presumably, had engaged in some rather vigorous sex—prior to Sal's heart attack.

But they were both adults, Nate had pointed out—just as he had to Channel 9's Naomi Winston—and neither one was married. So people could moralize all they want, he said, but there really wasn't anything sordid about the relationship. More important, Sal's death—tragic though it was—was merely a sidelight to the bigger story here: the possibility that Sal had succeeded in his attempt to contact his best friend from the afterlife.

Content that the article wasn't a hatchet job—he would devour it word-for-word when he got home—Nate laid the newspaper down and tried to appear upbeat. But he was dazed and struggled to keep his emotions intact. He still had trouble accepting that his image was plastered across the cover of one of the most highly-read publications in the country; meaning that by the end of the day, tens of thousands of people—in addition to the millions who'd already witnessed his appearance on *The Tonight Show*—will have learned about his hole-in-one and its potentially profound and eerie implications.

"You OK, Z?" Tyler asked.

"Absolutely," Nate said with a wave of his hand. "Really, I'm fine."

But his mind was swirling. He looked across at Doc and asked if he could borrow his cell phone. Then he shuffled to the clubhouse's side door and stepped outside to call Brigitte.

"Sorry to bother you at work, pal," he said, after a co-worker had tracked her down. "But I thought you'd want to hear it from me first. The *USA Today* story is out. I just read it—- Doc spotted it in a *USA Today* box this morning and bought a copy. I'm at Turtle Creek, and he showed it to me just a few minutes ago while I was having lunch with Tyler.

193

"I have no idea why they published it today. I was still under the impression it was going to be in Friday's paper."

"Oh no," Brigitte gasped, bracing for the worst. "And?"

"And, well, it's not bad. Nothing to fret about anyway—although it was a bit of a shock to see my picture on the front page."

"Oh my God, Nathan, I can only imagine. What shot did they use?"

"Just what you'd expect. I'm standing next to the tree near the third hole, holding up my 4-metal. And there are two photos inside. You're not in either one, unfortunately. But the Rev. Jerry Falwell is."

Brigitte's heart sank.

"Please tell me you're joking."

"I wish I were. But I guess I should have expected that, too. The other photo's an old black and white shot of Sal in his restaurant's kitchen."

"What else?" she asked anxiously. "We're understaffed today. Emily called in sick—I've got to get back to work."

Nothing that couldn't wait until later, Nate told her—other than that he was eager to get out of town and wanted to change their travel plans. There was no sense in waiting until Thursday afternoon to head up to Doc's cabin for their desperately needed getaway, he reasoned. Since the story was already out, he preferred to take off first thing the next day, Wednesday. Especially since the spring semester had officially ended at noon on Tuesday.

"Once the pundits start bloviating, I want to be in another galaxy," he said.

"You and me both," Brigitte concurred. She would ask her boss if she could take off a day early, she said, but didn't believe it would be a problem. "We're full-staffed the rest of the week," she noted, "and the new part-timer we hired started this morning."

As he hastily drove home, taking mostly back roads, Nate tried to anticipate the public's reaction to the *USA Today* article—especially that of the local media. The very thought caused his chest to tighten. Then again, maybe he was overreacting, he told himself. There'd been a grisly murder on the UW-Madison campus over the weekend. Chances were the local news hounds were preoccupied with that. Blood and guts always trumped other news stories—even stories as far out as this one.

But just as his mood was brightening, Nate turned up his block and noticed a white van with an antenna on its roof parked in his driveway. As he eased to a stop at the front curb, he noticed the words "WISC-TV Channel 9, Your No. 1 Local News Source" in large black letters on the side of the vehicle, and his heart froze.

"Jesus!" he screamed, choking the steering wheel angrily.

As he climbed out of his car, the passenger door of the white van swung open and a pair of long, shapely legs in a tight charcoal gray skirt appeared, and the next thing he knew Naomi Winston was standing in his driveway, flashing her magnetic smile at him. Then, on the driver's side of the van, the same rumpled cameraman who'd filmed the interview with Nate at Turtle Creek Golf Club emerged and trudged around to the front of the vehicle, camera in tow.

"Hi, remember me?" the news woman chirped, holding out her right hand as Nate warily approached her.

Unmoved, he shook her hand ever so briefly and tried his best not to appear rattled.

"Nice to see you," he lied. "Obviously you heard about the *USA Today* story."

"Actually, I just finished reading it. We get the paper delivered to the office. I must say, it was very well written. And all in all, quite positive, wouldn't you say?"

"Look, Ms. Winston," he said, but she immediately cut him off.

"Two minutes, that's all I'm asking," she pleaded. "I just want to find out what happens next. People love this story."

Nate was in no mood to negotiate. He could feel the hairs standing up on the back of his neck. "I'm sorry. But if I give you two minutes, then I have to give Channel 15 and all the other media their two minutes. And that's not going to happen.

"Look, that article was my last interview for a very long time. Seriously, you know how painful this is for me. I thought I made that clear when we met at Turtle Creek. I'm not into publicity."

Undaunted, she tried a different tact.

"Mr. Zavoral, no disrespect. But this isn't some huge blockbuster, and I'm not out to ruin your life. It's a fun story, an enchanting human interest story. All I'm asking for is two minutes. You can time it on your watch if you'd like.

"I mean, c'mon, you can't just drop off the end of the Earth now. You know that. So why not get out in front of the story and control it—instead of letting the 24-hour news cycle dictate how this thing plays out? I mean, you teach this stuff. You know how the game works."

Nate smiled, then promptly turned his back to the news woman and proceeded toward the front door of his home.

"Have a nice day, Ms. Winston," he said, dismissing her with a wave of his hand. Then, without looking back, he hurried onto the porch, twisted his key in the lock and shoved open the door.

"Despicable parasites," he mumbled under his breath as he stepped inside and slammed the door behind him.

Hurricane Sal was rapidly gaining speed.

18

His eyelids had just flipped shut when Nate felt his body jerk.

Startled, he sprung straight up and stared at the red and white bobber floating motionless in the still blue waters of Big Pike Lake.

Had he gotten a bite? he wondered as he surveyed the lake from his chaise lounge chair, which was perched perilously close to the edge of the long, rickety pier at Doc Flanagan's cabin. Puzzled, he sank back in the chair, his fingers still loosely wrapped around the bamboo pole that was secured in his lap. He began to nod off again when he heard a commotion at the far corner of the small, teardrop-shaped lake.

He squinted into the glistening sunlight and realized what had aroused him from his nap: a family of loons that was yodeling madly near a weed-bed less than 100 yards away. And the reason for their distress, Nate discovered, was a monstrous bald eagle that was dive-bombing them, claws extended, hoping to snare one of the little ones for a mid-afternoon snack.

Nate sat mesmerized as he watched the scenario unfold, then felt the urge to shout triumphantly after the mother loon had coaxed her babies into some tall reeds just a few feet from shore. Frustrated, the eagle retreated to the top branch of a nearby white pine, then flew off moments later to seek out a less savvy adversary.

The spellbinding little drama was yet another reminder to Nate of how much he enjoyed spending time at Doc's cabin, which sat isolated from the other dwellings on the 110-acre lake in sparsely populated Adams County, just a 90-minute drive from Madison. It spoke to the loner in him. And he was convinced that, like Thoreau-wannabes everywhere, he could scratch out a reasonably happy existence were he to live here year-round—totally dismissing the fact that even Thoreau had needed social stimulation on a semi-regular basis.

He even drew comfort from the fact that the cabin was more of a fishing shack than an actual cottage. And he liked that it existed on what was undoubtedly one of the few lakes left in Wisconsin where the cottages weren't stacked upon one another like tinker toys.

The cabin had just one bedroom, a cubbyhole of a kitchen, a small living room with an old recliner, foldout sofa and wood-burning stove, and a tiny, claustrophobic bathroom with a shower that spewed lukewarm water—if it worked at all. Which is why Anna was so elated when her parents agreed to her request to remain in Madison the next four days, providing she stayed with her best friend, Cassi Nguyen.

Still, as idyllic as the setting was, Nate couldn't shake the sentiment building inside him that he needed to honor The Pact and let people know he was virtually certain that his hole-in-one couldn't have been a mere coincidence; that as disconcerting and frightening as the implications were, people needed to know that he'd recently concluded that his deceased friend had, in fact, communicated to him from the darkest reaches of the universe.

After all, it was here, at this very cabin, that he and Sal had concocted their scheme five years earlier. And even though they were both half in the bag at the time and hadn't discussed what actions Nate would take if Sal somehow kept his promise, it was certainly implied that Nate not only would inform his friends and family about what had transpired at Turtle Creek, but that he'd go public with the revelation as well.

Of course, he never even considered in his inebriated state that there'd be a rather significant downside to Sal's plan if it actually played out the way Sal predicted it would. That his life would never be the same, that he would be perceived by many people—especially cynics like himself—as either a nut case or a charlatan, and that he would lose the one thing he cherished above all else: his privacy. Worse yet, his wife and kids would be forever haunted by his actions.

Now wide awake, Nate lifted his bamboo pole out of the water to make sure the night crawler was still attached to the hook. As he pulled the line close, he heard his stomach growl. He hadn't had much of an appetite since arriving at the cabin the previous day, but now he was famished. Then he remembered that the refrigerator was empty, save for a bottle of pickles, a couple cans of Lake Louie beer and a small chunk of Swiss cheese, and that he'd promised Brigitte—who'd taken off on her bike to pick strawberries at a nearby farm—that he'd drive into town and purchase some groceries.

He carefully laid down the pole, then grabbed his suntan lotion and empty beer can and paraded down the pier to the narrow sand path that led to the cabin. Once inside, he exchanged his swim trunks and flip-flops for a clean t-shirt, jeans and running shoes. Then he was out the door again and, no more than 10 minutes later, was driving along the main street of Carson Springs (pop. 1,431), one of those atypical Wisconsin small towns that seemed trapped in a time warp—like something only Norman Rockwell could've created. Except that in Rockwell's day the only ethnic minorities that existed in towns like this were seasonal migrant workers; whereas Hispanics who worked mostly in the town's four restaurants, two area resorts and a still controversial $70-million sparkling-water bottling plant that opened in the mid-1990s, now accounted for nearly 10 percent of Carson Springs' population—a development that had stirred up considerable hostility and resentment among the town's older residents.

Nate parked his sedan in front of Bethke's General Store, then strode inside and swiftly loaded a small plastic basket with enough food to last for two more days. After chatting briefly with the middle-aged Chicago couple that had recently purchased the store, he stepped outside and deposited his bags in the trunk of his car. As he did, he noticed a new coffee shop across the street, in the spot where Star Video used to be.

And something else caught his eye: a blue and white sign in the right-hand corner of the window that announced, "We Have Internet."

Intrigued, he stared at it for several seconds, trying to decide whether to give in to temptation. Ah, what the heck, he finally decided.

"Bless me Father, for I'm about to sin," he said with a chuckle while closing the trunk. Then he trotted across the street and entered the coffee shop.

He glanced around and was pleased that there were just two gray-haired gents, both donning baseball caps and sipping coffee at a window table, in the establishment. That meant the only two computers in the place were available.

After paying $2 for 30 minutes of Internet to a geeky, soft-spoken young man behind the counter, Nate plopped into a chair at the computer closest to the door and entered his password, mj41jfk. Then he quietly sighed and accessed his Gmail account.

It appeared seconds later, and as Nate scanned the dusty screen, the butterflies in his stomach instantly vanished. There were just seven new e-mails, all from people he knew and, judging from the subject lines, not a single one appeared worrisome.

However, there was an e-mail from Doc tagged "fyi" that made Nate balk.

Should he open it and risk spoiling what remained of his revitalizing four-day mini-vacation? Or should he forget he even saw it—at least until he returned home? Then again, maybe the contents were perfectly harmless. What if Doc was merely suggesting Nate check out a little-known fishing hole on the lake, or recommending a new area restaurant?

Against his better judgment, Nate clicked on the e-mail—and immediately wished that he hadn't. It was just three paragraphs, but those three paragraphs were enough to cause Nate's blood pressure to jump:

"Hey Z-man, hope you're having a good time. But you probably should know that things are as crazy as ever down here. Will save most of the gory details for later, but if you haven't heard, Falwell ripped you again, this time in *The Washington Post*. (Hard to believe, I know, but I saw it on their website.) And you are still a hot item on radio talk shows. Also, the Cap Times' editors want to know if you'll grant the paper an interview—I think they want Adam Sweeney to do the honors—when you get back.

"Zanier yet, *The National Enquirer* (!!) contacted Tyler, Luckovich and me to get our versions of what happened on April 24. No, I'm not kidding. We declined, of course. (And yes, you owe us big-time.) But thought you should know.

"My advice: Kick back and enjoy yourselves. And just so you know, nobody's using Camp Flanagan till the July 4th weekend. So you're welcome to extend your R&R another week if you'd like."

Gosh, if only he could, Nate moaned as he closed the e-mail and fell back in his chair. Unfortunately, next week was the end of the semester, so taking even a few extra days off was out of the question. As it was, he suspected he was already in Milt Wilcox's doghouse.

As he continued checking the screen, there was one other e-mail that stood out—from the Rev. Mitch Crandall. It was tagged "How goes it?", and as Nate opened it, he was relieved to see it was even shorter than the one from Doc.

The reverend said he'd read the *USA Today* article and was impressed by how balanced it was, and that he was both surprised and pleased that Nate now appeared to see the hole-in-one in a different light.

"Please stop by to see me in the next day or two," Crandall wrote, unaware that Nate had escaped to Doc's cabin for a few days of leisure. "I've got a proposition for you."

"Great—just what I need," Nate muttered.

He pounded out a brief response, noting that he was out of town, but that he would pay a visit to Crandall's church on Monday morning, two days after he returned to civilization.

As disconcerting as the two e-mails were—especially the one from Doc—Nate felt oddly encouraged as he drove back to the cabin. Yes, the news about *The National Enquirer* was troubling. But at least his golf partners had done the honorable thing and rejected the magazine's request. And if it was dirt the tabloids were after, well, good luck, because there wasn't much; certainly nothing that *The National Enquirer's* readers would be interested in. (Well, OK, outside of the raucous, X-rated 50th birthday party his brother Paul had thrown for him in Panama—with Brigitte's consent.)

So maybe the worst *was* behind him, Nate told himself; and maybe if he continued to stay cool and not overreact, the whole thing eventually *would* pass and he could resume his laid-back, largely uneventful life.

Fifteen minutes later, he turned his Saturn into the long snake-like driveway that led to a small gravel circle behind Doc's secluded getaway. As he eased to a stop, he was happy to see Brigitte's mountain bike propped against a nearby tree.

He shambled through the back door and carefully set the two bags of groceries on the kitchen table. His wife was on the opposite side, slicing a large pile of dark, ripe strawberries.

"How does strawberry shortcake for dessert tonight sound?" she asked cheerily, without looking up. "And strawberry pancakes for breakfast tomorrow?"

"Wonderful and wonderful," Nate said, gingerly removing a carton of organic eggs from one of the bags.

"Uh, I do have a confession," he added, slightly chagrined. "I stopped at a new coffee shop in town. They have Internet service, and I checked my e-mails."

Brigitte's head flew up.

"Shame," she scolded. "Anything interesting?"

Nothing to fret about, Nate assured her. In fact, there were just seven e-mails, he noted, including one from Doc offering to let them use the cabin for another week.

"Ho boy—wish we could take him up on that," Nate said, shaking his head.

He purposely did not mention the Rev. Jerry Falwell or *The National Enquirer*, knowing it would set her on edge for the rest of their stay.

There was also an e-mail from Crandall, Nate disclosed. The minister actually liked the *USA Today* article, he said, and asked if Nate could pay him another visit once he got back.

"Hmm. Wonder what that's about," Brigitte mused.

"I have no idea," Nate said, purposely avoiding any mention of the "proposition" the reverend had mentioned.

"Actually, I've got a confession of my own," Brigitte said with an embarrassed half-smile after slicing the last of the strawberries. "I checked my voice messages."

Nate glared at her with a feeling of dread.

"And you'll be happy to know," she said, "there were just four—including one from your son."

Nate's face lit up. "Really? He actually got through?"

"Yep—although he got cut off after a minute or so. Said he's doing great and that their team's been going from village to village for those AIDS training sessions he told us about and that the people seemed surprisingly receptive to their recommendations—even the men."

"But mostly," Brigitte said with a bemused grin, "he wanted to know how *you're* faring. Somebody on their staff apparently heard about the *USA Today* article—and the stuff that was said about you on Larry King. Unfortunately, his team's going back out into the field again—at least, that's what it sounded like. The connection wasn't real good.

"But he wants you to e-mail him with all the details. And just so you know, Nathan, he sounded concerned—said something to the effect that he hopes you know what you're doing."

Nate smiled at how downright comical the situation had become. Sean Zavoral was living and working in eastern Mozambique, where AIDS and malaria were nearly epidemic, amid abject poverty—and *he* was worrying about his father's ability to cope with a media blitzkrieg instigated by some ludicrous golf shot?

"Anna called too—twice, in fact. She's fine," Brigitte said. "And there was also a call from Sophie Magestro. She didn't sound upset, but she did ask that you call her—said it was urgent."

Before Nate could answer, Brigitte stretched her right arm across the table and passed him her cell phone.

"So please don't put it off, like you usually do," she said in a gentle but explicit tone. "Call her."

Nate scowled as he took the phone from her. Then he obediently marched to the front door, pushed it open and trotted down to the pier, where he figured he'd get the best reception.

He walked to the very end and, while gazing out at a mass of lily pads that nearly surrounded the neighbor's swimming raft, dialed Sophie's number. He had a pretty good hunch what this was about: she'd probably seen the *USA Today* article and wanted to express her opinion. Nate assumed she was OK with it. Then again, it had been just six months since her son's death; perhaps it had torn open a still fresh wound.

He was surprised when Sophie picked up on the second ring. However, there was considerable static, just as he'd feared.

"Hi Sophie, it's Nate Zavoral. I'm calling from a cabin about 80 miles north of Madison, so I don't know if we'll be able to maintain a connection. But how are you?"

"Nate, it's so nice to hear your voice," she answered. "But, sorry to say, I'm not so good."

There was an uneasy silence, and Nate could tell she was having a tough time getting the words out.

"Nate, I've got cancer—pancreatic, the worst kind. My doctor says I've got three or four months, at most."

Nate went numb. Jesus, is there an end to this madness? he wondered.

"Oh my gosh, Sophie, I'm so sorry. Is there anything I can do—anything?

"Unfortunately not, honey. But don't worry. I'm at peace with this. I'm a Catholic, you know, and besides, I've had a rich and full life. At least, that's how I look at it.

"And I'm at home, and I don't feel any pain. Father Ryan just left. He's stopped by every day since I got the diagnosis last week."

Nate was thankful to hear she was handling it so well. But the cynic in him wondered if Father Ryan had an ulterior motive. After all, it was widely known that the Magestros' liquor store—which they'd sold in the 1990s—was once the biggest in Madison and had been a virtual goldmine.

"Nate, there's another reason I called," Sophie said. Her voice faded in and out, and Nate strained to hear her. He pressed the phone hard against his ear.

"Nobody else knows about this except Tony and Father Ryan," she continued, "and they're both OK with this.

"You know all the time that Sal spent the last few years trying to raise money for that new swimming pool at the Boys and Girls Club? Well, I'm leaving most of my estate—almost $2 million—to the club, to be used for the pool.

"I talked to the club director, Brian Grindrod, yesterday, and he was very excited, of course. They've raised about $4.5 million so far, and this should put them over the top."

Nate's jaw dropped. He started to reply, but Sophie interrupted him in mid-sentence.

"And I'm doing it anonymously, Nate," she said emphatically. "I just don't want the publicity—not after seeing what you've gone through.

"It's just something I want to do. I think—I think Sal would be very happy with me, don't you?"

There was heavy static on the line again, and for a second or two Nate thought he'd lost the connection.

"Are you still there Sophie?" he asked.

"Yes, I'm still here, honey."

"Look, Sophie," he said, raising his voice so he could be heard above the sporadic buzzing, "I think that's extremely generous of you—I mean, just incredibly generous.

"And yeah, I think Sal would be very happy with you—or, I guess I should say, *is* very happy with you."

He pressed the phone to his ear to hear her response, but all he caught was a word or two. Then the line went dead.

He flipped the phone shut and stared out at the calm waters for a half-minute or so, trying to digest the ramifications of what he'd just been told.

Still stupefied, he turned in stony silence and, with his eyes cast down at the white wooden slats, marched back up to the cabin.

He didn't notice the giant walleye that leaped out of the water just inches from the end of the pier.

19

The fragrant smell of incense permeated the air as Nate slipped into a pew at the back of Lakeside Episcopalian Church, just a short walk from both the Capitol and Lake Mendota.

Beams of sunlight streamed through two giant stained-glass windows on the east side of the church, creating a warm, inviting atmosphere inside the stately, century-old building, which was even tinier than Nate had envisioned. The windows were creaked open at the bottom, and there were two large fans circulating air at the front of the church, which contained two sets of faded beige pews, each 14 rows deep.

All were empty now, save for Nate, who was seated in the very last row.

He peeked at his watch. It was nine o'clock, and Nate found himself thinking that this was the second time he'd set foot inside a church in six months—the first being Sal's funeral at St. Augustine

Catholic Church on Madison's near west side. Prior to that it had been at least a decade—for a young colleague's wedding, he remembered—and he couldn't recall the last time he'd actually attended a Catholic mass.

Just then, he felt a tap on his shoulder and heard a voice say, "If you need more time to pray, I can wait." He stood up and greeted the Rev. Mitch Crandall with a big smile and a loose embrace.

"I'm afraid I could pray 24/7 and it wouldn't save me at this point," Nate retorted as he followed the minister to his office, which was partially hidden in a side hallway at the rear of the building.

The reverend was dressed in casual attire—a sleeveless forest green v-neck sweater over a white shirt, and khakis. He asked Nate to have a seat in a blue, padded swivel chair, then pulled up a straight-back chair for himself.

Before sitting down, Nate sized up the room and was surprised that, outside of a large sterling silver cross directly behind the gleaming cherry-wood desk, there were no religious artifacts or holy pictures in the office. He excused himself momentarily and strutted over to study a framed photo on Crandall's desk of the reverend, his wife Holly and their four kids, with jagged snow-capped gray mountains in the background.

Then he noticed a larger framed shot on the wall of Crandall and several other religious figures, their tanned faces glistening with sweat as they marched down a dirt road in bold-colored religious vestments, with towering stands of bamboo behind them.

"Cambodia, 1997," the reverend explained. "The guy next to me is Maha Ghosananda, the Buddhist prelate of Cambodia. We walked for three weeks to promote peace. It was 114 degrees the day that picture was taken."

Beside that was the same poster of the indomitable Mahatma Gandhi that had graced a wall in Crandall's office when he was Madison's police chief.

"So, how are you holding up? And have things finally calmed down?" the reverend inquired earnestly as Nate finally settled into his chair.

"What do *you* think?" Nate said.

He informed the reverend that he and Brigitte had just returned to Madison after four stupendous days at Doc Flanagan's secluded cabin in Adams County, and that the mini-vacation had been even more satisfying than he'd hoped it would. It was so rejuvenating, in fact, that he really didn't mind the dozens of e-mails, letters and phone messages that greeted him upon his return. That included, Nate said, an offer to speak to the local Rotary Club, conveyed through his friend and golf partner Freddie Luckovich—an offer, he noted, that he actually might accept.

"Figure it's better they get the full story from me, rather than some contrived piece of garbage off the Internet," he rationalized.

He did not mention his phone conversation with Sophie Magestro. Nobody except Brigitte needed to know about that, Nate had decided on the drive back to Madison. Moreover, Sophie had specifically stated she wanted her donation to be anonymous, so Nate wasn't about to betray her trust.

The reverend peered at Nate inquisitively over his thick, wire-rim glasses. Nate had accepted an invitation to speak to the Rotary? This was an encouraging development, Crandall thought. Not just encouraging, actually—remarkable.

"So, in answer to your question, no, things haven't calmed down," Nate said ruefully. "But I guess—I guess that's OK."

Now he definitely had Crandall's attention.

"It is?" the minister asked, slightly mystified. "Uh, well, glad to hear that."

Nate had anticipated that very reaction. He shifted upright in his chair, placed his elbows on the table and pressed his hands together in front of his face.

"Look, Mitch, I'm not quite sure how to say this," he said haltingly, "and I'd rather not go into the details, but ... I guess you could say I've had a change of heart. I suppose someone in your line of work might even call it a conversion."

As Crandall listened intently, Nate mentioned all the soul-searching he'd done at Doc Flanagan's cabin and how it had given him a fresh perspective. More to the point, he'd concluded that his hole-in-one couldn't possibly have been a coincidence. And that meant, Nate said, he really did have an obligation—to Sal, if no one else—to fulfill his end of the deal, even at the risk of temporarily disrupting his life. That is, to tell his story to anyone who wanted to hear it and, along with that, to confess that Nate Zavoral—a one-time agnostic—was now virtually certain that the ace was a message from his deceased friend.

He assumed that's what Sal would want him to do, Nate said. Indeed, if he had one regret, it's that he and Sal never discussed—not in any detail anyway—the extent of his obligation after witnessing the ace. Undoubtedly because the very idea was so far-fetched, Nate added with laugh.

"But you know what, Mitch? I think you're entirely correct. If even a tiny percentage of people change their behavior and become better human beings because of this—even if it's out of fear that deceased family members might be watching them and judging their actions—well, that alone will be worth it."

"Now," he added, "I have no idea if some ridiculous golf shot could have that kind of profound impact or not. But I guess there's only one way to find out."

Pleased with his explanation, Nate settled back in his chair again, crossing his legs.

"Anyway," he said, smiling at the reverend, about that proposal …"

Crandall remained still for a long moment and stared at Nate with suspicion, trying to figure out what had triggered this startling change in attitude. Had there been a second signal perhaps? He decided not to force the issue—though there was no disguising his excitement.

"This is … very welcome news," he said.

With that, the minister stood up, strolled over to his desk and picked up a manila folder filled with letters and newspaper clippings. He handed it to Nate, then plopped back in his chair.

215

"Have you ever heard of an organization called the International Peace Council?" he asked. "It's been around since the 1990s, but, sorry to say, hasn't gotten much press."

Nate furrowed his brow and admitted he'd never heard of the group. He opened the folder and flipped through the clippings. He noticed that one of the articles, from *The Capital Times,* carried the same photo of Crandall and the Dalai Lama that was displayed on his office wall. The headline above the story read: "Crandall Returns to the Killing Fields."

The Peace Council, the reverend pointed out, was a relatively small group of renowned religious and spiritual leaders—it currently had 17 members, including Crandall himself—that was formed in 1995, as an outgrowth of the 1993 Parliament of World Religions in Chicago.

The group met biennially for a three-day conference at different locations throughout the world, and its intent, Crandall said, was to seek peaceful, enduring resolutions to some of the world's thorniest, under-reported issues—such as their prominent role in the Ottawa Treaty of 1997, which has resulted in the destruction of 44 million land mines in war-ravaged countries across the globe.

But it's still a formidable problem, the reverend noted.

"One hundred million," he said somberly. "That's how many land mines are still buried in the ground, mostly in fields and alongside rural roads, in about 60 countries. Staggering—absolutely staggering. People here have no idea."

216

Crandall got up again, scooted over to his desk and hastily browsed through a handful of documents before finding the one he wanted. Just two pages, it outlined the group's objectives and included a list of its members, along with their phone numbers and e-mail addresses.

He hurried back and deposited it in Nate's hands. Then he dropped back into his chair and waited for the reaction. He didn't wait long.

As Nate explored the list from top to bottom, his mouth dropped. Former South African Archbishop and Nobel laureate Desmond Tutu. His Holiness the Dalai Lama. Oscar Arias Sanchez, former president of Costa Rica, another Nobel laureate. Imam W. Deen Mohammed, former leader of the Muslim American Community. Archbishop Samuel Ruiz Garcia of Chiapas, Mexico.

Nate didn't recognize all the names, but it seemed like a Who's Who of the most revered spiritual figures on the planet. The Pope wasn't among them, but the list did include the name of a Vatican representative.

Crandall noted that he himself had joined the group in 2000, shortly after becoming a minister, at the invitation of both the Dalai Lama and Luis Mantilla, who was its executive director and who, incidentally, resides in Mount Horeb, the sleepy bedroom community 20 miles west of Madison, the reverend pointed out.

"He's actually a former history professor at the University of Wisconsin," Crandall said. "But that's another story for another day."

217

Nate arched his eyebrows as he continued to examine the list.

"I can't believe I haven't heard about the organization. And its director is based in Mount Horeb, Wis.? How strange is that?"

The reverend had assumed Nate would be impressed—especially being a former journalist. "As I indicated, it's a low-key, dignified group of holy leaders dedicated to world peace. There's no screaming, no demagoguery. None of them has been involved in lewd scandals. So why would you be surprised that it hasn't gotten much publicity?"

"Excellent point," Nate acknowledged.

"OK, so here's my proposal," Crandall said. "What have you and Brigitte got going on Saturday, June 27—11 days from today?"

Nate thought for a moment, but drew a blank. He and his golf partners played 18 holes every Saturday morning during the summer, but his participation certainly wasn't etched in concrete. Other than that he'd have to confer with his wife. She was the one who arranged their social schedule.

"Sorry," he said, wincing slightly. "I really don't know."

"OK, next question. Have you ever been to Seattle?"

"Seattle? Nope," Nate said, resting his chin on his right fist. "Spent a long weekend in Portland once, for a national teachers conference. But never Seattle. I hear it's a marvelous place—when it's not raining.

"So what's happening in Seattle?" he asked inquisitively. "Let me guess—you want me to meet Bill Gates?"

"Now *there's* an idea," Crandall retorted. "But, to be honest, I think mine's better."

The Peace Council's next conference was in Seattle on June 25-27, Crandall noted. Naturally, the minister himself would be among the participants. And he'd be honored, Crandall said, if Nate would be his guest for the closing session the morning of June 27.

Nate was dumbstruck. He tried vainly not to overreact but could feel his insides start to churn.

The reverend made it clear he had dual objectives in extending the invitation.

Though the Peace Council preferred to remain under the radar, so to speak—which was only proper considering the distinguished makeup of the group, he suggested—it nonetheless had been greatly disappointed by the dearth of media coverage following its previous meetings.

"But I'm guessing that might change if you show up," Crandall said—though he stressed the group would not publicly disclose Nate's appearance until after the three-day conference had ended. Otherwise, "It would be a circus, a big distraction—we wouldn't accomplish a thing."

The second reason for the invitation, the reverend said, was that, upon hearing of Crandall's initial encounter with Nate, a number of Peace Council members had asked for the opportunity to meet Nate personally. "Even the Vatican's representative expressed interest."

Nate flashed a look of astonishment—of utter disbelief.

"They've heard of my story?" he gasped. "Desmond Tutu knows about my hole-in-one? The Dalai Lama? Does the Dalai Lama even know what a hole-in-one is?"

Crandall laughed. "I can assure you he does." In fact, the reverend said, he'd recently e-mailed a link to the *USA Today* story to all 17 members.

He continued, "We'll pay your expenses, of course, and put you and Brigitte up at a nice hotel from Thursday through Saturday. But let me emphasize that I'm not pressuring you in any way. It's entirely up to you—assuming, of course, that you can get time off from your job. Although I'm guessing that now that it's summer, that won't pose a problem."

Nate felt slightly woozy. For an uneasy moment, he again regretted not only The Pact, but the fact that he'd shared it with anyone other than his wife and his close circle of friends. Granted, he'd recently vowed to set aside his concerns and continue to tell his story. But he'd done so under the belief that people's fascination with it would eventually dissipate. Now he anxiously wondered when "eventually" would be.

For cripes sake, he thought. He'd already appeared on *The Tonight Show* and had his lackluster, greybeard image splashed across the front page of one of the country's most widely-read newspapers. Meeting face-to-face with some of the most esteemed spiritual leaders in the world would elevate it to yet another level—the mere thought caused his heart to race.

Sensing the discomfort Nate was experiencing, Crandall leaned over and patted him on the knee. "Relax. It's no big deal—really," he said.

Then the reverend stood up and walked over to a mini-refrigerator that was hidden behind his desk. He opened the door and pulled out a bottle of spring water. As he returned to his chair, he playfully tossed the bottle to Nate, who was lost in contemplation.

Nate thanked him, twisted off the cap and took a long drink.

Still somewhat shaky, he finally looked up and began to think out loud.

"But what—what would I tell these guys, Mitch? I mean, what are they looking for? I guess I'm not sure what the point of such a meeting would be."

"Well, for one," the reverend said, "I think they want to hear the story in your own words—because most of them, I'm guessing, aren't sure if you're a phony or the real deal. Or some sort of media creation, if you will.

"Luis Mantilla, who e-mails the members almost daily, says they're very curious about the whole thing. Not all of them, mind you. But several of them believe it's something the group should investigate—to see if you're credible, if nothing else."

"And if they decide I'm not credible?"

"Well, if that happens—and trust me, they'll be very up front about that—there will be no mention of you in the press release after the conference ends. Nobody except the Peace Council members will even know you'd been there.

"Honestly and truly, that's the worst that could happen. And if that's the case, at least you and Brigitte will have gotten a free trip out of it, right? You'll have gotten to see Seattle. And by the way, it hardly ever rains there in the summer."

Nate hunched forward and tried to envision other possible scenarios.

"And the best that could happen?" he asked.

Crandall lifted his hands, as if to acknowledge that he didn't have the answer to that question. "Depends on the media, I guess," he said. "I think it's safe to say, at the very least, you'll end up changing some lives. The question is, how many?"

Nate didn't want to think about that. Like everything else that had happened in the last month, it seemed completely absurd—and nearly impossible for his overtaxed mind to comprehend.

"Now, I can guarantee you one thing," Crandall continued. "Nobody in this group is going to claim—as your friend Luckovich does—that you're the great Messiah or whatever it is he calls you; or that you possess some kind of mystical power. These people do not make rash or bold statements. So that's not going to happen. I want to be clear about that.

"Last I read, there are about a dozen places around the world where apparitions of the Virgin Mary have been validated by the

Catholic Church. But those were actual sightings—or alleged sightings, anyway—so your situation's very, very different.

"Still, if these guys find you credible, it's conceivable that they'd release a statement of support—maybe something along the lines that they've concluded you're an honest man and that your story warrants further investigation."

The reverend paused to study his friend's reaction. Then he leaned over and said soberly, "However, I don't want to mislead you. These are very intelligent, very savvy individuals. They didn't get to be such powerful and influential world leaders by accident.

"They'll be fair and respectful of you—but they'll also be blunt. They'll challenge you. But I think once they understand you're not a publicity seeker, and once they see The Pact and understand that this actually happened to you—well, then it gets interesting. And I mean that in a good way."

Crandall paused as Nate settled back in his chair with a strained look on his face and took another swig of spring water.

The reverend gazed out his window for a moment, then glanced back at Nate and flashed a wry smile. He probably shouldn't be saying this, Crandall thought, but it was imperative that Nate understood all the potential ramifications.

"One last thing—and this is off the record," he said. "As dignified as these men are, they also possess—with one or two exceptions—rather prominent egos.

"So if they do suspect you're the real deal and that you might actually be in a position to change the world, even in a small way ..."

Crandall peered out the window again and chuckled.

"Well, some of them, I dare say, may even be a bit jealous."

20

The flight attendant, a prim, pencil-thin brunette in a snug blue and white uniform, handed Nate the small pillow he'd requested.

"That will be $8 sir," she said curtly.

"Is that all? Gee, what a bargain," Nate grumbled as he dug into his pocket, then passed her a $10 bill. She ignored his snide remark and promptly gave him his change.

As she sauntered to the back of the plane, Nate, who was seated in an aisle seat near the front—so he could make a swift exit if his claustrophobia began acting up when the plane landed—heard someone call out his name.

"Mr. Zavoral—over here," the voice called out again.

Clutching the pillow, Nate turned his head and spotted a burly, ruddy-faced man in a gray pinstripe suit grinning at him from the row behind his, just across the aisle. The man, who was balding and appeared to be around 40, thrust out his right hand, and, without a word, Nate warily but instinctively reached across the aisle and shook it halfheartedly.

"You are Nate Zavoral, right?" the man murmured, cupping his mouth so that other passengers couldn't overhear.

As Nate observed the man suspiciously and pondered how to respond, the man said excitedly, "I thought I recognized you back at the gate. Anyway, I'm Patrick Gallagher from Naperville, Ill. And I just had to tell you—there's no way that hole-in-one was just a coincidence. I don't care what the talking heads and the religious nuts are saying.

"And for what it's worth," he added, "I'm hardly the only one who feels that way. Just thought you'd want to know that."

Slightly taken aback, Nate smiled faintly and thanked the man.

He then slid the pillow behind his head and returned his attention to the *New York Times'* op-ed page, which he'd been staring at mindlessly from the moment the plane had lifted off the runway at Chicago's O'Hare Field some 20 minutes earlier.

He glanced at Brigitte, who always drew comfort from the humming of engines—she'd once slept for seven consecutive hours, while pregnant with Sean no less, during a road trip to Glacier National Park—and had dozed off minutes after the plane had departed for the nonstop flight to Seattle's Sea-Tac Airport. He admired her ability to do that, but knew it would be futile to attempt it himself. He simply had too much on his mind.

Still, he was amazed at how relaxed he was despite all the turmoil in his life—and despite the fact that he would be stuffed inside a giant metal cylinder with approximately 120 sweaty, anxiety-prone strangers for the next five hours. Though he was severely claustrophobic and had suffered two debilitating panic attacks on planes in the last decade, he had yet to pop a single Xanax to help keep his emotions in check.

He suspected his contentedness was due in part to the fact that nobody could contact him while he was 30,000 feet off the ground. But he figured it was also because he'd pretty much come to terms with his predicament and what he needed to do next.

Yes, he knew perfectly well there was a potentially scary downside to his decision to meet with members of the Peace Council—a decision that undoubtedly would keep the Nate Zavoral saga alive for at least another week or two. Not only was he wading into a potential religious quagmire, he realized, but if his appearance before the group became public knowledge, he'd be opening himself up—and his family—to further scrutiny from a gruff and quick-to-judge media, particularly the shrieking ninnies who dominated cable talk shows and the blogosphere.

Still, he wasn't about to second-guess his decision now. He believed that the Rev. Mitch Crandall had summed it up best—that as terrifying as the future sometimes appeared, this thing was bigger than Nate Zavoral. So it was time to face that fact and put his own life aside—hopefully just temporarily—and do what was right.

227

After all, as amusing and irrelevant as it may have seemed in 1999, he'd agreed to the pact with Sal Magestro, he reminded himself for the umpteenth time. Nobody had put a gun to his head and insisted that he sign the document.

So, schmaltzy as it sounded, this really was about character now—Nate Zavoral's character. And, if asked, Nate would be the first to admit he'd made a ton of mistakes, big and small, in his life and that he'd done a number of things that, in retrospect, he wasn't particularly proud of—like his refusal to get a vasectomy after Anna was born. (Brigitte, who'd never wanted more than two children, finally relented and got her tubes tied, but Nate's act of cowardice had sparked the only serious spat—one that had lingered for several months—of their marriage.)

But even though he occasionally came up short, Nate had always tried to be a man of honor, and he wasn't about to abandon his principles now. Moreover, he couldn't shake the thought that his own father—who not only toiled in a monotonous and sometimes arduous factory job for much of his adult life, but worked odd jobs in the neighborhood on weekends to help feed and clothe his five kids—might be watching this whole dizzying drama unfold.

Was Sal watching as well? Outrageous as it seemed, Nate realized now that was a distinct possibility. There was even a slight ache in his heart as he thought about it, and it dawned on him for the first time how much he missed the guy.

Theirs truly was a special—if unconventional—friendship, Nate thought.

He remembered the time in his senior year at Madison North when a member of the school's wrestling team, Doug Snell, confronted him at a Marc's Big Boy restaurant—the school hangout—one Friday night. Just a few days earlier, Snell had broken up with his long-time girlfriend and, Nate later heard, had gone berserk upon learning that Nate had asked the girl out the very next day. (She declined, but that apparently was immaterial.)

Snell, who was roughly the same size as Nate and was known to practically foam at the mouth when provoked, demanded that Nate step outside to the parking lot to "discuss" the matter. And while Nate immediately accepted the challenge—his father had taught him how to box at an early age—he knew both of them would probably regret their macho, hot-headed behavior once it was over.

Then, out of nowhere, Sal appeared—just as the two young gladiators were about to square off in front of about 10 classmates under a dim street light just a few feet from the restaurant's front door.

This was during the roughly three-year period when Nate and Sal had grown apart—like characters in a real-life version of *Grease*, Sal had migrated to the "hair-boy" crowd, which worshipped fast cars and tough-talking floozies; while Nate gravitated to the "collegiates," who tended to be short-haired, self-righteous jocks who claimed the moral high ground.

But while he'd established his greaser bona fides by his junior year, Sal had also become a star tackle on the football team—he was a good 30 pounds heavier back then—and was not somebody you wanted to mess with.

229

So when he spotted the wrestler berating Nate and flinging off his Madison North team jacket as they prepared to do battle, Sal stomped out his cigarette and charged over from the far end of the parking lot. After forcefully separating the two combatants, he grabbed Snell by the neck with both hands, pinned him against a tree and calmly explained that unless he left the premises immediately, he would discover that his face had been rearranged when he woke up the next morning—*if* he woke up.

Nate smiled warmly at the memory. Then he glanced down again at Brigitte and gently patted her head. She was the real rock in their relationship, and he was delighted that she'd agreed to accompany him on the trip, to play the role of cheerleader if nothing else. That had been a tremendous relief, because Nate wasn't sure he could do this alone.

But then, they'd been a team from the beginning—from the day they'd tied the knot at Immaculate Conception Church on Madison's north side in 1974, just a couple of foolish, idealistic, baby-faced kids—and they remained a team now, exactly three decades later. Which was as it should be, Nate surmised, because it wasn't just his own future that was at stake here. It was Brigitte's future, too—as well as Anna's and Sean's—although his wife wouldn't be attending Nate's meeting with the Peace Council on Saturday morning, opting instead to meet an old high school classmate for breakfast and some shopping in Belltown, just a short jaunt from their hotel. She'd leveled with Nate that she couldn't possibly bear the pressure, and he was ok with that.

But while he was oddly at ease with the situation, there remained a small kernel of doubt in Nate's mind about Sal's ability—even if he had, in fact, ascended to a higher life form—to pull this whole thing off. Try as he might, Nate couldn't entirely dismiss the notion that his hole-in-one *was* just an extraordinary fluke—a nagging skepticism that Nate attributed to his days as a reporter, when he was required to question anything and everything.

Then again, as Crandall pointed out, even devoutly religious people occasionally have doubts. The minister had cited, as just one example, Mother Teresa, who reportedly questioned the existence of God during the final years of her life.

"But that's where the power of faith comes in," Crandall asserted.

Unable to focus on his newspaper, Nate reached inside his jacket and retrieved three note cards, along with a blue felt pen.

Then he jotted down a few key words on each one for his appearance before the Peace Council the next day—much as he did whenever preparing to address a large group. "Don't meander," he wrote. "Nate and Sal: two ordinary guys." "No interest in fame." And, most important of all, "JFK"—which he underlined twice, his customary reminder of how unflappable President Kennedy had been throughout the Cuban Missile Crisis.

As he inserted the cards back inside his jacket, the Boeing 747 jerked severely, causing several passengers to gasp out loud. It happened again a few seconds later, and Nate heard what sounded like plates and silverware crashing to the floor at the back of the plane.

Just then the pilot's voice resonated over the p.a. system, noting that the plane was experiencing some turbulence as it cruised over the continental divide, and requesting that passengers remain in their seats and make sure their seat belts were securely fastened until further notice.

"There might be a few more bumps over the next half-hour or so, but we don't expect anything too serious," the pilot said in a composed, reassuring tone. "But until things settle down, I need to ask that everyone stay put for a while."

Nate flinched and drew in a deep breath, but again was surprised that he wasn't panicky or even worried. He cast a look at Brigitte, who had yet to even stir, then squinted out the window and saw nothing but ominous-looking gray clouds.

He even entertained a brief dark thought: what if the plane was struck by lightning, burst into flames and everyone perished—and word got out that Nate Zavoral was among its passengers? Not only that, but that he'd been flying to Seattle to meet with some of the most prestigious religious leaders in the world.

What a field day the media would have with that story—in Wisconsin, anyway, he mused.

The plane again bounced sharply, and Nate closed his eyes tight.

Then he heard his name being called again. He turned his head and immediately spotted the man from Naperville, Ill., who was leaning toward the aisle with a dopey grin on his face.

"I'm a white knuckler—this stuff usually scares the crap out of me," he said, again cupping his mouth so that other passengers couldn't overhear. "But not this time—not with Nate Zavoral aboard!"

Nate smiled weakly, but he was annoyed, and the man immediately sensed it.

"Hey, I don't mean to be a pest," the man said apologetically. "All I'm saying is, if things get really dicey up here, it's nice to know you've got connections."

———

Nate had just stepped out of the shower following an early morning workout in the hotel's austere exercise room when the phone started ringing.

Still half-asleep, he waited several seconds for Brigitte to pick it up, then remembered that she'd rushed out the door some 30 minutes earlier to meet her old high school friend for breakfast. He hastily wrapped a towel around his waist, then scurried out of the bathroom to the nightstand to answer it. As he did, he eyed the clock radio next to the phone. It was 8:15.

He figured it was Crandall, reminding him that they were to meet for coffee in the hotel's restaurant at 8:30.

"Mr. Zavoral—Nate Zavoral?" the voice asked. "This is Brett Finklemeyer, reporter for *The Seattle Times*. I heard you were meeting with members of the International Peace Council this morning and I just ..."

Nate abruptly cut him off. "How'd you get this number?" he snapped, making no effort to mask his anger.

"Uh, from someone at your hotel's front desk. An anonymous caller contacted our city editor about 20 minutes ago and tipped us off about the meeting. And the editor ..."

Nate interrupted him again.

"Look, Brett—what was the name again?"

"Brett Finklemeyer."

Nate paused for a moment and tried to harness his hostility. He's a reporter, Nate reminded himself, just as you once were—in another lifetime. And he's just doing his job.

"OK, Brett, I don't mean to be rude, but nobody was supposed to know about my being here. But I'll tell you what. I'm going to be meeting with the Peace Council in about 45 minutes, and I can call you after that and meet you at a coffee shop somewhere in the neighborhood.

"I'll give you an exclusive. But you've got to promise to keep this under your hat. I don't want you mentioning it on your paper's website or in any stupid blog."

"I'll have to clear that with my editor," the reporter said. "But that works for me."

"Well, tell your editor that's the only way it's going to work," Nate said crisply. "So I'll be back in touch around 11 or so." He asked the reporter for his cell phone number and scribbled it on a notepad next to the clock radio. Then he slammed down the receiver and cursed loudly.

Was it too late to bail out? Nate wondered. He collapsed on the bed and, while hunched over, head in hands, waited for his rage to subside. After a half-minute or so, he abruptly stood up and headed for the door. Caffeine would probably just exacerbate his anxiety but he desperately needed some coffee.

There were only a few people in the hotel restaurant when Nate arrived there at precisely 8:30. He took a quick look around and instantly spotted Crandall, who was clad in a shiny white and maroon silk robe and seated at a booth in the far corner that was framed by an assortment of lush, tropical plants tumbling out of immense, orange clay pots.

He marched over to the booth and firmly shook the reverend's hand, then dropped into the bench seat across from him.

"My gosh, first time I've seen you in a suit," the reverend said while taking a bite of his hash browns. "Very impressive. I almost didn't recognize you."

"I got it two days ago—first suit I've owned in probably 15 years," Nate replied defensively, not at all comfortable with the image it conveyed.

"So, how are you handling all this, if you don't mind me asking?" Crandall inquired. "Did you sleep OK?"

Yes, amazingly enough, he'd enjoyed a long, nourishing sleep, Nate said, pausing to order a cup of coffee from a slender, nattily-attired waiter. But he was shocked, he noted, to get a phone call just minutes earlier from a reporter for *The Seattle Times*. And, of course, Nate said, the young newshound had wanted an interview.

"I told him I'd meet with him later this morning—providing that he not let anyone else know I'm here. No blogs, no breaking news bulletins—nothing else until I've left town. And he seemed satisfied with that."

Crandall looked across the table and grimaced.

"I'm dumbfounded," he said. "Seriously, I can't imagine how he knew—I mean, most of the local media were aware of the meeting this morning. I'm pretty sure we sent out a press release about it. But in the past, the media's always ignored them. And I made it clear to members of the Peace Council that we didn't want to publicize your appearance. So the fact that this guy knew ... It's very odd."

Clearly befuddled, the reverend took a drink of his orange juice.

"Other than that," he said with a chuckle, "how are you feeling? No last second change of heart or anything like that?"

"Nope. And, you know, strangely enough, I'm really not all that nervous. I mean, as I said all along, I'm just going to explain what happened and let the chips fall where they may.

"I mean, it's really quite simple, right? Sal and I had an agreement. So I really don't have any choice but to honor it."

Nate raised his shoulders as the waiter filled his cup with coffee. "If they buy it, great. And maybe my life changes." He lifted the cup to his lips and took several gulps. "If they don't—hey, at least I'll have gotten to see Mt. Rainier."

Crandall grinned and responded with a shrug of his own—though he was still somewhat mystified by Nate's willingness now to

236

share his story not only with the Peace Council, but apparently with millions of other people—assuming, that is, that the finicky national media didn't lose interest in the story.

"Terrific," he said. "That's exactly the attitude you need."

He took a last bite of his scrambled eggs, then wiped his mouth.

"Because," he added, "I just got some news that—well, I don't want you to overreact or anything, because it's not that big a deal."

Nate pursed his lips and braced for another jolt.

"Turns out the Pope himself wants to hear your story, outlandish as that may seem. So he's going to be taking part in the meeting through a video hookup."

Nate remained still as he glared at the minister.

He didn't know whether to laugh or scream or call the whole thing off right now. No big deal? He could feel the color draining from his face.

"Let me get this right," he said incredulously. "Pope John Paul II wants to hear my story?"

He turned his head, surveyed the room, then slumped back in his seat.

"And is the Pope aware that I refer to myself as a recovering Catholic?"

"I believe he is," Crandall said. "He also knows you're agnostic—or *were* agnostic. So do all the others. They've all seen the *USA Today* article, and I think it's fair to say it piqued their interest even more. They want to know who this Nate Zavoral character really is."

237

"But again," the reverend said in an earnest tone. "I want to be totally up front. They'll probably grill you a bit—and they won't hold back.

"I think the bottom line for many of them is trying to decide if God would communicate in such a peculiar manner.

"I'm guessing most of them are highly skeptical—perhaps even cynical. At the same time, if you tell your story exactly the same way you did to me—and if they're convinced some good may come of this, that it might, for example, make people think twice before committing crimes—who knows?

"Maybe they'll issue a statement saying that God sometimes works in unorthodox ways, and that they're open to the possibility that what happened to you was a—well, for lack of a better word, miracle."

Nate felt more confused than ever. He still had trouble comprehending that he was actually here, in Seattle, about to appear before the Peace Council. It was like something out of a two-bit hokey novel.

"Frankly," the reverend added, "I'm intrigued myself to see how they react to this—especially the Pope. But if they issue a statement that essentially says your story may have merit—I mean, my gosh, do you realize what that would do for your credibility?

"It might even silence the buffoons like Falwell. So in that respect it would be huge. Huge!"

Nate checked his watch and adjusted his tie.

"It's almost 8:50," he noted coolly—having long ago accepted his increasingly zany plight.

Crandall nodded and wiped his mouth a final time as he reached for the bill, which the waiter had placed on the table seconds earlier. Then the reverend stood up, slid a hand under his robe and pulled out his wallet. As Nate waited patiently, Crandall tossed three crisp $5 bills on the table, then wrapped an arm around his friend as they strode toward the elevator.

"Just be yourself," he said heartily.

21

The 17 members of the International Peace Council, resplendent in their diverse, colorful religious garments, were gathered around a large oval table and engaged in warm, jaunty conversation as Nate and the Rev. Mitch Crandall entered the hotel conference room.

Nate immediately felt invigorated. It was the sort of atmosphere, he thought, one might encounter at a high school reunion—which wasn't that surprising seeing as how the Peace Council had been meeting every two years since its inception, and its members were now like family.

Almost as one, the prestigious figures stopped talking and shifted their attention to the two men approaching the table. Nate had been expecting a polite, cautious welcome, but instead was greeted with welcoming smiles and strong handshakes as Crandall led him around the table and introduced him to each member, almost all of whom were in their 60s and 70s, and were either white-haired or balding. The lone exception was Luis Mantilla, the group's affable director, who still had a full head of wavy, black hair and, Nate guessed, was in his early 50s.

Perhaps, Nate surmised, they'd gotten the weighty issues out of the way in the first two days of the conference. Whatever the case, the effusive greeting gave him a much-needed emotional boost as he sat down next to Crandall near the end of the long table, across from Mantilla, who was casually dressed in a mauve silk shirt and light dress slacks.

Still, it was hard not to feel intimidated. Archbishop Desmond Tutu of South Africa and the Dalai Lama were seated side-by-side at opposite ends of the table. And immediately to Nate's left was Oscar Arias Sanchez, the former president of Costa Rica and winner of the 1987 Nobel Peace Prize.

The instant he was seated, Nate discreetly searched inside his sport coat and pulled out his note cards. While he was doing that, Mantilla rose from his chair and formally welcomed Nate to the conference and thanked the Rev. Mitch Crandall for arranging Nate's appearance. He noted that the meeting was running late, for which he apologized, and said that while the group couldn't wait to hear Nate's story, he needed to first turn on the giant flat-screen TV behind him that would allow Pope John Paul II to witness Nate's remarks via a video hookup from the Vatican.

The director informed his colleagues that the Pontiff was battling the flu but nonetheless had insisted on watching the proceedings from his bedroom.

"I'm told he's as curious about Mr. Zavoral's story as every person in this room," Mantilla said.

He strolled over to the large entertainment cabinet that had been brought in for the occasion, picked up the remote and turned on the TV. Suddenly, the Pope's larger than life image appeared on the screen. He was clad in a sparkling white cassock, smiling broadly, his thin silver hair partly concealed under a white skull cap. He was seated in what appeared to be a large rose-colored stuffed chair.

Almost immediately, Nate felt butterflies in the pit of his stomach—not unlike the butterflies he'd experienced on the third tee at Turtle Creek Golf Club two months earlier.

"Your Holiness, can you see us all right? Are we coming through clearly?" Mantilla asked, his eyes focused on the screen.

"I can indeed," the Pontiff responded in perfect English. He extended a greeting to the members of the Peace Council and congratulated them for their continuing efforts to make the Earth a better, safer, more humane place—particularly their efforts to improve the plight of the poor and the sick and the frail. He issued a special welcome to Nate, stating that it took courage and "a great eternal awareness" to appear before the religious leaders. And he apologized for "not being there personally" to meet Nate and learn more about his background.

Mantilla graciously thanked the Pontiff. He explained that Nate that would speak for about 15 minutes and then take questions. Unfortunately, they'd have to keep an eye on the clock, he noted, because there were still other pertinent issues to discuss before the conference officially ended at noon.

"That sounds reasonable. I am anxious to hear Mr. Zavoral's first-hand account," the Pope said. "You know, I did some kayaking and skiing when I was younger but never tried golf. There weren't many golf courses in Poland when I was growing up and, of course, nobody would have had the time or money to play anyway—this was during the war years, remember. But I understand it's an extremely humbling game.

"Anyway, please proceed."

Mantilla turned to the Peace Council members and observed that they too were anxious to hear Nate's account of what had happened on April 24—and the trials and tribulations he'd experienced since the story became public. It seemed, Mantilla said, that most Peace Council members had yet to form an opinion on the question of whether Nate's deceased friend, Sal Magestro, had actually sent Nate a signal from the hereafter—or, for that matter, whether such a thing was even possible.

But even the doubters among them were interested in what ostensibly had occurred, Mantilla acknowledged—especially after reading the *USA Today* article and knowing that the story had taken on a life of its own and become the subject of contentious debate throughout the United States.

And of course, they were especially interested, Mantilla said, directing his eyes at Nate, because the high school English teacher had openly admitted that he's an agnostic.

"So without further ado," the group's diminutive director said, gesturing with his left hand, "Nate Zavoral."

Nate rose slowly, cleared his throat and took a quick glimpse at the top note card in his left hand, which simply said: "JFK"

He raised his head and, while scanning the faces assembled around the table, thanked the religious leaders for their invitation. After nearly 20 years as a teacher, Nate was fairly confident when speaking before large gatherings. This was a little different, of course, and, as he made eye contact with each of the dignitaries, he couldn't help but feel awed.

He inhaled slowly to help dispel his jitters, then began by explaining in a calm voice that although he'd been raised Catholic, he'd left the church during his teen years—as the *USA Today* article had mentioned—and had never been a fan of organized religion as a whole. In fact, as the article also pointed out, he sometimes referred to himself as a "recovering Catholic," Nate confessed.

He noticed Crandall cringe as he said it, and assumed it had struck a nerve with the Pope as well. He half-expected the Pontiff to interrupt him at this point and possibly admonish him, but upon hearing only silence swiftly moved on.

He did not, Nate made clear, rule out the existence of a Supreme Being "of some sort." Moreover, he said he had enormous respect and admiration for the members of the Peace Council, and praised them for their vision and for seeking honorable and lasting solutions to the violent conflicts that plagued far too many countries on the planet. He was particularly impressed, he said, by the role they'd played in the United Nations' treaty to rid war-ravaged countries of land mines.

In recent years, Nate said, he'd come to appreciate that organized religions did much good in the world—that without the churches, the homeless situation in the United States, to cite just one example, would be even more abysmal than it is today. That's why, he said, he was so encouraged to learn from Crandall about the existence of the Peace Council, which he'd been unaware of, even as a onetime journalist.

Nonetheless, he was still largely old-fashioned, Nate said, smiling for the first time. That is, he felt that people's religious beliefs were a private matter and nobody else's business—unless, of course, those beliefs infringed on other's rights and beliefs. And unless they incited bloodshed and mayhem—and in many cases, even war, which Nate maintained was the ultimate hypocrisy for anyone who claimed to be religious.

What's more, Nate continued, he'd always been suspicious of anyone—religious leaders included—who claimed to know what God was thinking. If in fact there was a God.

And yes, he quickly added, it was true. He'd long been an agnostic—which, he suggested, was another reason people were so captivated by what happened to him on the morning of April 24.

How did he himself explain the—for lack of a better word—"incident"? Well, at first, he wasn't sure what to think, Nate told the men. And, to be honest, he was more caught up in the actual achievement—the first hole-in-one of his life—than the possible supernatural implications. But now, some eight weeks later?

He surveyed the faces of the religious leaders, then gazed across the room at the luminous, daunting image of the Pope on the massive TV screen just beyond the end of the table.

In the last few weeks, he'd gone over it again and again in his mind, Nate said. And he'd recently come to the conclusion that it couldn't possibly have been an accident. The odds were just too great, he said, particularly when you consider that he and Sal Magestro had this ... this so-called pact.

At that moment, Nate reached inside his suit coat and retrieved a small cellophane baggie that contained one of the two copies of the pact—slightly crumpled and bent at the corners—that he and Sal had signed in the summer of 1999. The Peace Council members all broke into wide smiles.

It had been Crandall's suggestion to bring it to the meeting; if the members could view and touch the actual document, the reverend had suggested to Nate, it might help validate his authenticity.

Nate carefully removed it from the bag, then handed it to Crandall to pass around the table for the other sacred officials to examine.

"For obvious reasons, I don't share this agreement with just anyone," Nate said. "After Sal and I typed it up five years ago, I showed it to a couple of golf buddies—and to my wife Brigitte, of course. But ever since the *USA Today* article—and I'm sure you can appreciate this as well—I've been keeping it in a lock box at my bank."

Sal had kept the only other copy, he noted, and Nate had no idea what he'd done with it, or whether it still even existed.

"I'm told you've all seen the *USA Today* story, so I guess there's no need to rehash what transpired on April 24," Nate said, as the members continued to listen intently while briefly examining the document as it was passed from one to another.

"The only thing I'll add is that ..." He looked up and observed the faces of the religious leaders. "I don't know how many of you have played golf, but believe me when I say what happened that day was, well, there really isn't a word for it.

"Seriously, I wish each one of you could stand on that tee and get a glimpse of the hole—the flagstick waving in the breeze at the top of a rather steep hill, and the massive oak tree about 10 feet to the right of the green. I think then you'd understand just how implausible this whole thing was."

As he glanced around the room, it dawned on Nate that every member of the group—the Pope included—seemed mesmerized by his presentation. Their expressions ranged from disbelief to bafflement, but to Nate's astonishment they seemed to be hanging on his every word.

He shot a peek at his next note card, then paused momentarily to take a gulp of water.

"I do want to mention one other thing, and then I'll answer any questions you may have," he continued. "I really am not in this for fame. If it were up to me, I'd run back to my simple life as a teacher and more or less try to disappear—similar to what the esteemed author Harper Lee did after writing *To Kill a Mockingbird.* For which, as many of you know, she won the Pulitzer Prize for fiction way back in 1961."

That comment elicited chuckles from several Peace Council members, including Mantilla.

"No, I'm dead serious about that," Nate said firmly. "For me, having to deal with the media is about as appealing as undergoing a lobotomy—and I say that as a former newspaperman. I happen to cherish my privacy. And my biggest fear right now is that I may have lost that, forever."

He stopped to take a breath, then peered down at the next note card in his left hand: "Don't Meander," it cautioned.

"So why, you may be asking yourselves—why do I continue to promote my story? Well, mainly because the Rev. Mitch Crandall convinced me that some good might come of this. That if even just a small percentage of people who learn all the details are convinced Sal Magestro *did* send me a signal from heaven or wherever else he might be—in other words, that there is, in fact, a life after this one—maybe it will strengthen their resolve to be good, honest, compassionate human beings. Or, in some cases, maybe it will frighten them into being good people. Either way, the impact could be significant."

"This friend of yours, this Sal Magestro," one of the religious leaders abruptly interrupted. "Did you ever discuss with him what the person still on Earth should do if, in fact, the deceased succeeded in sending a signal? In other words, what the surviving friend should do with the evidence?"

"No, never did," Nate replied with a slight frown, an acknowledgment that he deeply regretted that they hadn't. "I mean, a couple times we joked about how our closest friends—and our wives— might react if it actually happened. But other than that, no.

"And I think that's because—well, although we both vowed we'd always honor this pact, we pretty much considered it a lark at the time. At least I did.

"I mean, the thought that this could actually come true was utter nonsense as far as I was concerned. So we never talked about what the surviving friend would do with this information—although it seems obvious to me that Sal would want me to share it with others. Otherwise, what's the point?"

From the back of the room came another question: "And did you ever discuss what this life after death would be like?"

"Oh, we'd joke about that too, but nothing very profound, I'm afraid," Nate said. "To me, of course, it was a non-issue because I totally dismissed the possibility. Sal had the traditional Catholic view that you spent the rest of eternity in God's kingdom. Only in Sal's mind, the kingdom was mostly a bunch of golf courses—all resembling the famous Pebble Beach course in California—and pristine lakes, all stocked with 50-pound muskies.

"Oh, and there were women, of course. But in Sal's version of heaven, they all looked like Halle Berry."

Nate looked up expecting to see smiles, but instead noticed expressions of bewilderment all around the table.

"You know, Halle Berry, the movie actress?"

After a brief, clumsy silence, he peered down at his note cards and promptly shifted direction.

"We did agree on one thing, however," Nate said, determined to make this final point. "That if there truly is a God, that God almost certainly is a woman. We were both troubled by all the violence in the world—almost all of it instigated by men, from the beginning of time. And we agreed that if it weren't for women, the entire planet would be engulfed in chaos and hatred and bloodshed.

"So it just seemed obvious and logical to us that if there was indeed a loving God out there—a God who in the end would make things right—that God in all likelihood was female."

He again studied the faces at the table, waiting to be challenged for this bold—and, perhaps to some of those present, boneheaded—observation. But again, there was only quiet.

Then all at once came a loud voice, and those in the room turned their heads and shifted their eyes to the TV screen at the back of the room.

It was the Pope. He was smiling, like many of the others, which suggested to Nate that he was amused not only by Nate's nonconformist beliefs, but probably by Nate's audacity as well. In any event, His Holiness now wanted to be heard.

"My friend, Mr. Zavoral," he said. "I am convinced—as, I presume, most of my distinguished colleagues are—that you are an honorable and modest man. I do not doubt your sincerity."

He paused for effect, his hands clasped in front of him.

"So let me be frank with you. Before your appearance today, I was almost certain that your sensational golf shot was some sort of hoax. Now I'm convinced that's not the case.

"That said, allow me to be candid—and I assure you, this has nothing to do with your naïve, shallow, uninformed opinions of the Catholic Church. I don't believe for one moment that your hole-in-one was a miracle or anything close to it. I don't care what you claim the odds were. It was, it seems to me, a mere stroke of luck, pure and simple.

"Granted, you are a common man, a good man," he went on, "but God does not communicate in this manner. And if you knew anything about the Bible or the church's teachings, you would recognize as much."

The room fell mute now. The terse admonishment had caught everyone by surprise and seemed jarringly out of character for a man known for his gentle, reserved demeanor. For a disturbing moment, Nate had a flashback to his days in catechism class, when speaking one's mind often led to a severe rebuke by one of the nuns—sometimes even expulsion.

Thank goodness the Pontiff wasn't actually present in the conference room, Nate thought, because he'd probably march over to where Nate was seated, jerk him by an ear and deposit him in the lobby.

Then, just as quickly, the tone in the Pontiff's voice shifted again, and in an instant the smile returned.

Skeptical though he was, the Pope said, he agreed there was some merit to the argument that Nate was in a position to do some good in the world—possibly "an extraordinary amount of good."

He pointed out that the Peace Council was not an officially recognized world body and that it possessed no powers to pass laws or forcibly enact change. Nonetheless, it was so widely respected and its members so revered, he said, that it was capable of influencing the behavior of millions of people—providing it possessed the means of reaching such a large audience.

"So if the Peace Council's members decide to issue a statement declaring that they believe you are genuine and that they are keeping an open mind about your golf shot and its potential divine implications, I can support that."

He grinned at the camera and added in a soft voice, "That is the most I can offer at this time."

The Pontiff thanked the council members for allowing him to take part in the exchange, and praised Nate for his courage and perseverance, and for traveling to Seattle to meet with the council.

Perhaps one day Nate could visit the Vatican and meet with the Pontiff personally, he suggested. "Maybe you could even teach me the golf swing," he joked.

"Just remain righteous, Mr. Zavoral," the Holy Father advised, "and do not become intoxicated by all this attention. You will be in my prayers."

He smiled again and made the sign of the cross. Then the screen went blank. The moment it did, Mantilla rose from his chair and waited a few moments so that the council members could fully absorb the Pontiff's remarks.

"Well," he said, staring at the Vatican's representative, Bernardo Antonelli, who was seated next to the Dalai Lama. "I'm sure I speak for all of us when I say that we're grateful to the Holy Father for his astute observations and for sharing his time with us this morning, despite being a bit under the weather."

Mantilla checked his watch, then informed the luminaries that while he wished there was time for more questions, they were slightly behind schedule and still needed to discuss some important issues before adjourning at noon. "And, of course," he said, turning to Nate, "we need to decide whether we want to release a statement to the media about Mr. Zavoral's appearance here today."

The leaders all nodded.

Echoing the sentiments of the Pope, Mantilla thanked Nate for his "enlightening" presentation and promised he would get back to him before the group took any further action. In any event, he wished Nate a safe return to Madison and said he hoped Nate found his appearance before the Peace Council to be beneficial and perhaps even inspiring.

"Maybe," he surmised, "it will even help you cope with the myriad pressures you continue to endure in your personal life."

Nate was beaming, unable to conceal the enormous relief and elation he was feeling. It had gone well—shockingly well, he believed. Crandall felt it too, and after getting up from his chair, the two of them made their way around the table, ardently thanking each official for not publicly dismissing Nate and for allowing him to meet with the leaders personally and explain exactly what had occurred on the morning of April 24.

Crandall then flung an arm around Nate's shoulders and led him to the door.

"Perfect. Absolutely perfect. I wouldn't have changed a thing," he said in a hushed voice.

"Thanks," Nate said. "But it really was hard to interpret their feelings."

"Oh, trust me. They were impressed. No, not just impressed—enthralled!"

As Nate shoved open the conference room door, he let out a yelp. In front of him stood four reporters, all holding tape recorders, plus a TV cameraman.

Before he could react, one of the reporters—a hulking young man with a large bulbous nose and reddish hair—rushed forward and pressed a small microphone inches from Nate's chin.

"Tim Lavalette, News Channel 15, Mr. Zavoral," he said forcefully. "Just had a question or two about your meeting with the Peace Council ..."

No sooner had the words left his mouth than the other reporters barreled forward and pointed their microphones at the school teacher's face.

Nate was aghast.

"Who scheduled this meeting—and what did you talk about?" the TV reporter stammered. Slightly shaken, Nate flashed a look of alarm at Crandall, who was as incredulous as Nate and unsure how to respond.

Nate reacted spontaneously, throwing up his hands and telling the reporters he was sorry, but that he had no comment for now. He and the reverend then hurried past them to the elevator.

The reporters followed close behind, continuing to spit out questions as they pursued the two men. Luckily for Nate, the elevator door opened almost instantly, and he and Crandall leaped in.

When the door finally closed, Crandall immediately apologized.

"I am so sorry—I have no idea how they heard about it," he said. "I mean, we sent out a press release about the meeting, as I told you, but there wasn't one word about you being here."

Nate stared at the floor glumly. He did his best to laugh it off.

"Mitch, I'm a former reporter, remember?" he said, still looking down. "Twenty years ago, I'm embarrassed to say, that might have been me."

As Nate entered his hotel room, his wife was posing before a full-length mirror, admiring the new calf-high leather boots she'd just purchased at a downtown boutique.

"So—how'd it go?" she asked, her eyes fixated on the fetching image in the mirror.

Nate tried to appear composed, even optimistic.

"Pretty good, actually. At least they didn't compare me to Satan or anything like that. They're still talking, but I think there's a chance they'll issue a statement that says I'm not just some goofball—and that my story may have merit. At least that's Crandall take on it."

"Really?" Brigitte said. "Wow. That's—that's wonderful, Nate."

She waited for a moment, not wanting to be the purveyor of bad news. But she knew she had no choice.

"Uh, sorry to have to tell you this, honey," she finally blurted out. "But the media knows you're here. You've got two phone messages from reporters requesting that you call them back."

Nate rolled his eyes and flipped up his arms in exasperation.

"I know," he said angrily. "Somehow the word got out—don't ask me how.

"A reporter for *The Seattle Times* called just a few minutes after you left this morning. I didn't know what to tell him—although I did end up agreeing to meet him for coffee later this morning. That was stupid— it just caught me off guard.

"And that's not all. There was a bunch of reporters waiting for me when Mitch and I left the conference room just a few minutes ago. I essentially told them no comment and jumped on the elevator."

Brigitte crumpled her nose. She felt thoroughly overwhelmed.

"What time are you meeting the Times' reporter for coffee? And where?"

"Screw coffee!" Nate snapped, fighting to contain his mounting rage. "Let's just pack and get out of here. I'll call the guy from our taxi. Maybe give him two or three minutes. But that's it as far as interviews go—for now anyway."

Brigitte tried not to panic, but felt exactly as her husband did. She did not care to be trampled by any media brigade. When Nate had asked her to accompany him on the trip, he'd never even hinted at such a possibility. In fact, he'd told her that outside of the Peace Council members themselves—and, of course, his golf partners—she was the only one who was aware of his appearance before the group.

She plopped down on a chair and kicked off her boots. Then the two of them began stuffing their suitcases. At that moment, the phone rang. Brigitte looked at Nate for guidance, and when he nodded, she picked it up.

It was Crandall. Without uttering a word, she passed the phone to her husband, who listened intently and, except for a few curt responses, said almost nothing. Then he abruptly hung up.

"Well?" his wife said.

Nate got up from the bed and paced back and forth for several moments. This is absolute madness, he thought, shaking his head.

"Welcome to the future," he growled.

Crandall, he explained to his wife, found out that two local TV stations had already posted stories on their websites about Nate's appearance before the Peace Council. Crazier yet, a small crowd of people had gathered in the front of the hotel, apparently hoping to catch a glimpse of Nate as he left the building.

Nate scowled after noticing the look of sheer terror on his wife's face. He had trouble believing it himself.

The good news, he told Brigitte, was that Crandall had arranged for a taxi to pick them up at the hotel's back entrance in approximately 10 minutes. Crandall would meet them at the door.

"We need to be there," Nate said firmly.

A frantic 15 minutes later, Nate and Brigitte were hurtling down the stairwell just a few steps from their third-room floor, the wheels of their suitcases clanging noisily on the concrete steps as they made their way to the ground level. When they reached the glass exit door at the bottom, they immediately spotted Crandall leaning into the passenger-side window of a lime green taxi no more than 20 feet away. He was conversing with the driver.

As Nate and Brigitte shoved open the glass door, lugging their suitcases behind them, Crandall noticed them out of the corner of his eye and motioned for them to get into the vehicle. He rushed over and gave them each a hug, profusely apologizing for the chaos.

"I'm still not sure how this happened," he said.

Crandall said he'd explained the situation to the cabbie—a young, swarthy man whose curly, black locks were spilling out from under a Seahawks cap—and that the ride to the airport would take 20 minutes, at most.

"That means you'll have almost five hours until your flight," the minister said. "But it beats waiting here."

Nate wasn't about to protest.

As the cabbie clambered out of the car and tossed their luggage into the trunk, Nate thanked the clergyman a final time and suggested they get together as soon as Crandall returned to Madison later in the week. Then he and Brigitte scurried into the back seat, pulled the door shut and looked at each other assuredly. Without uttering a word, they instinctively squeezed hands for luck.

A second or two later, the cabbie hustled back into the front seat, closed the door and stepped on the accelerator. Then he abruptly halted the vehicle after moving just a few feet.

"Uh-oh," he said.

Nate sprung up and, as he peered out the windshield, was shocked to see a crowd of about 30 people—several of whom were pointing excitedly at the cab—parading toward them. Those at the front, clutching mikes and assorted cameras, clearly were members of the media. But most of the others—including one carrying a large placard that proclaimed, "Seattle Welcomes The Great Messiah!"—appeared to be mere curiosity-seekers hoping to catch a peek of Nate and his wife.

Nate turned to Brigitte, whose hands were pressed to her lips and was watching in stunned horror as the crowd closed in.

"It's OK—don't overreact," he said, calmly placing a hand on her left knee.

"Any suggestions?" the cabbie asked anxiously.

"Yeah, pull over. Just give us a few minutes," Nate said.

"Nathan, what on earth are you doing?" Brigitte gasped as the taxi eased to a stop.

"We'll be fine, honey. Trust me," he said.

As he watched the mob gather within inches of the vehicle, Nate remembered what Nelson Mandela once said about fear—something about how the brave man isn't he who doesn't feel afraid, but he who conquers that fear.

Feeling surprisingly self-assured, he pushed open the door and, while still clutching his wife's left hand, hopped out onto the pavement. "Just stay with me," he murmured to her.

Then the two of them edged past the TV cameras and strode valiantly into the advancing throng. "Just give us some breathing room!" Nate pleaded loudly as he waved and acknowledged the shouts of adulation from the crowd, which had formed a large semi-circle around the taxi.

"God loves you, Nate!" a dowdy, middle-aged woman yelled as she brushed past several reporters and thrust a pen and small scrap of paper in his direction. He immediately reached out and snatched it.

He'd never signed an autograph before. It felt right.

22

Six years later: July 2010

After sliding off his goggles, Nate hoisted himself out of the deep end of his backyard pool and grabbed a striped towel at the bottom of his mesh lounge chair. He peered up at the glittering, blue sky and grinned, knowing it was going to be another sweltering July day—the hotter the better, as far as he was concerned.

There was no better way to start the day, Nate believed, than with a vigorous workout in his Olympic-size pool—which is why he often wondered if he'd be better off living in Panama or Hawaii, or some other tropical nirvana rather than in Wisconsin, with its depressingly long winters. But the practical side of him understood that Wisconsin, being in the Midwest, was ideally located for the many speaking engagements he had throughout the country.

After an uncertain start, he was now enjoying his new career as a much-in-demand spiritual advisor—and the many perks that went with

261

it—and knowing full well that, at least based on the feedback he was getting, he *was* having an impact on people's ethical behavior.

A few criminologists had even publicly suggested that the phenomenal saga of Nate Zavoral may be one reason the violent crime rate had stabilized in a number of major U.S. cities in recent years. Nate was skeptical about that, but flattered that the law enforcement community had been so receptive and supportive of his work in the inner cities. The only negative was all the travel involved; with his claustrophobia still acting up on occasion, he dreaded having to fly to many of his speaking engagements—although it certainly helped that he could now afford to sit in first-class.

As he dried himself off, he heard the sliding door to the sunroom open. He turned and saw Kenneh Roberts, his dapper, sinewy security guard and all-around confidante, calling to him.

"Sorry to bother you, sir," shouted the Liberian native, who attended night classes at Madison Area Technical College and dreamed of one day starting his own software business. "But there's a young man at the front gate who asked if he could talk to you. Says his name is Seth Gilbertson—or something like that.

"Anyway, says it's important."

Nate frowned as he tossed his towel on the chair. He was suspicious, as always. He did not know anyone named Seth, and his first reaction was that it was some born-again Christian type or somebody from one of the local charities seeking a donation.

Having worked for Nate for almost three years, Kenneh knew instantly that Nate wanted his own assessment of whether the guy was legitimate or not. He took several steps toward his boss, so that Nate could hear him more clearly.

"He rode up on a bike," Kenneh shouted before Nate could pose the question. "Looks clean-cut, normal. Claims he's a Marine and that he's leaving for Afghanistan next week, which is why he needs to see you."

Nate remained silent as he finished drying himself off. Then he leaned over and took a gulp of his sport drink.

A young Marine? That's odd, he thought.

"Fine," he said finally. "Let him in."

Nate set the drink down next to the lounge chair and strolled to a round white table just a few feet away. He flipped on his sunglasses, then leaned forward and cranked open a billowy mint-colored umbrella so that they'd both be in the shade. Just as he finished, he turned to his left and saw a small, wiry, baby-faced young man with a buzz-cut standing in the patio just outside the sunroom door. He was clad in a button-down white shirt and khakis—and, from afar anyway, looked like he was just a year or two removed from Little League.

Nate got up and sauntered over to greet him, being careful not to slip on the limestone rocks that formed a path to the sunroom and glistened with small puddles of water.

"Nate Zavoral," he said, extending his right hand. "Pleased to meet you."

263

"Seth Gilbertson," the young man replied tentatively while pumping Nate's hand. "And believe me sir, the pleasure is mine."

Nate accompanied him to the table, then asked if he'd like a sport drink—or maybe a beer? The young man politely declined, and the two of them sat down, opposite one another.

"So you're leaving for Afghanistan?" Nate said as he slumped back in his chair and took another swig of his drink. "Got to admire that. But, no offense, you hardly look old enough."

"I'm 19, sir," Seth said. "I enlisted in the Marines two months ago, after completing my freshman year at UW-Whitewater. My grades weren't very good though, and I wasn't sure about a major.

"And, well, this war's been going on for eight years now, and I just felt … Oh, I don't know. I'm a graduate of St. John's Northwestern Military Academy in Delafield, and I just felt—I know it sounds cheesy, but I just felt I owed it to my country to do whatever I could to help end this thing."

Nate nodded, but refrained from commenting on the wisdom of that decision. He'd heard essentially the same line before—mostly from former students, both male and female. Each time, he privately admired their bravery, but felt they were appallingly naïve, not realizing they would become faceless pawns in yet another senseless U.S. war.—a war, in this particular case, that continued to drag on despite President Obama's and the U.S. military's repeated public assurances that progress was being made.

"Do you know where you'll be stationed?" Nate inquired.

"Uh, Bagram, sir—where the big airfield is. About 30 miles north of Kabul. I'll be part of a replacement unit that defends the base against insurgent attacks. In the beginning, anyway. Guess I'll have to stay on my toes."

"I would think so," Nate said, gritting his teeth in empathy.

"So, how can I help you Seth?" Nate asked. "Let me guess. You're headed off to war and you're probably a little frightened right now—well, maybe not frightened. Concerned."

"Uh, not really, sir," Seth said. "I mean, yes, of course, I'm a little nervous—maybe even frightened. But that's not the reason I'm here.

"To be honest, sir, I've wanted to talk to you for several years now. And I just decided that now's the time—you know, not knowing what's going to happen to me once I'm over there."

He looked across the table at Nate and paused to clear his throat.

"I mean, it would just be terribly wrong if I got killed and—and you never knew the truth."

Nate knitted his brow and cast the young man a puzzled look. The truth? What in heaven's name could he be talking about? Maybe the kid *was* a wacko, Nate thought for a moment, just like the dozens of others who'd shown up at Nate's door in recent years. There'd been so many, in fact, that—much as they hated abandoning their old neighbors—he and Brigitte decided in 2007 they needed to a find a home in a safer, more upscale setting; a home that not only was equipped with a sophisticated security system and was separated from the street by a gate but required the presence of a security guard as well.

But Nate also felt sympathy for the young man, realizing that he was straining just to get the words out.

"You're sure you don't want something to drink?" Nate asked.

"No, but thank you."

"OK then, Seth," Nate said while settling back in his chair. "I'm certainly intrigued. What is this truth I need to know about?"

The young man cleared his throat again, then looked directly into Nate's eyes before shifting his eyes downward at his hands, which were folded neatly on the table.

"I know you're a busy man, Mr. Zavoral, so I'll try to keep this as brief as possible," he said. "But first, I want you to know I have tremendous respect for you, sir. What you've done with your life since your hole-in-one, the positive effect you've had on people ..."

He glanced up and noticed that Nate was smiling warmly, although he could also tell Nate was growing impatient and was anxious to hear about the secret Seth now felt compelled to share with him.

So the young man laid it all out: How he'd just turned 13 when Nate got his ace, and how April 24, 2004 turned out to be one of the most important days in his life as well.

"Because I was there, Mr. Zavoral—I was at Turtle Creek Golf Club when it happened," he said, peering across the table at Nate, whose hair was still dripping wet, and forcing himself to make eye contact.

Nate cocked his head to the side and eyed the young man somewhat skeptically. Now Seth definitely had his attention.

"You were there?" he asked curiously. "You took up the game at a young age obviously."

"Well, no sir. I've never been much for golf—except for hitting balls at Fensin's Golfland once in a while with my buddies. Soccer's always been my game."

Actually, Seth went on, the reason he was at Turtle Creek that day was pure happenstance. He and his best friend at the time, Matt Dupree, had gone swimming earlier in the day at Sheridan Pool, the indoor public swim facility just a couple blocks from the golf course.

Matt had moved to Madison the previous fall and was somewhat of a troublemaker, Seth explained. "You know, dumping garbage cans, spraying graffiti on walls, throwing eggs at girls' houses. My parents weren't thrilled that I was hanging out with him."

Nate understood. Typical kids stuff. "Go on," he said.

Seth squirmed in his chair. "This next part is rather painful for me to admit, sir," he said with a wince. "But after we were done swimming, we ransacked two lockers in the dressing room that had been left open by kids who were taking showers. We didn't even know them.

"We took money, a watch, a new baseball glove—which was stupid because neither one of us even played baseball. And then we took off.

"It was Matt's idea. But ... I went along with it."

Nate sat mute, fully absorbed in the narrative. He felt a bit like a Catholic priest in a confessional booth and it made him uncomfortable. He was also growing more impatient by the moment and motioned for Seth to proceed with his story, still trying to figure out why he should care about any of this.

Sensing Nate's frustration, Seth bowed his head again and continued his story. After stealing the items, which they stuffed in a duffle bag that they'd scooped up at the foot of one of the lockers, he and Matt dashed out of the swim facility and didn't stop running for two blocks. Then they darted up a wooded hillside until they found a small clearing between two large bushes beside the No. 3 green at Turtle Creek Golf Club. Only they didn't know it was the No. 3 green at the time, Seth said.

"Not that it mattered."

All they really cared about, he said, was the money. They dropped to their knees and poured it all out, laughing hysterically as they counted every penny.

"It was a little over $8—and we used it to buy lunch at Dairy Queen."

Nate continued to listen in stony silence. He was nonplussed.

He heard a noise behind him, then turned and noticed Kenneh standing aside the sunroom's sliding door, holding up his cell phone.

"It's Mrs. Zavoral, sir," he said loudly. "She's calling from the tennis club and wants to know if she should make a reservation for dinner tonight."

"Not now, Kenneh," Nate replied irritably with a wave of his hand. "Tell her I'll call her back in 10 minutes."

He returned his attention to Seth and, as he did, a feeling of dread began to rush over him. He sensed for the first time that the story wasn't going to have a feel-good ending—and that, after seven years of relative calm and contentment, life was about to throw him another nasty curve ball.

Seth waited until the security guard pulled the door shut, then took several seconds to collect himself before continuing. He was determined to get this out and be on his way, not wanting to prolong Nate Zavoral's apprehension any more than necessary.

As he and Matt were counting their loot, Seth said, they heard something hit the ground nearby—almost like an egg splattering on the floor. Worried that someone might be coming, they pushed some branches aside and spotted a golf ball on the far side of the green, maybe 40 feet away.

Sure, Tyler's tee shot, Nate determined.

"We didn't think anything of it," Seth said.

For the next minute or two, he continued, they just sat there and laughed—and marveled that they'd actually gotten away with their deplorable little crime. Matt would keep the watch, they decided, and Seth would try to sell the baseball glove at school.

"That's when it happened," Seth said.

He and Matt both sprung up upon hearing a loud crack—similar to a firecracker exploding, he said. Or a rifle shot. When they turned their heads again, they saw a golf ball scooting across the green directly toward them. To their astonishment, it rolled into Matt's lap—"Hit him right in the crotch," Seth said, breaking into a half-smile.

Nate was dumbstruck. His whole body went numb. He gestured for Seth to continue, but a part of him was already rebelling over this obviously ludicrous tale.

The moment the ball came to a stop, Seth said, he and Matt looked at each other in disbelief. Then, in an instant, he said, Matt jumped up, flashed a perverse grin and said, "Watch this!" Stooped close to the ground, he dashed to the flagstick, which was no more than 10 feet away, and dropped the ball in the hole.

Then he raced back, Seth said, and the two of them dived on their bellies behind one of the bushes and waited.

Nate listened stoically, not saying a word. He wasn't sure he wanted Seth to finish the story. He really didn't need any more details—assuming, of course, that Seth was telling the truth.

Was this some sort of sick gag? Or maybe a setup? No, not likely, he quickly surmised. He could grasp the sincerity in the young man's voice—and see it in his face—as he related the story. The kid was legit.

Nate paused to take a gulp of his sport drink, but his eyes remained fixed on the bright-eyed, square-jawed young man across the table who bore a striking resemblance to the choir boys Nate remembered from his pre-teen days when he attended mass every Sunday at Immaculate Conception.

Seth looked down at his hands again—he was fidgeting now—and shrugged. "And then, well—we heard some voices. And then we peeked through the bushes and saw some guy walking toward the flagstick—you, Mr. Zavoral—and then we saw you reach down and lift the ball out of the hole.

"And then," Seth peered across the table and forced a smile. "And then we heard you swear, sir—quite loudly actually. I think you were just so shocked to see your ball in the bottom of the cup."

Nate's face turned red. "Uh, yeah, you're absolutely right, Seth," he said timidly.

"And then, all of a sudden, your buddies were screaming and slapping you on the back and acting crazy. We were scared out of our minds that you'd see us, but the next thing we knew all four of you were headed down the hill to the next tee. And as soon as you were out of sight, we got the hell out of there."

Nate was momentarily paralyzed. He felt a myriad of overwhelming, conflicting emotions surging through him—shock, fear, rage, confusion. Even resentment.

"And you never told anyone about this?" he stammered. "The thought never crossed your mind?"

"No, not really," Seth said. But there were a few other things Nate needed to know, he said—and then perhaps he would understand why Seth had kept the whole thing a secret all these years.

Keep in mind, he'd just turned 13, Seth said. He and Matt pulled pranks all the time—sometimes two or three a day. "Most of our friends did, too," he said. "But it was mostly little stuff. You'd pull a joke on someone and laugh for a minute or two, and then you were on to something else. But you never thought about the implications."

And like most 13-year-olds, Seth said, he never paid attention to the news. In fact, he didn't even know who Nate Zavoral was until about three years later, after Nate had become famous, he explained. It was only then that he read an article about Nate's hole-in-one in 2004 and began to make the connection.

"And, of course, I was absolutely terrified when I realized what Matt and I had done—I mean, I honestly thought for a while that I might go to jail if anyone found out."

"What about Matt?" Nate inquired.

"Well, that's the other thing you need to know about—at least, so you understand why I kept this whole thing to myself."

Two weeks after their Turtle Creek prank, Seth said, Matt was riding his bike home from Elver Park on the west side and was hit from behind by a woman in an SUV who was talking on a cell phone. The force of the collision flipped him over the handle bars and he landed on the curb, breaking his neck, Seth said. He was pronounced dead at the scene.

"He wasn't wearing a helmet, but police said they doubted it would have helped much anyway. The woman was going about 40 mph when she hit him."

Nate grimaced. He rested his chin on his left hand and tried to jog his memory. Then he remembered. Of course, the Dupree kid. Then he recalled the emotional funeral and the intense anger in the community and the long, acrimonious debate in the state legislature on whether to ban drivers from talking on cell phones—a debate which, unfortunately, went nowhere.

"His death really hit me, as you can imagine," Seth said solemnly. "It's all I could think about for months. It even affected my school work. Which is one of the reasons my parents sent me to St. John's."

Nate slumped back in his chair again. It all made perfect sense. As flabbergasted as he was by the startling revelation, he understood Seth's decision not to share the story with anyone else; and why the young man felt compelled—for so many reasons—to come forward with it now. As painful as the facts were, this was something Nate needed to know. And he was profoundly grateful that Seth had decided it would be Nate's prerogative whether to divulge the information to others or to lock it away forever.

Seth finally looked up and exhaled quietly. "Well, that's really about it, sir," he said peering across at Nate, the weight of a thousand water buffaloes no longer pressing down on his shoulders, the angst now gone from his eyes and his voice.

Was there anything else Nate wanted to know? The young man asked.

Nate shook his head ever so slowly. There were, in fact, dozens of questions twirling through his head, but he was too discombobulated to present them now.

273

Wearing a look of utter relief, Seth rose from his seat and thanked Nate not only for meeting with him but for allowing him to tell his story—and, he added with a smile, for not reacting in a hostile manner.

"I know it's probably going to take a while for you to digest all this, sir," the young man said, "but I just want you to know that whatever you decide to do—even if it's nothing—I will respect that.

"Seriously, sir. As far as I'm concerned, what happened that day will always be a private matter between the two of us. But if you decide to go public with the story, I'm OK with that, too.

"Obviously, I'd prefer to put this behind me, now that I've finally gotten it out. But I've given it a lot of thought and, well, I wholly trust that you'll do what's right."

Nate smiled appreciatively, then got up, walked around the table and wrapped his right arm around the young man's shoulder. "That *is* quite a story, Seth—even better than the original," he quipped.

They strolled together down the path to the sunroom, and Nate nudged open the sliding door. When they reached the breezeway, he stopped abruptly, pulled the young man close and gave him a long, tender hug.

"Thank you, Seth—and I truly mean that. I know how difficult this must have been for you. And for gosh sakes, good luck in Afghanistan. You will be in my thoughts often."

Seth wanted to respond, to say something meaningful, but the words were stuck in his throat.

His eyes welling with tears, he nodded to show his gratitude, then stepped outside and began heading down to his bike, which was propped up against the giant wrought-iron gate at the entrance of Nate's driveway.

He'd taken just a few steps when Nate called out to him.

Seth stopped in mid-stride and spun around.

"I'm just curious, Seth. Are you religious?" Nate asked.

"I am, sir. Devout Methodist."

"Good," Nate said softly. "Good."

Seth smiled and studied Nate's expression. Was he being sincere? Seth wondered. Or was that a look of disappointment—maybe even pity? He couldn't tell.

Nate closed the door, then slowly strode through the house and back to the pool. When he got there, he kicked off his flip-flops, plopped down in his lounge chair and stared blankly at the glistening turquoise water. After five minutes or so, he lifted himself up and strolled around to the deep end of the pool, but he was too numb to do anything but just stand there, his toes curling over the edge.

He gazed upward and half-expected to see storm clouds rolling in. But the sky was benign, totally devoid of clouds, and there was nothing but brilliant sunlight.

Acknowledgments

The idea for this book came to me while I was touring the Panama Canal on a giant catamaran in 1999. I'm still not sure what inspired it—I was on my fourth pina colada—but I remember thinking it would be fun to attempt a novel, and figured it would be a nice diversion from my job as a newspaper columnist. It turned out to be just that—fun. However, I never fathomed it would take 12 years to finish it, even though I'd been warned by other authors that life's challenges would intervene repeatedly along the way.

Now that the journey is finally over, I want to express my utmost gratitude to those who kept me on track, despite all the detours. Foremost, I want to thank Jerry Apps, a highly successful Wisconsin author and creative writing instructor at the University of Wisconsin Extension, whose expertise and encouragement were the chief reasons I decided to revive the project—after a lapse of several years—in 2010.

He wasn't my only cheerleader, of course. My wife Cindy and my daughters Jessica and Kerry performed that role admirably. Jessica was also my sounding board whenever I altered the manuscript, and Kerry helped me overcome my woeful computer deficiencies. In addition, there were many friends—too many to list here—who constantly prodded me to keep going whenever I'd hit a lull; my sincere thanks to every one of them. And throughout the process I relied heavily on the insights and editing skills of several former colleagues: Samara Kalk, Natasha Kassulke, Dennis Punzel and Frank Ryan.

To my astonishment, I produced the first rough draft—aided by numerous pots of coffee and rejuvenating walks in the woods—in just six weeks in the spring of 2000, while living in a renovated farmhouse in rural Dane County owned by longtime friends Dr. Victoria Vollrath and Steve Schumacher. I'm guessing they'll be equally astonished to find out I've actually completed the book a mere 12 years later.

Perhaps fittingly, I wrote the final few chapters in another country home—this one on a pristine lake in northwestern Wisconsin—owned by friends Don and Annie Smithmier. Don was one of the first people I shared my idea with in 1999, shortly after he'd graduated from the University of Wisconsin, and he never wavered in his support for the project. (Even more important, he promised to remain friends even if I don't sell a single copy.)

Sando Johnson, who has a small software business in Milwaukee, helped me format the book digitally and transfer it to amazon.com, for which I'm eminently grateful. Malynn Utzinger also provided valuable publishing advice, and my longtime chum John Ferraro offered some terrific promotional ideas. My nephew, Mark Giaimo, an enormously talented artist who works for the Washington Post, designed the book's cover, which far exceeded my expectations.

I was told early in the process that, in addition to putting in long hours—or, in my case, years—and overcoming seemingly endless obstacles, luck is often a factor in completing a first novel. I can't remember who said it, but I did feel extremely lucky when Karen McQuestion, one of Amazon's budding stars, agreed to meet over coffee in Hartland, Wis., one morning last fall and convinced me that, due to the mushrooming interest in e-books and the demise of small publishing companies, the most promising market for my novel was the tens of thousands of readers who download books every day on Amazon's Kindle.

It seemed like the logical final step—even for an old technophobe like me.

About the author

Rob Zaleski is a freelance writer who spent three decades in the newspaper business, including 23 years as an award-winning columnist for The Capital Times in Madison, Wis. He also worked for United Press International, the Green Bay (Wis.) Daily News and the Idaho State Journal in Pocatello. He and his wife Cindy have three daughters and reside in Madison.

Made in the USA
Monee, IL
06 July 2023

38753276R00166